THE DAMNED LOVELY

THE DAMNED
LOVELY

ADAM FROST

THE DAMNED LOVELY

DOWN&OUT
BOOKS

Down & Out Books
3959 Van Dyke Road, Suite 265
Lutz, FL 33558
DownAndOutBooks.com

Cover design by Zach McCain

ISBN: 1-64396-253-1
ISBN-13: 978-1-64396-253-5

For Nora, Dashiell, and Emmett.

She wasn't pretty.

She sat quiet and across the tracks. On San Fernando Road, north of Colorado. On the wrong side of the 5. All innocent between a cheap tile store and three rotten mechanics.

She had a lone black brick wall facing west that was hot to the touch by four p.m. There were no windows. Only a small sign. And a gutter. A sun-bleached, rusted-out reservoir thirsty like the rest of us.

She wasn't pretty but she was *ours*.

Jiles called her The Damned Lovely. He never told us why but didn't much need to, either. We all had our theories. Jiles used to be a cop. He aged out and they kicked him to the curb. His wife told him he needed to get out of the house. Said he needed to stop drinking and take up a hobby. So he opened a bar. Set up shop for his team. Someplace the men and women in blue could deflate. Bang around cases with a ripe shot of booze. A place for the soldiers to sing. A room for heroes to mourn. Away from the cameras and glare of backstabbing headlines. Where really, Jiles could feel like a cop again. Where everyone knows your name, rank, and demons.

It was dark.

It was dank.

And it was my kinda slice.

It wasn't just a cop bar. The Lovely had *character*. And history. Eleven black-padded stools with their own personalized bruises and dents. There was a worn-out, stained mahogany bar with the perfect brass rail and a soft cushion for our arms. There were wood stains. Water stains. Stains inside and out. Initials, hearts and skulls etched with knives. Memories and heartbreak slashed in wood.

Around the edges were seven private booths with updated red padded benches that looked tight and outta place. Like a bad eye job on an aging starlet. They made the place look better and I guess prettier, but a little crooked, too. Jiles said it kept asses in the seats and whiskey flowing so we best shut up about 'em.

There was even a battered piano in the corner because of course there was. And a piano man who came around some Thursday nights we called Billy. No one knew his real name cuz he wouldn't tell us like he was embarrassed or some shit. But most of the time we hit the Seeburg, which Jiles had paid extra for. A vintage 1963 Chrome Seeburg SC1 Stereo Hi Fi he put some real money into so we could tap the old school classics on vinyl. Sam Cooke. Nina Simone. Otis Redding. Lou Reed. Wilson Pickett. Carole King. Joe Cocker. Roy Orbison. Jackie Wilson. Tina. Bowie. Janis. Smokey. He wanted rhythm. And horns. Brass. Soul and all its beautiful parts he claimed were for us.

We weren't unhappy.

We weren't depressed.

We were *hardpressed*.

That was our handshake. Our secret bent. Our *hey we're not alone after all* when the door cracked early at eleven a.m. Or when the sun seeped in, trying to distract us at three in the afternoon. After all, we were deflecting tomorrow *together*.

We were bound by our fix. Cocktails. Spirits. The *grape*. Hops and IPAs. Glowing ambers. Frosty glasses. An endless reservoir of old school booze and the bliss of that second sip. When the splash sits just right. Drowning out the poison of our real life. The inbox. The monsters at work. The kids. The latest STD. The drive at five. The tomorrow grind. Pick your poison cuz we got the fix for tomorrow.

After all, this wasn't Los Angeles. No, ma'am. This was Glendale.

This wasn't even close to Hollywood.

This was fuck you and your tasty Santa Monica oxygen. Your perfect ocean sunsets.

Your pretty Venice tans and Abbott Kinney gloss.

Your Beverly Hills's plastic faces and dark money.

Your WeHo happy Sunday Fundays.

We never made it *that* far west...

No. This be Glendale. The land of Chevy Chase Boulevard. That hurricane of car dealerships and sparkling ribbons promising the American dream. *Oh, and while you're here—have you been up the street?* It's the Americana! The Grove without a soul. Without the gloss but all the function and cheaper parking. Just take San Fernando Road, that endless pipe to nowhere.

Glendale. That bland ugly open secret, where nothing ever *happens.* Nothing wild. Nothing wonderful. Wedged between the trendy boulevards of Silverlake. The Los Feliz hills. The cute bungalows of Atwater Village. The historic Pasadena mansions. The Santa Anita horse track. The JPL. Roofs with a pulse. With history and feeling.

Glendale. That tasteless grid of flat streets and relentless, punishing sunshine in search of a soul. The shrug of a last resort: *I mean, I guess we could live in Glendale...*

Glendale. My home for nine years. I'd accepted this. Like some kinda dull splinter. Like one of these days this pain would figure itself out. Take a page from her neighbors and stop being such a sad sack single kid with cooler cousins named Echo Park and Silverlake and Mount Washington. *If they can do it, why can't we? Why can't we, fellas?* Because, cous', you be Glendale...

Glendale. That ugly chore we're gonna fix up one of these days.

Monday, July 6th, 2:04 p.m.

It was only two p.m. Worse, it was a Monday, two p.m.

But I needed a burst.

When I stepped inside, Pa hit me with a nod. Ah, Pa. The soft soul at the bar with stringy shocks of white hair and an unquenchable thirst for Beefeater on ice. I'm guessing three hours of drinking and the old coot probably hadn't nudged from his perch or even thought about takin' a piss. He had a crooked smile. Dirty glasses and rank breath. Pa was a disgraced surgeon outta Eagle Rock. A lonesome kind man with an ugly past and if I had to guess, very little love left in his life. But he was a welcome fixture in the joint. Small, soft and gentle, content with his failure. You could always lean on Pa for a piece of kindness or a burst of something brighter.

And then there was Jewels. Thank god for Jewels. She was twenty-three. Skinny as a pin, with a neck like a flamingo and long black hair. Sleeves of tattoos with demons and flowers and pyramids she had to regret by now. Jewels spun jewelry. It was garbage. Globs of metal and jade for hundreds of bucks a piece. Who the hell was she kidding? No wonder she was slinging a tray six days a week. She was a scrappy love. Forced to put up with us. But Jewels kept us straight. Jewels smelled pretty and reminded us to be kind to each other.

Jiles was standing behind the bar. Jiles was our king. He was sixty-seven years old. A tough and bruised retired cop who probably had to put up with entitled knobs like me growing up. Bustin' heads in the San Fernando Valley for thirteen years. He

4

failed backwards and transferred to Central LA. Worked Homicide for twenty-two years after that. Twenty-two years scraping bodies off the ground. Knocking on doors, spilling pain to strangers. Tangling with the worst demons in the city. You could see it behind his eyes sometimes. The darkness he'd seen. But he kept his cards close and never complained. Still, I'd wedge in when no one was around and press out some of his war stories. You could smell the pride buried deep.

Yeah, Jiles was our king.

Hardened, wise, and uncompromisingly loyal.

Jiles liked me. I have no idea why. He had a room in the back and cut me a deal. I even paid rent. Just sixty bucks a month with a few commercial breaks cuz sometimes an off-duty detective would drag in a perp and untangle the lies. We called it "the box." Two chairs, an '03 phone book, and no cameras. Where the truth spilled out. It wasn't right. It was antique. History happening now. Old school justice even I was surprised still existed...

Anyway. The box smelled sour. The box had no windows. There was a desk and four ugly grey walls. But it was quiet. And it was mine. The rent was cheap. And the booze close by. So I could bury myself for hours on end. Just me and Benny, my scratched up 2012 MacBook Pro. My feed to the world at large. My cohort. My therapist. My reflection. My only true asset. All that I aspire to be jammed into a sliver box. I named him Benny after my all-star friend in high school. Benny was the kid with promise, the guy we all wanted to be. Benny was the man who OD'ed on fentanyl and reminded me to live better now.

I landed at the bar and ordered a Bulleit bourbon from Jiles. Two fingers. Neat. I picked up the newspaper at the bar. Jiles still got the *LA Times* hardcopy. Bless him.

Dodgers intel.

Calendar drivel.

The City Hall fires.

Business blah.

California crazy.

Pa read her cover to cover. Jiles pinched pieces. Jewels could care less. I usually hit the front page and the sports. Crumpled and wet by eleven a.m. Shredded by two. Soggy and recycled by four. Rinse and repeat.

Jiles dropped off my pal. *Cheers*. Heaven, here we come.

I caught a piece of the Rooster in my glass's reflection. That pale thirty-something mystery in the black hoodie we called the Rooster cuz two years in, no one knew his real name. Be we knew that rooster decal on his computer. And crack of our dawn, he was steady, day in day out. The ultimate outcast. A man with an ugly crutch for Diet Coke with no ice. A man who spoke to no one, crouched in a back booth behind his stickered up PC. We all had our theories. On his name. Where he came from. What he did. Who he had kidnapped and kept bound in his basement this very moment. Most of us figured he was a demon on the web, making the world an e-scarier hell. Jiles earned some actual cred and discovered the Rooster worked as a dedicated day trader. It made sense in a lot of ways. Where he got his cake. But the screen was lit well beyond market close, so none of us really bought the angle. As the full story, anyway. At the end of the day the man kept to himself, paid his bill, and Jiles was more than okay keeping him around.

"It's a free country, right?"

Or as Slice would say, "Because you just never know when you're gonna need a friend to hack the shit outta someone, eh, Jiles?"

That was Slice. Slice was an original. An opinion man. A sidelined ex-cop with a dirty past and toothy snarl. A sneaky bastard with a decent heart who liked to ply us with dirty stories and pizza at one a.m. It worked. Jiles had met him on the beat in '94. Told me Slice was a wreckin' ball back when, but the soldier crossed one too many lines and they kicked him to the curb without a pension. Jiles went easy on him. They buddied up. I'd still never got the full story. No matter how many times I tried to weasel out the truth the copper would shake me loose. He was the kind of drunk who was broken to the core but flashed an infectious Jack Nicholson smile so you still ended up inviting him to the party. Yea. Everybody loved Slice. But nobody trusted the man. Including me.

I took a sip and checked my phone. Waiting for the screen to *siiiing*. Praying. Hoping.

She held her ground and I lost the fight.

The empty telephone. Reminding me, I had no excuses. To be in a better place. To be successful.

I was an American.

I was white.

I grew up safe and surrounded by love.

There was money for birthday parties and proper schools.

I had a college degree in communications.

I'd traveled to Southeast Asia. Seen Europe. Touched down in South Africa. I had a sweet girl who liked to cook and wanted a ring. We had an apartment in West Hollywood with good light.

I'd found a marketing gig early and wrote ad copy for seven years. Logos. Corporate promos. Internet ribbons. Microcopy drawl. Quippy garbage that paid the rent and then some.

I was on the right track.

Until I broke. Crashed the cart and pulled the plug on my world of California lies.

Staring at those smiling faces across a Doheny dinner table that night.

The masquerade of happiness.

The Instagram sham.

There was no substance. No truth. No intent for anything more than gain.

I had sealed the truth for years. Locked and bottled that depression south, convinced I could kick it. Convinced the gnaw would pass.

Things are great, I kept saying. *Things are great.*

But something about those faces on that very Doheny night

popped the cork and shattered the glass. I called it out. I let it rip ugly. These weren't my friends. They were assets. Nothing more.

This wasn't love. This was compliance on rails.

I needed something pure. Something with purpose and mine all mine. That I truly adored.

So I quit the girl who liked to cook. Lost the apartment with the light and moved to Glendale. Where it was cheaper. Where there was no good light.

And worst of all. I was compelled by a force inside my bones to write something real. Something long and from the heart. Something maybe even wise.

This, more and more it seemed, may have been a grave mistake.

It was in no way working out.

Still, I refused to believe in misery. *An honest rut is all.* It'll turn around soon. It *has* to. Because when you're going through hell in Glendale, keep going. *Right?*

So. Soldier on. Live with intent and drown those voices out.

Drown. Them. Out. Soldier!

Swish. Swish.

A red Trojan alpha bro was swipin' right at the bar. Americana run off sipping a sea breezer with a skinny lime. Slice and I shared a healthy glare of disdain when Jewels crossed behind me and nodded to stool 9.

"She's baaaack," Jewels cooed.

And there she was. Hiding her green eyes under a black felt fedora and a worn-out paperback of *To the Lighthouse*. She had dark brown hair pinned low at the back. Wore a simple tight white V-neck tee exposing that soft skin around her collarbones. She sat straight. With her legs crossed in black jeans that pinched in at her waist exposing a band of flawless smooth lower back. She kept her face down. Never spoke to a soul beyond ordering a drink. And never looked at her phone. Not once. Not once had I seen her look at her phone. Instead, she just buried her eyes in that book. Drowning out the world with a Negroni and

Woolf's words like some kinda mystery from a different era. She'd been in four times now by my count. And it was consistent. Early in the afternoon. Same drink. Same book. Alone. Like an oasis in this godforsaken Glendale desert.

I'd already plied Jiles for credit card intel but the unicorn paid cash.

I rehearsed my ways in.

Hard to believe Virginia Woolf was only fifty-nine when she walked into that river...

There's no WAY you live in Glendale...

They say the Negroni was created by a Count in Florence looking to spice up his usual cocktail...

I could never pull off wearing a fedora like that...

Drivel.

Desperate rank sure to piss her off. I mean, how was I supposed to compete against the Woolf?

Jiles snickered wise, but I didn't care. I was hooked hard and caved after watching her for an hour and twenty-seven minutes. Hopped off my stool and crossed behind her. Hoping to catch a scent of something as magical as she looked. It paid off when I caught a piece of something simple and sweet and beautifully feminine.

When I got back to my stool, I tried not to stare and failed magnificently. She pulled a worn-out denim shirt from her bag and wrapped the sleeves around her waist. Closing the gap on that lower back.

She had to know I was watching her. The way she shifted her legs. Spinning that black straw on the bar, clawing it round like a cat with her thin, slender fingers. Those polished nails.

She loved it.

Or did she? Maybe she just liked to read.

Or maybe she *wants* you to talk to her.

Or maybe she wants to be left alone in peace.

Roy Orbison cooed from the jukebox, singing for a better tomorrow.

No shit, Roy. *Maybe tomorrow...*

The Trojan stain put down his phone. Swilled his vodka cran and chewed crude on some ice cubes, taking in the room. Clockin' that fedora now.

"Virginia Woolf, huh?"

Fedora piss-off smiled. Nearby, Slice grinned on his stool.

Round 1.

"*To the Lighthouse?* What happens at the lighthouse?"

It all burned.

"Lemme buy you another drink and you can tell me what's so special about this lighthouse, anyway," he blathered. "What is that...Campari?"

"No, thanks," she said softly.

She spoke. I was enthralled, hoping for a few more magical syllables but the Trojan kept barking.

"Come on, you look like you could use some company instead of that stupid old book."

He left me no choice.

"I think she just wants to read..."

Fedora craned her face my way, curious.

The Trojan twisted.

I held my ground and stared down his ugly red University of Spoiled Children sweatshirt.

"Just sayin', man. Look at her body language. I don't know this woman, but I know this—see her fingers? Those little white tips at the end. Pressing into the table like that? That means she's uncomfortable. They weren't like that before you started barking at her."

She flashed a sweet smile my way. Like she might have been impressed or possibly even thankful.

"I don't remember asking you."

I could feel his fight-boner starting to grow—

She smiled and mouthed the words, *Thank you*, rattling my heart some. Then, she turned back his way.

"I'm really just trying to read."

"See? Just leave her alone."

The Trojan stood up and walked towards me, barking his way down the bar. Fedora squirmed. Those fingertips still burning white.

Maybe tomorrow, Roy belted.

Eat shit, Roy. Maybe NOW you prick.

I barked back.

I took my swing and cracked his jaw.

The world went cold and slooooowed way down.

His fist ripped into my gut. I doubled over, and then his fat fingers slammed into my nose.

Blood hit the bar. Blood sprinkled the limes.

Slice cackled.

Pa groaned.

Jiles roared.

Fedora smiled sweet.

I hit the ground fast and hard.

But I was a hero.

For a moment. I was her goddamn hero.

And then my world smashed to black.

Monday, July 6th, 5:19 p.m.

Pa's gin-soaked breath blew in and dredged me back to life. The disgraced doc smiling victorious all up in my face.

"There he is."

I pushed a bag of ice off my nose and sat up, finding myself in the box with Slice and Pa staring down on me like a cheap piece of entertainment.

"Didn't know you had it in ya, Sammy." Slice chuckled and held up his soft worn-out fists like a prizefighter. "Keep those elbows up next time, champ!"

I could still taste the blood in my mouth.

"You okay, slugger?" Pa genuinely wanted to know.

"Yeah."

Then I remembered her. The Fedora. The Woolf.

"She still here?"

"Don't think so," Pa offered softly.

I said thanks and got to my feet, pushing outta my corner back towards the bar where Jiles was still mopping up the wreckage.

"You're alive." He looked mad as hell but like he understood the greater good.

I scanned the bar but only found the usual slugs. Jiles pegged the glance. He knew.

"She's long gone."

I pretended it all made sense.

"She said to say thanks."

"You talked to her?"

"Yeah." Jiles shrugged it off like no big thing.

12

"And?"

"She asked your name and I told her." He shrugged again.

"That's *it*? You get her name?"

Jiles looked annoyed, like he shoulda thought of that. Or shouldn't have to at all given he was cleaning my blood off his limes. "All happened pretty quick, Sammy. There wasn't a lotta talking."

I looked around, trying to remember her. Trying to play it all back.

Then, Jiles remembered something and pulled that denim shirt of hers from behind the bar.

"She forgot her shirt. Or maybe she just didn't want it anymore."

I could see the bloodstains. *My* bloodstains soaked into the fabric as I took hold of it. The blue denim was soft and worn thin. It had snap buttons running up the middle and on the cuffs. The elbows were worn down. Like one of those shirts you just can't throw away. Wash after wash. Year after year.

"She put it under your head when you were out cold on the floor. Kinda nice of her," Jiles added.

I couldn't stop staring at those stains like we were bound by fate now.

"What happened to that frat boy?"

"We kicked him to the curb," Slice bellowed as he straddled back up to the bar. "That chump learned his lesson. Won't be coming back here."

My face swelled fierce. I bought the lie.

Jiles handed me a Bulleit. "Take it outside next time, bruiser." Then he smiled like an older brother.

"I got one punch in, Jiles. One good one," I muttered. "Never done that before."

I swallowed the liquid gold with pride. Holding that shirt in my hands, catching the scent of a woman. I wanted to drown in that smell. And planned to all alone. But right now, I held my head high.

My first fight. Ever.
I went down swinging. I went down noble.
She had to be impressed.
She had to come back.

Tuesday, July 7th, 9:06 a.m.

"You don't look so good," said Nick.

Nick was an asshole. But Nick was an asshole who paid his share of the rent on time, so was worth the pain and dirty dishes. Nick felt better than the world. Entitled just for landing. This man was gonna be rich someday.

Guaranteeeed.

Nick bought good hipster coffee. He liked to TALK. Gab empowered radical right-wing bent. Conspiracy-infused intelligence. We sparred incredulous:

"How can you be so stupid?"

"How can you be so naïve?"

Rinse and repeat. Coffee coffee coffee. Three dirty cutting boards for one egg and some spinach, which he wouldn't clean for days so it fell on me. I buried the pain.

He could tell I was in a bad way and dug in his hooks but there was no way I'd tell him about the girl. My hero moment. That belonged to ME.

"I had a rough night."

I blamed the booze.

"You're all cut up and bruised..."

I blamed the booze and some crooked concrete.

Nick told me I drank too much.

Nick was spot on.

Nick suggested I get some exercise.

Nick was spot on.

I needed to get away from Nick's logic. I wanted to lock myself

15

in the box but my reality alarm smashed back hard. The voices calling out:

(The money's running out, Sam.)
(The money's running out, Sam.)
(The money's running out, Sam.)

So instead I vacuumed out my wimpy Chevy Volt. Punched the ignition. Lit up the app. Strapped on a smile. Five stars shining bright. Welcome to my pain...

Thursday, July 9th, 11:13 a.m.

Hi, Margaret?
   Hi, Derek?
   Hi, Hon-ji?
   How long have I been driving? Oh, about a year.
   Too hot? Got it.
   Too loud? On it.
   Too cold? For real? It's like ninety-five degrees outside?! *You got it!*
   Woodland Hills? [in six o'clock-traffic?!] *Sounds good. Would you like a water?*
   Are you kidding, who doesn't like soft rock?
   Please, do not vomit in my car.
   Well, the GPS says to go right...
   Do not vomit in my car. PLEASE.
   I'm not TRYING to go around but the road is literally closed so...
   That's weird...I was waiting at that address...the one you entered!!!!
   Don't puke!
   SMILE. Soak it up and EARN those five-star bourbons.
   One day I'll strike it rich...you'll see, Dad. One day.

Friday, July 10th, 3:19 p.m.

You need to think bigger.

I was back in the box, staring at the screen. Blinking cursor. Cursed blinking. All that white. What the hell am I going to write now? I'd already put it all out there. Seventeen months. 102,133 words. My novel. An epic psychological narrative about a man reeling from heartbreak who reclaims his life as a vigilante.

It never took off.

That's what my agent Daphne told me. The only agent in town who'd even consider reading me cuz she went to college with my old man.

It's too dark.

It's too small. You need to think bigger. You need to excite a wide audience.

It's not supposed to *be* for a wide audience. It's supposed to be good.

What's something only YOU can write? What's original to YOU? What do YOU have to say about the world?

I'm thirty-five years old.

I weigh one hundred sixty-three pounds.

I'm five feet nine inches tall.

I grew up in Oregon surrounded by loving parents.

I spent the best seven years of my prime writing ad copy and living with a girl I was supposed to love.

Now, I live in a shoebox apartment with a soulless fascist in Glendale.

I had opportunity.

I squandered my privilege.

Sam I am.

And now I was tapped. Burnt with nothing left in the tank. Come on, Benny. Sing to me. Just one. Just *one* compelling idea. *Sinkholes*. Maybe. Where do they lead? Who falls in?

Blinking Cursor. Custard. Cucktard.

I could hear Joe Cocker wailing about friends from the other room. A little help from my friends, right, Joe? Waxin' poetic on someone else's words. Tsk tsk. See, but Joe had an angle. Joe could sing.

Forget original.

I'll just be me.

...I need the Bulleit

You need NO Bulleit.

I need water.

You need protein and a tan.

Cancer with a spin. Good cancer?

Mercy.

No, I really do need water. I stood up and cracked the box.

Slice hit me up with a toothy snarl at the bar. "Jesus. You been in there this whole time? Christ, kid. Why don't you go write at a Starbucks or something."

"I DESPISE Starbucks."

"How can you despise Starbucks? All that green. And they got those Frappuccinos." The old man licked his lips like a bad commercial.

"There's no soul in a Starbucks, Slice. I can't write someplace without soul."

"So you stick yourself in that rat hole all day? That place is poison. There's blood on that table. Literally. And you got no oxygen in there, kid. You gotta breathe. No wonder you're all jammed up."

"I'm not jammed up, I'm pushing through a block."

"They got a new Coffee Bean on Colorado. With one of those cozy outdoor fire pits. How's that for your soul, Sammy?" Slice cackled and even Pa chuckled at my expense, listening in as he sucked back the *Times*.

"What's the latest, Pa?"

"Dodgers are down again. Three straight."

I got tight. "We still got a lotta months left."

Slice cut in. "Bellinger's broke."

"Don't say that."

"They oughta juice."

"Please!"

Pa was feeling gracious and changed the topic. "Your nose looks better."

Jiles was deep into the California section. I asked him for water. He piled ice into a pint, hosed it down with tap water, and handed her off. It tasted important.

Cold and necessary.

Maybe something about Demons. Priests. Demon Priests. Who fall down a sinkhole?

Jiles went back to his section and shot me a look.

"What?"

"You read the paper today?"

"No...why?"

Jiles crunched his brow like he'd read something uncomfortable. Jiles had been a cop for twenty-five years. Jiles didn't get uncomfortable easy. He looked me in the eye and told me to sit down. Then he handed over the paper. The headline blasted:

3RD WOMAN ABDUCTED IN EAST LOS ANGELES
Authorities have released the name of the woman abducted Monday night in Glendale as Josie Pendleton. The 22-year-old Pasadena native was found strangled to death in a stolen Camry—

Josie Pendleton?

I stared at the picture of the woman and ran it down. I *knew* the face. But who was Josie Pendleton? The dots weren't connecting. There was a shot of a beige Camry. The yellow tape and first responders. A dark red stain in the back seat. A smashed fedora in the corner, broken on its side.

The Fedora. The Woolf.

I stalled out. Like something choked me from inside. Jewels crossed behind me and caught the spread.

"Oh my god. That's that girl who was..."

Even Slice got oddly quiet. Pa, too. Curious and still. My eyes drilled down on the article, desperate for information: Josie Pendleton was last seen on Monday, July 6th. *Monday?* That was my hero Trojan day. She was found by a jogger early Tuesday morning and had been strangled in the back of the stolen Camry. Authorities believe she was sexually assaulted but were awaiting autopsy results. Detective Lou Pinner of the Glendale Police Department was running point on the investigation.

Jiles handed me a Bulleit on the house. I wanted the skinny on Pinner.

"You've met him. Big, fat bald guy. With the crooked glasses...Angry most of the time. Obnoxious as all hell but a damn good detective."

Of course. They give it to the ugliest, messiest trainwreck of a cop, Lou Pinner.

"If you want, I'll talk to him. See what he can tell us."

"Yeah, thanks." I nodded and tried to hold my feelings together. But breathing got hard. Jiles nodded back, almost worried, like he'd babysat this face before.

My world started spinning. Josie Pendleton. Her name was Josie. Those fingers. Those lips whispering *thank you* my way. That fedora. *To the Lighthouse.* She was here. She was just here. Now she was never coming back. I still had her shirt. My eyes were about to break. I needed oxygen. I needed to escape. I stepped off the stool and made a break for the door.

Outside, the heat off the concrete hit me hard in the face. I stared at the train tracks.

"I never even talked to her." I said it out loud. Quiet but out in the world. *"I never even talked to her."*

My face cracked with pain. Eyes breaking. Tears pouring out. I never even talked to her. Like I had all the time in the world, like maybe tomorrow. Who was she? I didn't even know her. Think about her family. Think about her mother. Her father. Brother. Sister. Friends. Her lovers.

You got no grieving rights.

But I had to know more. I had a new rash. A new itch to scratch. Inside, burning bright, determined to know everything there was about Josie Pendleton.

Who was this girl?

Friday, July 10th, 3:58 p.m.

J-O-S-I-E P-E-N-D-L-E-T-O-N

Back in the box.

Armed with a fresh Bulleit I hit up Facebook for intel on Josie
Pendleton. Turns out we shared one mutual friend. A girl named
Allison Hager. *Whothehell is Allison Hager?* Pin it. I'd circle
back but meantime: Josie was a SoCal native. Grew up in South
Pasadena and, according to her homepage, she lived in Eagle
Rock and attended Pasadena City College. Her public profile was
lean. Personal details scant. The pictures were mostly reposts of
assholes smiling proud over dead lions and other cruelty to
animals banners. Oceans of plastic. Save the world stuff. Along
with some events connected to her college art fair. But that was
about it.

Her Instagram account had been frozen and Twitter was a
bust. She wasn't on LinkedIn. A Google images search turned
up a bunch of shots of her at what looked to be some kinda
charity event for an organization called Backyard Dreams. And
there was a spattering of other pics. Smiling at a charity run.
Wrapped in the arms of her friends at a high school party.

Smiling. Beaming with life.

I stared at her denim shirt lying on my desk and pulled it
close to my face, smelling it like a piece of treasure. Sweat and
perfume fused right. I hoisted it up high and the sleeves dropped
down on either side. Swinging all lifelike.

I thought about her skin inside those sleeves.

Then I laid the shirt out on the desk carefully, gazing at the only tangible piece I had left of her.

I needed more. So I dug into Allison Hager. Based on our lack of mutual friends, I ruled out any high school connection. Same with college. And on account she looked almost ten years younger. Or maybe she just aged right. Better. Wait, was she the obnoxious girl I met at Andrew's play three years ago? Or was it at the Barnsdall wine tasting event? I volleyed the theories until there was a knock on the door and Jiles stuck his head in.

"He's here."

Detective Lou Pinner landed large and sweaty at the bar. Pinner was fat. He wore broad glasses that were too wide for his face and deflected his eyes. He looked like an angry lost man who ate too much meat and boozed big.

Jiles squeezed him for details with a fresh pint and his word we wouldn't tweet or talk to the press. Slice, Jewels, and I were already leaning in for details on Josie's case.

"Sonofabitch stole some lady's car outta Eagle Rock. We don't know where he abducted her but looks like he raped her in the back seat. Put a plastic bag over her head then strangled her with an extension cord."

It was ugly concise. Jewels peeled off. Guess she'd heard enough. But Jiles didn't skip a beat and fell back into step.

"Got any leads? Witnesses?"

Pinner grunted. "Nothing so far. No actionable prints. We're still sourcing traffic cams, ATMs. And running DNA...so far no hits in the system. But...we think there's a connection to two other recent murders."

"What other murders?"

"Girls. All in their early twenties."

Slice chimed in. "Like some kinda serial killer? In *Glendale*?!" I had to agree. It sounded impossible. But Pinner didn't flinch. Just shrugged it all off.

"The morons down at the station are calling him the Glendale Grabber. So far he's targeted three random women on the east side, if we include Josie Pendleton. All of them in their early twenties. Same MO. First he steals a car, abducts them at night, then rapes them in the back seat and finishes them off with a bag and the cord."

"The Glendale Grabber? What kinda stupid name is that?" Slice shot me a look. Amen, Slice.

"What's the time spread?" Jiles asked.

"First murder was May 4. Natalie Johnson—nursing student working after hours. Just moved out from Ohio. The other, Janet Pacci was abducted on June twenty-third on her way home from a shift at Burger King around nine p.m. No witnesses. They found her crumpled in the back seat of a stolen red Toyota in a parking lot off Fletcher and San Fernando."

Slice hung off every word, charged at this local development. Pinner slammed back his pint and his phone chimed with a text. He glanced at the screen, all impatient.

"You said you had something, Jiles?"

"Josie was here the day she was killed." The cop sparked up from his phone, intrigued. "She was getting hassled by some guy until Sammy the bull in shining armor over here stepped in and got his ass handed to him."

Pinner twisted my way, trying to square it. Slice jumped in, eager to lay out the sordid tale that ended with him and Pa pulling my broken face off the floor. The fat cop howled with laughter like some kinda drunk hyena. "Anyone get a picture of this guy?"

We all chimed *no*.

"He pay with a credit card, Jiles?"

"I'll check."

"We'll run it down. But honestly...doesn't feel like our guy. Whoever killed these girls was sick. Back alley peeper scum. Not some college punk." He swallowed back the rest of the pint. Lumbered off the stool and made for the door. "Gotta go. Autopsy results on Josie just came in. Thanks for the beer, Jiles.

Send me that guy's name."

"Can I come with you?" The words just spewed out. I'd never seen a dead body before and I didn't want to begin with Josie Pendleton. But I didn't have a choice. I'd never see her again. This was my last and only shot. And something dark and unhealthy inside me compelled me to step up.

The fat man stopped and looked me in the eyes, searching to see what kind of sick person wanted to see this murdered girl on a slab.

"I'm...I'm going to write an article about her."

"You can't write shit," Pinner barked. "This is an open case."

"Not *now*," I countered, "but after you find the guy...I'm gonna write an article about it. I'll write about you, too, if you want."

I prayed his ego would cave but Pinner shook his head. All dubious.

So I pointed at my broken face.

"I didn't even get a chance to talk to her."

He shot Jiles a look.

"He's good people, Lou," Jiles remarked. "Trust me. The kid wants to be a writer. Show him the thing. Show him how the world really works."

This brought Pinner an ugly kind of joy. "Think you can handle it?"

I felt a push deep in my gut.

I did not.

I was terrified. "Of course."

The cop grinned like a bully in a schoolyard.

"Better make me a hero," he said as he pushed open the door. "C'mon. Get in the car."

Friday, July 10th, 4:39 p.m.

Red lights flared and the alarm screamed as Pinner stormed through the metal detector, waving at a security guard he called Gordon.

"He's with me."

Gordon sized me up some.

Gordon was black with a smooth cracked face that had to be over seventy years old.

Gordon looked frail for any kind of security detail but you could tell he'd been at this gig a long time. Guarding ghosts and their shells. He caught my wide eyes. The short steps. He looked at Pinner.

"Tosser?"

Pinner nodded and Gordon smiled, like they were in on some kinda inside joke. "Well," the guard added, "welcome to the Los Angeles County Coroner."

I pretended not to care or understand as I emptied my pockets into the red plastic basket and passed through the gates of the morgue.

Pinner laid it out.

"We call first timers tossers cuz they always toss up their lunch."

"Swell."

"Be sure to check out Skeletons in the Closet on your way out," Gordon chimed in.

"Skeletons in the closet?"

Pinner shook his shoulders. "They got a gift shop now. Body

bags. Crime scene tape. Any chance to make a county buck."

Pinner stormed down the hallway without waiting as I scrambled to collect my phone and wallet. I nodded thanks to Gordon and marveled at how simple and quiet his life seemed. Standing guard above the shelves down below.

We hit the elevator.

We went down.

I felt that push in my guts again.

The doors opened.

The hallway was bright. Brighter than I expected.

The air smelled raw. Ugly and still.

Pinner grinned.

"You okay?"

I shrugged it off, all no big thing. On its face the joint was no different than a hospital. Sterile. Bright. Some people ambling around in scrubs. Looked like scrubs, anyway. There was no smell of death. There was nothing profound or touching or at all intriguing. Just sterile calm. A hallway filled with sour sadness and the spirit of rot.

Pinner rounded a corner and we walked into examination room 3A. The sight of the shelves hit me hard. Those steel covered human filing cabinets. Stacked on top of each other. Just as I'd expected but still my mouth slipped open a bit, taking them in.

"Hey, Marge."

Pinner spoke to a woman slouched over a sink washing something I didn't want to see with one of those huge wobbly overheard faucets that looked like they were going to blast out of control at any time.

"Hey, Pinner." She turned to dry her hands and saw me. "Jesus. On this one?"

"Relax. He's good."

"Good how?"

"Trust me, Marge."

"Is he an actor?"

"I'm not an act—"

"It doesn't matter what he is. He's with me. He's good to go. Come on, let's do this."

Marge huffed away and pulled a file from a wall holder. She shoved it in Pinner's chest and stepped up towards those damn steel shelves. Then threw her weight into the handle and hauled it open.

The feet came sliding out first. They looked almost soggy and blue as they came ripping towards us. The rest of her naked body followed suit and lodged tight with a click that sent a shimmer through her, jostling her skin and breasts as if there was life in there still.

But there wasn't.

And there she was.

Josie Pendleton.

Still. Silent. Naked and dead.

I stepped back like this was all some big violation, some big car accident of a mistake. I had no right to see her like this.

Pinner's eyes bore into me like that massive frail ego of his was on the line and screaming, *I vouched.*

I muscled up and stepped forward.

Her mouth hung slack and open. Her lips purple. Soft and saggy. Abandoned. Her eyelids were shut but there was a gap under her right side exposing a piece of her yellowing eyeball. I got a bit closer and stared at her skin. The light made her look almost green. You could see the veins in her breasts, broken and starting to rot under her skin. There was a tattoo on her upper right thigh. Some sort of a cloud shape with a hand and an arrow piercing through it. I needed to remember it. Carbon copy this image. This privilege. This part of her...

Staring at her naked body felt wrong.

It felt like a betrayal.

I looked away but it burned my memory like a sin. I felt that push in my guts. Something deeper and stronger inside me pushed back. Like I was here to help her.

Pinner crouched closer to her throat, eyeing the blue and purple bruises, curious.

"Premortem bruising from suffocation." Marge said flatly.

"Same cord?" he asked.

"The ligature patterns match but we didn't find any black fibers like the others."

Pinner kept it in neutral like nothing more than a math problem. "And these? Defensive wounds?" He motioned to three dark red scratches on her arm—like someone's fingernails had raked her forearm.

"No. Those are older. Based on the scabbing, I'd say about three days before she was killed. But we didn't find any trace DNA in the tissue."

"Three days?" I barked at the inconsistency. "I thought this was a random attack?" They looked surprised to hear my voice, or that I was even there.

"There's more on her back, too," Marge carried on, then rolled her over like Josie was just some hundred-pound loaf of bread. Someone's fingernails had raked at her soft flesh, leaving a collection of crimson scratches across her back.

"So she was bangin' Wolverine? Doesn't track with our timeline." He scanned her file, uninterested.

I played it through in my head, trying to catch up to with the game. "So someone else did those?"

Marge just nodded.

Pinner kept at the file. "And she was raped? Like the others?"

"Yea. SAK's already been sent to the lab but...I didn't see any semen. And there was considerably less tearing."

I burned inside. Buried it down. But Pinner perked up at this headline.

"So he wears a rubber this time?" The man twisted his head, curious.

"Comb turned up some disparate hairs," she added. "We'll run 'em, see if they match the other two."

"Maybe it's not the same guy," I said.

30

"Or maybe he's just getting smarter," Marge pointed out. "Covering his tracks."

Pinner wasn't sold. He stared at her body and a sliver of emotion pushed through his face. His thin lips growing tight. I could tell he was grinding his teeth. So the fat man was human, after all.

I fell into step and looked at her broken shell. Pinner caught my gaze. "You wanna touch her? Go ahead."

"Chrissake, Pinner," Marge rightly objected.

This was way wrong. But this was also my only chance. I reached out and touched her fingers. They were cold and felt almost wet. Steel waves shot up through my arms. Rippled down into my gut. I buried the push. The push pushed back.

"Ya tosser."

And then Pinner smiled like he'd won some ugly bet, watching my guts spray all over that steel sink.

Monday July 13th, 3:06 a.m.

They weren't nightmares.

Those images of Josie's slack mouth. Those cold fingers crawling along my skin. Her body surrounded by darkness. The denim floating without a head.

They were just flashing and spinning inside me. Smashing to the surface any chance they got.

I refused to be haunted.

No.

I was *absorbed*, that was all. And it was too damn hot and the AC hissed every nine seconds, so I stared sweaty at the ceiling in bed letting the drips hit the pillow. I stared alone. Stirring. Swirling. Like the more I thought about her, the more alive I became and refused to sleep.

I dressed and drove to Fred 62 in Los Feliz, smashing a black and white milkshake.

Three a.m. medicine.

Tomorrow was a new day.

Tomorrow I'd flush this crush and start fresh.

Monday, July 13th, 11:19 a.m.

Tomorrow ranked worse.
Josie's obituary flashed fierce in the California section.

Our hearts are broken...
It is with the utmost sadness...
A beautiful soul...
A life cut short...

In lieu of flowers I had to do something with this pain.

Wednesday, July 15th, 12:04 p.m.

Broken souls in dark clothes crowded the Forest Lawn grass around Josie's coffin. The punishing California sun flared. It was hot and sad.

I stood far back in the shade of an oak tree. The ultimate outsider. A peeping tom with noble intentions. A hundred sixty-three people surrounded the box. Josie Pendleton was dearly beloved.

I searched for a familiar face and came up empty. I couldn't tell who her parents were, though suspected her father was the sixty-five-year-old looking guy at the front in a heavy wool suit. Punishing himself in the heat. His expression stone cold, old school stoic. The kind of man who was saving the pain for later. All for himself, alone. Clasping his elbow was a tiny and tidy conservative looking woman in her late fifties. She wasn't crying now, but even from far away I could see she'd been at it for days. The mother. Wiped clean from anguish. Bone dry.

A minister garbled out some bullshit about God. As if Josie might be better off with *him* now. Ranting and pretending like she wasn't rotting inside that box only fifteen feet away.

Him. The collared hypocrisy.

Next up was a twenty-something girl in a spaghetti strap dress clinging to a guitar and a plastic red stool. She perched herself down near the flowers and started strumming some melody meant to destroy people's hearts. It worked. Something about angels and love and always being together. C minor pain. This wasn't a celebration of life. This was a cruel reminder of the monsters among us.

The service broke up and people ambled around the green, so I figured this was my window of opportunity. I stepped out of the shade and walked towards the congregation. Head hung low.

I kept sad and played the good soldier. No one paid me much attention. But I wanted them to see how I understood. How I felt a fraction of their pain. Hungry for just a slice of empathy I knew I didn't deserve...

I stared at the beautiful flowers.

A woman with fierce bangs and big red lips locked on me, looking lost, and she wrapped me in a hug like some crazy aunt. She moved on, her work complete. I ambled undercover and caught the gaze of a woman staring at the flowers. She looked about thirty. She looked like a skinny sea gull, ruffled up in the flock with gangly long stems, blinking hopeful and lost.

Wait.

It was my Facebook amigo. Allison Hager. Who the hell was Allison Hager? Mike's friend—? Coachella—? From the Lovely—? I rolodexed hard but came up empty. Nevertheless, I had a lead. I had an opening. It was time to dance.

"Allison?"

"...Sam?"

I opened strong with a hug. Wrapped her tight, and she doubled down with a tight squeeze in what felt like ripped yoga arms. I held on for a moment too long in part because I wanted to be on Team Josie Sad, in part because I hoped maybe holding onto this woman might shake some memory loose. And if I'm being honest because she smelled so damn pretty. Blindsiding me, reminding me, I really do need to hug people more often.

She stepped back and looked me in the eye. We rocked the appropriate sad-doesn't-this-suck-we're-here looks then I bled into the awkward defense maneuver.

"It's good to see you. Been forever."

"How've you been?! I didn't know you were even friends with Josie..."

I shrugged and shaded the truth. "We weren't all that close

but I was...well...I really wanted to be here."

She shook her head like it was too awful to even comprehend the events that led us to this graveyard. I volleyed it right back as if I had the right to.

"That's sweet of you. Are you coming to the reception?"

"Are you going?"

"Yeah, of course."

"Where is it again?"

"Her aunt's house in South Pas'."

"Right." I pulled out my phone—aka the bait. "My car's getting worked on...I guess I could Uber there."

"Oh." She looked surprised and caught off guard. "Well...I'm driving. I can take you."

"You sure?"

"Yah. We gotta catch up...I wanna hear all about Karen. I haven't talked to her in ages...How is she?"

Bam! KAREN. Crystal now: Allison and Karen. The connection made. The world's foremost perfect sister. Karen had perfect teeth. A perfect husband. A perfect life. A nurse mending souls and making the world a better place. A genuinely kind and beautiful person. I hated her. But mostly, really, I loved her. She was my younger sister, after all. I hadn't talked to her in a while, either. I was sure she was fine. She always was.

"I haven't talked to her in a while, either. I'm sure she's fine. She always is."

"I miss her. Is she still in Portland?"

"Yup. Still with Paul. Workin' at the hospital."

"She's the best. And what about your parents? Everyone good?"

My parents *were* good. Better than good. They did everything right. Provided means. Taught me manners. Filled me with twenty-first century promise.

You can do whatever you want in this world, Sam.

Work hard play hard, son. My father hounded the mantra which only made my current slump all the more distressful.

36

They failed to understand my creative fueled U turn. *How could you pull the plug? After all that hard work. Abandon your paycheck. Your health insurance. A pretty girl who cooked.* I was an island to them now, drifting further and further away from reason into a sea of trouble.

But they *were* good, I assured Allison.

She smiled, happy to hear it.

And I smiled, buzzing victorious. It was probably wrong. But I had a lead. An asset in Josie's world, and one I intended to heartlessly exploit.

We hit the 110 speedway, snaking out the east side of downtown towards South Pasadena. Allison drove her tight grey Audi fast like she knew the bends well. I gave her the boring scoop on Karen. Happy fine. She hammered me with questions about my own life since I quit advertising. I lied my ass off bandaging my failure with fake gigs. Magazine articles, upcoming potential TV shows and important deadlines. Padding my ego just long enough til she got quiet and I could ask her about Josie.

"So, how did you know Josie?"

"We volunteered at Backyard Dreams together."

"Backyard what?"

"It's a charity. They fix and design playgrounds for kids with disabilities. We worked a lot of the same events. Like fundraiser galas. Charity walks."

"Sounds noble."

Allison shrugged it off, like she didn't want the props. "How did you know her?"

"I met her at The Damned Lovely."

"You mean that nasty dive bar in Glendale? I went there once." The girl winced. "That place is creepy weird."

Eeeasy, Allison. I smiled bright with defense. "I live nearby so I like to grab a drink there once in a while."

"Why was Josie there?"

"Probably why most people go to a bar. Grab a drink. Actually, she was reading a book at the bar."

"Wait. Josie went to *read* in that dump?" I shrugged the truth. "That doesn't sound like her. When was this?"

"She was there a bunch. Last time I saw her was on the day she was, you know…" I trailed off, unwilling to voice the obvious.

Allison gripped the wheel and I could see her fingers clasping white and tight. "So…wait. *That's* where she was coming from the night she was killed?"

I shrugged, compliant.

"You were one of the last people to see her alive?"

"It was earlier in the day, but I guess in some ways."

The car weaved right, like she was having a hard time staying in the lane. "What did you guys talk about?"

"We didn't really talk much. Like I said, she kinda kept to herself. I mean, I…" Her eyes dug in. "Some guy was buggin' her and I told him to back off."

"What guy?"

"Some frat boy asshole. He was hitting on her and I asked him to back off."

Allison was concerned and I could see her spinning out inside. "Did you tell the police? Maybe that was the guy who—"

"I really don't think so, Allison. But I did talk to the police and they're looking into it, but they don't think so, either. This guy at the bar was a total douche. There's no way he was a serial killer."

The Audi swerved outta the lane now. "Serial killer? What are you talking about?" A white Lexus blared her horn from behind.

Shit. Right. No one outside the department knew that.

"Nothing. Nothing. I'm…I just think crazy sometimes."

She regained control of the vehicle but the air got tight. Allison drove in silence. I tried to take the stink off it all and opened up about Karen and the good ol' days back in Oregon, but I'd poisoned some kind of well and Allison clammed up hard and uncomfortable.

We parked on a steep side street and walked up to a South Pas mansion on a hill in complete silence.

We stepped inside and found the buzzing crowd of well-dressed mourners sloshing booze and eating hors d'oeuvres. Allison said she was going to use the restroom, disappearing like she was eager to part ways.

I kept my head down and eyes up. You could feel the old school Pasadena money in the room. Bold fat beams of wood overhead. Old fart art on the wall like rip-off Constables and Degas. Pictures of grandkids smiling on sailboats.

The rooms were filled with healthy, happy people.

I smashed three deviled eggs for fuel. It was time to dig in. Time to investigate. Time for a burst. I slinked to the bar and pinched a glass of the Cabernet on offer. Sweet dark swill, baby.

I looked around the room: fancy suits. Beautiful faces stuck in an ugly present.

I was an imposter.

I was a spy.

I felt glorious.

I *was* the inner circle.

I worked the room, eager to soak up every piece of Josie's backstory and caught some shreds of conversation about her Women In Art classes at college. Her love of eighties' sitcoms. Her passion for charity work. That trip she took to Paris right after college. Her infectious laugh. Nothing but the good.

I caught a framed picture of a teenage Josie clasping a snowboard on a mountain, surrounded by two people I recognized from the service. One of 'em was guitar girl. The other was a tall, good-looking guy I pegged as her brother.

"I took that picture."

Some whiskey-soaked air blasted my flank. I craned to see the source: a tired and worn-out mouth attached to a saucy

Mrs. Robinson smile.

"We were in Mammoth over Thanksgiving weekend. Those three were at each other's throats the entire holiday."

"They *look* happy."

"I'm Gloria, Josie's aunt." Then, she whispered like some kinda conspirator, "The fun aunt."

"I'm Sam. Nice to meet you."

"How did you know Josie?"

"To be honest, I didn't really." Her eyes got tight but since my ride with Allison I'd rehearsed the new angle in my head. "They say you show up to funerals for the people who are there, not the ones that are gone, right?"

She bought it and smiled saucy again. "Nice to meet you, Sam."

We kept up the pleasantries. She talked close and reeked boozy. But it wasn't tragic, it was endearing. My kind of sorrow. She kept clawing at my shoulder with perfect glossy nails like a predator.

"What do you do?"

Goddamn LA. Even at a funeral.

"I'm a writer."

"What do you write?"

Something about her boozy glare made me feel comfortable enough to tell her the truth. Like my kinda people. "I just finished a book."

"What kind of book?"

"The unpublished-on-my-hard-drive kind."

She laughed with a bellow that stung my gut but I wheeled restraint, reminding myself to be professional. On a mission, after all.

"So...tell me about Josie."

She stared at that picture on the wall, drifting into it. "Josie was a force. That day on the hill...She had just taken up snowboarding. Her brother, David, was outshining her on the slopes but she refused to back down when he dared her to go down the Grand Gully—this nasty black diamond run. So she spilled over the edge of the slope, fearless, completely out of control, and showed him up. And she also broke her wrist. Daring. Bold. Courageous. That was Josie. She wasn't afraid of anything—" She started welling up with pain and tears, trying to fight it all off with a plastered smile. "They better find this monster."

"They will." I reassured her as she drifted off to find something to wipe away her tears.

I ambled through the crowd, hoping to find Allison and buy back some charity. I couldn't find her and the room was thinning fast. I could feel the glares and stares coming in hard. *Who's that guy?* So I called a car and picked up the Volt from the cemetery. But I was charged. Compelled to report back to Benny and the slugs at the bar about the day.

They were gonna love this shit.

Wednesday July 15th, 6:12 p.m.

The Pluckin Strummers were flappin' when I walked through the door. The City of Angels' foremost ukulele club. Of all the joints in all the cities I gotta pick the one who hosts the bloody Pluckin Strummers.

Foremost, my ass.

Jiles caught my snarl and smiled. The man loved the Strummers and forced us regs to put up with the scratch every week. How does a badass ex-cop, a man with taste and experience, a man who understands the importance of Sam Cooke, put up with this squeal?

Slice hit me with a collegiate nod. He hated this scratch, too. I ordered a Bulleit and unloaded my tale. He was rapt. The perfect audience. A sucker for an ugly hero. Then I hit the box. I needed to write. I needed to expel my experience.

The players.

The place.

The ride.

The backstory on Josie.

I'd had no right to be there, but it only made it more exhilarating. Soaking up the pain under that cloak of a lie. Pretending to be a member of the broken Josie club. I felt like I belonged.

An hour later, I cracked the box and braved the Strummers. Ordered another burst that slipped down speedy and smooth. I caught Lily on the corner barstool with a stack of papers. Lily was our resident council. We called her Lily the Lawyer cuz she wore floral patterns. Roses. Tulips. Irises. Never lilies. Had to hand it to Slice for that ingenious tag. She came in most nights after nine.

"Heya, Lily."

"Sam."

"Working late again?"

She shrugged it off like she didn't have a choice. Lily was like bad scotch—a little strong and off putting upfront but once she got into your bones quite the delightful presence.

"How's the little one?"

"Sleeps, shits, and eats."

Lily was tough, tight, and liked to booze. Rum and Diet Coke with lime. She worked cases hard through the night with an office three blocks down, and a luckless stay-at-home-husband who looked after their kid. We got the feeling she didn't take to being a mom much. We got that feeling because she told us last Christmas when Jiles bought us a round and we all got drunk singing "Silver Bells" together. Lily was cold and fierce and I adored her. She floated me gigs once and a while. File this. Write some copy. Paralegal blather that paid straight.

The Strummers broke the set. Slice and I burst some claps.

"Hey, Lily, how can we get Jiles to stomp out the Strummers?"

"I'm sick of that jukebox. You need to open your mind to new things, Sam."

I nodded to her stack of files. "How's the law?"

"She's a bear."

"Got anything for me?"

"Maybe in a few days."

"You know where to find me."

I swilled my drink dry and felt my reality piss back in with a whisper. *The money's running out, Sssssammy.*

I hadn't hit the Volt in days. I needed to earn some cake. I ordered one more shot of Bulleit, slammed her back, and pulled out my car keys.

Jiles shot me a crooked look.

I blamed it on the Pluckin Strummers.

43

Thursday, July 16th, 3:11 p.m.

Hi, James? I'm Sam.
 Hi, Rebecca? I'm Sam.
 Hi, Yolanda? I'm Sam.
 I drove and slept and ate and dreamed of Josie on the slab.
 Rinse and repeat this punishing obsession.

I hit the box. The silence was strict. The bar was empty until eleven. I needed product. I needed pages. I needed content. I needed a goddamn idea. The tank was dry so I wrote about Josie. About her funeral. The faces and pain. The uncomfortable delight derived from it all. I steered clear of the booze. I called it discipline.
 I drove and slept and ate and dreamed of Josie on the slab.
 I hit the box.
 I wrote scratch.
 I was a hack with discipline.
 Rinse and repeat.

Monday, July 20th, 3:13 p.m.

Finally, Pinner rolled in and grunted hello to Jiles. He saw me and shot over a cold look. He could tell I was hungry for an update and needed to feed.

"Where you at on the case, Lou? I haven't heard from you. There's nothing online. It's like nobody cares, like they've just moved on to some other—"

"Jesus, Sammy, let the man sit down first. Back off a little," Slice barked.

"Back off? I've been backed off for like a week. Even I know the chances of solving a homicide after forty-eight hours without a lead suspect only get worse and worse. I mean, I figure you got someone you're looking at, right?"

"Go fuck yourself, Sammy," Pinner snapped.

Jiles stepped over with a glare that screamed louder than words. It wasn't nothin when Jiles stepped up. I could tell he understood the look behind Pinner's face. Attuned to the pain.

"Trail's cold kid."

"Already?"

Pinner swallowed his lager and laid it out. "Rape kit's a bust. We're still waiting on the DNA but no matching prints. Forensics take time. But there's no witnesses. We've been all over it. Checked cameras within a three-block radius of where we think she was abducted. We checked cameras outside her apartment. Up the street. Down the street. We checked all of it. It was a random attack. All three of them were. You know what random means? It means there's no pattern. Whoever this guy was, was smart cuz he picked an area that *had* no cameras. No pedestrians. No *trail*."

"But what about those scratches?"

"What about 'em? She wasn't killed by some crazy ex-boyfriend. We already cleared it. Talked to her family. Friends. Checked her phone records. She wasn't seeing anyone. Nothing regular. Forget the scratches. That happened three days before she was murdered..." Pinner's nails dug into the bar. He pushed off hard and lumbered into the pisser.

Jiles waved me over. "He's into it, Sammy. You gotta trust him. Pinner's good. Sometimes these things take time."

"I just think there might be more to go on—"

"Cuz you don't know what it's like," Jiles snapped. "These are the hardest ones. Attacks like these? We have to go on evidence. Evidence a bunch of morons on a jury can't push back against. So we work the DNA. Fingerprints. Cameras. Witnesses. Without those? We gotta cast wider. Look at motive. Drill down on lovers. Ambition. Cash. She drops—who stands to gain? When that runs dry, we're in real trouble. Because now we got a predator. We know these guys, they're a species. A type. Something in their brain, like a switch snapping circuits on and off, on and off and it's all they can see. Wired tight, fixin' a target. Brunette. Soft brown eyes with tight tits. And inside, this monster says: THAT ONE. They think about her. They follow her. They jerk off to her. It's all they can do until they snap and say now. *Now* I need the skin. With any luck they get impatient. And leave a trail. But the good ones know better. They cover their tracks. They know the roads we'll take. So they lay in wait. Quiet. Which means it's harder to source. We get spun around. Running leads that feed into nothing. And then guess what happens?"

"What?"

"Another one drops. Only now this one burns bright. Worse even. Just when you think it wasn't possible but now we got *another* one and she was only fourteen and he ripped her into pieces with a Cutco breadknife.

46

"And then another.

"And then they stack and stack and something inside us cracks so we pound booze and weave home willing ourselves, PRAYING—praying on all fours, on our cold bathroom tile, alone, where our wife won't catch us, where PLEASE GOD our kids won't witness the pain we're in—rambling for a break, a lead, a tell, any goddamn thing, praying into some godless space that maybe tomorrow…maybe tomorrow we'll ache a little less. Just a little less and find these monsters."

Jiles stopped talking and took a deep breath, like he needed to step outta something dark, and I could hear the air spewing out of his nose. "So back off, a little. He's workin'." Jiles stepped away to fix a Manhattan for table twelve.

It was speeches like these, bursts of his past and little shrugs of hard-fought acceptance, which reminded me why I loved this man so much.

Pinner lumbered back to the bar. The poor bastard was run tight. Like he was burning underneath. I skated the case and talked Dodgers. It all felt soft and sad. Pinner was a dick, a contemptible glutton with terrible morals, but even I felt bad for the guy. After all, he stood up for something that still mattered.

Justice. Old school, beautiful justice.

We didn't talk about Josie.

I bought him some more booze.

Tuesday, July 21st, 4:55 p.m.

Life pressed on.

Word went public about the Glendale Grabber. The world's worst named serial killer. Three girls so far.

My fixation only festered.

That denim shirt burning bright.

Those scratches.

Three days *before* the attack.

Whothehell scratched her like that?

Maybe in my heart I knew it wasn't connected to the murder. But somehow I didn't care. I wanted the truth. Even if it was just some guy she was sleeping with, I felt compelled to know who. Who got the goods? Who got to touch her warm skin?

This was a private obsession.

My envy was disgusting and I was more than okay with that.

I refused to clean it up. To tailor the edges.

This was pure. And I was going to dig deep into the root of my obsession because it was mine alone. I mean, I needed something to believe in. Something to wake up to. Something to want.

I took action and texted our Facebook friendly Allison Hager.

I opened formal. *Despite the circumstances it was great seeing you the other day. Wanna grab drinks sometime?*

Those three promising dots flared instantly.

Love to! when/where?

How about the Damned Lovely? I was gonna go there in

honor of Josie. Maybe this Thursday at 8?

k

She hit me back with a "k." The lowest common denominator of digital communication. Maybe she was driving. A moment with her boss. On a call. I gave her the benefit of the text doubt.

Look forward to it.

☺

A smiley face rebound. An uptick of respect. This was victory.

Thursday, July 23rd, 7:56 p.m.

I decided early on it was important not to sleep with Allison Hager.

It would only complicate things.

I needed to think straight with intention and boozy charisma.

I was pretty sure she didn't want to sleep with me either, but then again, those three dots popped up so fast I couldn't help but smell a whiff of want.

The door slipped open wafting heat and sunshine, and Allison rolled in wearing a slim red sundress and a loose ponytail. She had broad shoulders and seemed taller than the last time we met. Formidable. Her collarbones were on magnificent display. I played it cool like, like I didn't want to devour every piece of her, and we smiled like friends as I offered to buy her a glass of wine.

"I think I need something a little stronger. They make a good rusty nail?"

This was going to be harder than I thought.

"The best."

Jewels rolled up to our table, sizing up Allison. She shot me a look, almost surprised I was sitting/knew/able to talk to a woman like the one so poised sitting across from me but god bless her, reserved her comments for later.

We ordered up. Settled in with that awkward look in the eye ready for battle. I flared more lies about my any-minute-now successful writing career and steered back to tangibles like my annoying roommate and appetite for Cronenberg films in December.

"How long have you been out here?"

"Like seven years," she said.

We danced the veritable LA checklist. Zip codes, jobs, and whether we'd come to terms with living in this beautiful beast.

Lou Reed's voice bubbled out into the air calling it *a perfect day,* and Allison looked a little confused like she knew the song but couldn't place it.

"Lou Reed."

"Is that who this is? I know this song, but I didn't know the name, you know? Like I've heard it before but…"

"If you're ever looking for music that can ignite something inside you, I highly recommend Lou Reed."

She smiled skeptical.

"Seriously. His *Transformer* album is astounding. I mean…at first it sounds, kinda awkward and glam but then, it gets into your bones. Listen to it loud and alone and when you want to just break away from something. It'll move you, trust me."

Allison smiled. She had a dimple on the right side of her chin. But it didn't peek out when she laughed, only when she was mildly confused about something, like she looked now. Curious. Like—why the hell are we listening to Lou Reed in this nasty bar, anyway? Then, as if she couldn't contain it any longer, her eyes danced around the tired room and sad faces.

"So…*this* is where you met Josie?"

"Yeah. She came in from time to time. Sat at the bar. By herself usually."

"She came here all alone? That's so weird."

"Why?"

"It just doesn't seem like her."

I shrugged. "She usually read a book at the bar."

Allison shuddered a little like none of this made any sense. So I pounced.

"This might sound kinda weird but when she was here, I

noticed she had some pretty big scratches on her arm. Like three big ones right on her forearm—" I dragged my hands across my arm to indicate the pattern and severity.

She shot me a confused look. "Scratches?"

"Yeah. They looked pretty deep...I just got to wondering...was Josie in any kind of trouble?"

"No, not that I know of."

"Do you know who might have scratched her like that?"

"I have no idea."

We stewed in that oddness, staring at each other. Allison squirmed, uneasy at the line of questioning. But then she tilted her head, like some jagged memory came flooding in.

"I guess she had been acting kinda weird lately. At the charity, I asked her if anything was wrong and she skirted the question, but I could tell something was bothering her so I didn't let it go."

"What did she say?"

"She played it off like I was crazy to even ask. Except...at one point, she looked sad. Like, off. She turned and said the weirdest thing. She said: 'This place is rotten.'"

"What place was rotten?"

"The charity. She said Backyard Dreams was rotten. When I asked what she was talking about she got pretty cagey—didn't wanna get into it. That was all I could ever get out of her. It was so strange. I mean. They fix playgrounds for kids. What's so rotten about that?"

"Wait, you think this has anything to do with what happened to her?"

"I don't know. I guess not. I mean, the police all say it was this crazy rapist on the loose."

"Yea, but did you tell them? Maybe there's more to it, maybe she discovered something and someone found out and so they pretended to kill her like this guy's been doing..."

I trailed off cuz Allison stared at her rusty nail with wide sad eyes that suddenly filled with tears. She sat there frozen, letting them well up and break, flooding down her cheeks. Then she looked at me, coldly.

"Why are you asking me these questions, Sam? Why did you want to have drinks with me tonight?"

Over at the bar, Pa and Slice caught her sharp tone. Even Lily looked up.

"I wanted to see you."

"To talk about Josie?"

"Not just Josie. I didn't mean to upset you—"

"Why did you want to meet me *here*?"

"I seriously like this bar. I thought it would be nice to…I don't know…honor her a little."

"Honor her. Here? This place is depressing. What happened to Josie was sad and horrific and I don't understand why you're talking about scratches on her arm, why you're asking me about her…"

"I'm sorry."

Allison's eyes bore into me. Like they'd figured out some ugly truth. "Did you even know her?"

Fuck it. Time to bleed the truth. "No. I never even talked to her. I hardly said one word to her. I sat here and stared at her, wondering what kind of person she was. Who she was in this world…Then some guy started hitting on her and something in me snapped so I stepped in and my got my ass handed to me. I'd never even been in a fight before, but I felt proud of myself for the first time in a long time, like I'd done something meaningful. I never saw her again. Kept hoping she'd come back here and then I heard she'd been killed. That's when I got sucked up in all this, and to be honest, I just haven't been able to put it away or think about much else."

"There's nothing about this place that honors who Josie was or what she stood for in this world."

"It's not just her, I wanted to see you too, Allison."

She grabbed her purse, and stood tall. "I don't believe you."

She crossed past the listless seals soaking up the drama at the bar and burst outside.

The room got quiet.

Lily straightened up and represented, "She's got a point, Sam. She was friends with the woman and all you wanna do is talk about her murder. What do you expect?"

Slice chimed in, "Yea, why do you care so much? You didn't even know this girl."

"Because I *wanted* to know her, Slice. Because I didn't get a *chance* to know her. Why's that so hard for people to understand?"

"You had your chance when she was sitting right there at the bar and you let it go. You're just bitter that you didn't do anything about it sooner."

"The hell I didn't! When that chump was hitting on her I was the one who stepped up."

"The guy knocked you flat on your ass, Sam. You weren't some hero, some knight in shining armor. You just feel guilty—guilty that you sat there and ogled her, hiding in that back room instead of manning up and speaking to her. It's your own fault. You can't take it back. And now, she's dead. That's that. So let it go already, get on with your life. You can't go back…"

I wanted to scream and kick Slice in the face for being right. But instead I walked outside into the heat and hit the tracks along San Fernando. I walked angry and lost. Like I should have been ashamed of my obsession, but instead, instead in that stifling dry heat, walking along those train tracks with no destination in sight or mind, felt an unyielding conviction that Josie Pendleton's murder was not just a flittering fancy but rather a defining cornerstone that had the potential to redefine my life.

I needed to know more about this rotten charity.

Friday, July 24th, 9:12 a.m.

I swilled some coffee and three ibuprofens for breakfast. My head was in a vise but I refused to let it rule the roost. The apartment wouldn't get hot for another two hours and with Nick magically out, I chose to work from home.

I spooned peanut butter and fired up Benny and began digging into this charity online.

Backyard Dreams was created by an entertainment lawyer named Glenn Royce who had a four-year-old nephew named Cole. Some negligent doctor botched Cole's welcome into this world and the poor kid missed his first burst of oxygen. One day Glenn took his nephew to some swings in Burbank and the lil' tike slipped off the strap, and smashed his cheek in half. His lawyer uncle pegged an opening and with the winnings from the lawsuit against the city, opened a charity that worked to fix all playgrounds for special needs kids. What I pegged as nothing more than a feel-good romp for rich white folks looking for a tax break was actually a pretty decent racket. They had expanded all over the city—slapping bucket style seats on swing-sets and wheelchair accessible ramps. The board of directors was made up of glossy celebrities looking to pin their name, and excessive earnings, onto something that made them sleep smooth past midnight.

They seemed to be pushing the needle in the right direction and I could see why Josie would want to help their mission.

There were no ugly headlines. No breaking scandals, no shady secrets exposed. Just fundraising balls with has-been low-grade celebs. Charity walks. Galas. They were making good money and putting it back into the parks so damaged kids could swing safe. A venerable hats off...

So what was so rotten about that?

According to their website, a woman named Susan Glasser ran the day-to-day operations. I grabbed my phone and called Miss Glasser. She sounded tired and overworked like the rest of the world, especially put off by the cold call interruption.

"I'm sorry, but why are you calling?"

I planted my ace up front: "It's something I've been putting off for too long, figured I'd stop dragging my heels and"— injecting some legit enthusiasm—"start today...Do you have a need for any volunteers?"

Miss Glasser perked right up. "Oh yes. Yes, for sure."

She tested the waters on skills and schedules. How I could be of most help. How best to pluck my time. She told me they'd been downsizing and just moved offices from Beverly Hills to North Hollywood. I bent the truth and told her I lived in the neighborhood. She said there was a lot of grunt work still to be covered. Unpacking boxes. Putting up shelves...She let the request hang long and hard.

"Happy to help in any way that I can."

She wolfed up the bait and we were suddenly best friends.

I shaved smooth and showered. Stole three of Nick's bagels, slapped on a collared shirt, and hit the Volt.

I was going in.

Sunday, July 26th, 2:06 p.m.

Backyard Dreams had an office in North Hollywood off Lankershim. Deep in the valley of displaced dreams and runoff satisfaction. A cross-section of start-up families, second gen' immigrants, and struggling actors. A land of faux happiness you could smell driving down the main strip. I mean, does anyone move to Los Angeles, California with dreams of living in North Hollywood?

I rolled up to an ugly beige building with eighties' stucco and clay tiles on the roof. Walked up some stairs to the second floor and rapped on 206. A woman on the weathered side of forty-five opened the door and I pegged Miss Glasser for what she was. Tired and spent. She greeted me with a wary handshake and a distrusting smile. Who could blame her? I mean, who the hell picks up the phone on a Tuesday morning, hears from someone who says they just wanna help, then actually shows up an hour later with some freshly stolen bagels and a smile.

A man with an undercover bent.

A man with a zeal for intel.

Me. All glorious me, now.

She welcomed me inside the space. We waxed pleasantries. We danced courteous and well intentioned. Smiling. I needed to be patient and play the long con if I was gonna find out what was so damn rotten here.

"Put me to work, Miss Glasser...I'm all yours."

She showed me around the office. It was smaller than I expected. And, frankly, not as nice given the scope of their celebrity rolodex chippin' in all that cash. She made excuses for the state of affairs and I pretended to care. There were boxes lining the walls. Paintings parked against the walls.

This is going to suck.

She showed me around and got right to it.

"What I really need help with is getting this place organized. The kitchen. Unpacking Glenn's office. Oh, and hanging some of these frames so I can get them off the ground. I've marked spots on the walls where I want them with that blue tape. Think you could do that?"

"Of course."

She was already digging out a hammer from a toolbox and showing me which frames went where until a phone rang in the distance, so I seized the opportunity.

"Looks pretty straightforward. I'll just jump in and if I have any questions, I'll come find you."

"Okay, great. Great. And *thank* you," she muttered, like oddly reassured.

Glasser seemed genuinely relieved as she hustled off to get the phone. I grabbed the hammer and one of those picture-hanging hooks. The first framed photo was a shot of a large man in bold black glasses celebrating with a bunch of broken smiling children at a ribbon cutting ceremony. I recognized the guy from my research—Glenn Royce—the founding lawyer.

He looked rich.

Happy and genuinely fulfilled. I hated him immediately.

I hammered the wall and hoped for the best. This was me making a charitable difference, baby.

Next up was a poster-sized picture of a large crowd of volunteers at a fundraising walk. People filled with pride, making the world a better place—

Josie.

There she was. Smack in the middle. Smiling. Ripe with life.

Her arms wrapped around some fellow volunteers. She looked happy. Proud. Beaming like I'd never seen before, and it knocked me on my ass. I stumbled back, tripping over a metal lamp, sending us both crashing to the ground.

Glasser came bounding around the corner with a terrified look on her face, as I scrambled to get on my feet. She furrowed her brows, rightly wondering just who the hell did she entrust this office to, anyway?

"Sorry. Tripped on the cord. All good."

I bumbled up and tried to steer her eyes towards my formidable work hanging on the walls so far. "Look good so far?"

"Yes. Fine. Good. Good."

Glasser approached the wall and leveled off each corner as if she needed to put her own stamp on them. Marking her territory but still wary.

"Are you going to be alright back here?"

"Right as rain, Miss Glasser. Seriously, I just tripped is all."

"Okay." She lumbered off, uneasy.

The instant she disappeared, I locked back on that image of Josie. A wave of emotion smacked me and that dry crackle in the back of my throat swelled. This girl staring back at the world that destroyed her.

So, what the hell was so rotten about this place, Josie? And just how the hell was I gonna find out?

There were stacks of boxes at the foot of a built-in filing cabinet in the back corner of the room. I skipped the lids off and flipped through the beige folders. Gala invite lists. Manuals and warranties. Donor lists. Associate holdings. Certificates. Insurance statements. City permits.

Dreck.

It immediately occurred to me how insurmountable and poorly strategized my plan was. *What the hell I was expecting to find?* A secret red dossier labeled *Rotten Holdings*? I needed backstory and understanding of the ins and outs of the charity. I was gonna have to dive deeper, suck it up with my new pal Glasser, and suspected those bagels were my ticket in.

* * *

Glasser smashed a quarter of her bagel unwilling to wait for it toast properly. I couldn't tell if she loved the taste of it or loved the fact that someone finally brought her something. Anything. The woman seemed starved for attention. Recognition. Respect. And apparently a cinnamon and raisin bagel did wonders for her loneliness.

I pegged her for an aged-out actress. Yeah. A college theater major with a bucket of commercials under her belt who never even came close to success. Someone who desperately needed to pivot against those tireless auditions and incoming wrinkles. Those untenable leads. Those fading bit parts. The hustle run ragged and flat flat broke. Crying on the inside of her car, locked in 101 traffic. The Lankershim runoff type. Yeah, you could smell the noble tragedy on her.

But I played positive. After all, she turned it around. She found purpose in a charity. What's so terrible about that? When she asked me about my own life, I began throwing out the usual bent on my successful writing career. *Making it work so far!*

She volleyed it back with her own tale. Miss Glasser was long divorced. No kids. Just a green parakeet named Montgomery. She crooned on about Montgomery's magnificent plumage. I rocked a marvelous job of pretending to care until a quiet down beat enabled me to lob out a baited hook.

"How many people does it take to run an outfit like this?"

"Glenn hired me to run day to day operations so I'm kind of in charge of it all. But we have a stable of regular volunteers who chip in. Accountants. Student interns. Lawyers. Friends of friends. Favors! You'd be surprised how generous people can be with their time when you ask them to help for a good cause."

"In LA? Yeah, that kind of does surprise me," I joked.

Glasser smirked. The joke didn't land. I was tired of trolling and went for the goods.

"Have there been any problems at the charity recently?"

She looked at me wide-eyed like a goose. "Problems?"

"I thought I read a while back about some scandal here? But I might be mixing that up with some other charity. I do a lot of research for my writing."

"We had one bad apple—a teenage volunteer who was stealing our petty cash. He wasn't very smart. I caught him red-handed in the office. But that was two years ago."

"Hmmm. Yeah no, that wasn't it. For some reason I thought I heard about this charity in the news recently."

Glasser shifted in her seat, like I'd pressed a fresh bruise. She looked at the floor and spoke slowly. "Well...that's possible. Have you heard about this...Glendale Grabber?"

I played it cooool and neutral. "Sure...why?"

She got awful quiet and I got awful happy.

"One of the girls, she...she volunteered here. Josie...she was a lovely girl. It's been very sad for our team..."

"Oh my god. I'm so sorry. Josie—yes, of course, I mean, I read about her."

"We were all so devastated. She'd been helping out for about a year and a half. She was a real gem."

Glasser welled up.

Shit.

The hook ripped too hard and I was dragging her down. I tried not to dwell on this collateral damage. I tried to think about Josie screaming for help, for justice from the grave. And I, her unyielding soldier.

It didn't work.

Glasser kept crying. Deeper now. Heaving hard for oxygen. Like this was almost her first time letting it out. She apologized for crying and I legit burned inside to see her so cut up.

"I'm sorry. It's just been hard...how could someone do something so horrific...?"

"I know it's terrible. Horrible."

I nodded and before thinking better of it, reached out my hand in condolence, putting it on top of hers. The gesture caught her off guard, like she'd not been touched by someone that way, or anyway, in far too long a time. She looked at me with quiet and awkward appreciation.

"I'm sure the police are on it and are going to find this man soon," I reassured her. We chewed bagels in silence. I gingerly powered on.

"I can't imagine how hard that must've been for you."

"For Glenn, especially. He was absolutely devastated. Broken. We hosted a beautiful brunch for all the volunteers who knew her. It was touching how people came together. Celebrating her life."

"Glenn...the founder?"

"That's right. He's a wonderful man. A visionary. Glenn was only twenty-eight years old when he started this charity. He cobbled together an army and look what we've accomplished. Fourteen specialized playgrounds in LA County, all started in his basement, and look at us now..."

She looked around the room as if to take in some kind of splendor of this NoHo shell.

"Glenn's been a wreck, to be perfectly honest, but we've all been there for him. That's part of the reason why this move has been so hard. Usually I'd have Glenn to weigh in but he's so been so crushed. I couldn't even get him on the phone for days."

"Tough stuff."

"I couldn't really blame him, given how awful and sad it is...But I mean, at the end of the day, he's the one who has to make all the decisions. Pay the bills. I couldn't even pay the moving company on time."

As we finished up our bagels, Glasser pointed to three cans of midnight blue latex paint looming in the corner next to a roller and brush in a tray like a ticking time-suck grenade.

"Sam, are you any good at painting?"

My guilt for dragging her down took over my scorching hatred for all things manual labor.

"Any good? I'm like a goddamn Bob Ross, Miss Glasser."

She hit me with another pigeon blank stare. And as the joke blew cold, I quickly realized I'd be stuck here in hell for hours with that paintbrush in my hand.

Tuesday, July 28th, 3:11 p.m.

I was a devoted bastard.

The kitchen was painted.

File cabinets filled.

Pictures hung.

Windows cleaned.

I burned up two more afternoons helping Susan Glasser establish Backyard Dreams' new office in NoHo. Part of me felt rewarded for giving back to the community—offering my services to help prop up a good charitable cause. The other—and let's be honest, way larger—part simmered with fury.

I had nothin'.

On the third day I even plied this woman with Proof bakery's orange and cranberry scones and the most delicious goddamn croissants at four bucks a pop, but was still nowhere closer to understanding what Josie found to be so sordid about the charity. By now my snooping game was sharp. I'd rifled through entire stacks of any and all documents that might source this reputed shadiness—bank statements, insurance papers, lawyer correspondence. I'd even managed to discern when lil' miss Suz' pushed back her metal chair to come find me, easily covering any trail of suspicion. What's more I smashed this poor woman with endless questions about the ins and outs of the operation. Needling for any kind of breach or misdoings. And all I had to show for it was a mountain of volunteered goodwill.

By day four, she had me putting together the big cheese's office. Glenn Royce, aka Mr. Charity himself. A man with a beautiful family who, by the looks of the pictures I placed on his desk, vacationed regularly in Hawaii and had a successful law firm outside of these walls. A man evidently waaay too awesome for grunt work. A man with an ass-heavy new wood desk that I was stocking back up. Lining the top drawer with his beloved silver pens and daughter's adorable homemade bookmarks.

I was fried and ready to call off this demented search until I found it.

Lodged inside a worn-out Tom Clancy paperback called *Rainbow Six*.

A picture of Josie.

Her arms were crossed against her bare breasts, as if protecting against the sudden offensive lens. The side of her back twisted away from the camera, exposing a few perfect ribs couched in a swirl of bedsheets. Her eyes sparkled—half-smiling, half-incensed at the breach of privacy. Like she didn't want the picture to exist but was flattered that whoever took it, whoever she was with, insisted this perfect woman, this moment, be captured.

I stared. Transfixed. My obsession uncaged. But what the hell did it mean?

It meant Glenn was fucking Josie. Why else would he have the picture hidden in his desk? Maybe, I'd been staring at this puzzle all wrong. That it wasn't the charity that was rotten, it was the host. The man behind the curtain. Glenn Royce was the scratcher. The man who took her down. She was in bed with him and—

WAIT.

Roll it back.

I could hear those blowhard ex-cops at the bar, wailing in my skull. *Doesn't mean anything. What do you really know? How do you even know it's Glenn's picture?*

Likelys don't count with a jury.

Evidence. Cross them t's, kid.

How do you know that it was *his* Tom Clancy book? What if he found it? What if he bought it at a goddamn garage sale?

What if Glasser tossed the book inside his desk accidentally cuz she was the one behind the lens?

What ifs rippin' through my head.

Buzzing on the inside, I jammed that paperback and its piece of treasure in under my belt and told Glasser I had to split. *Pronto.* She seemed confused, like I'd broken some unspoken grunt work covenant.

I felt bad about that.

But I was emboldened with a compass pointing directly at Glenn Royce. Because no matter those damn cops' voices in my head, something inside my bones told me I was right.

Glenn was the scratcher.

I turned on my app and picked up a ride on my way home to earn back some of the cake I'd spent on Glasser. Thankfully, my customer wanted nothing to do with me and sat silently in the back allowing me to plug into this discovery. These crosshairs aimed at Glenn Royce. The founder of the charity. The big lawyer cheese with the corner office. Here's what I knew so far about Glenn:

The man was wealthy.

The man was smart.

Put those two together and you have a specimen who soars with desire in the eyes of a woman.

Add to that: he started a charity. Major bonus points.

People follow those they believe in, and here was a man who'd built an empire of diligent soldiers to lend their time to his charity.

The man had *sway*.

The man also had a wife and kids.

And now I had a theory: Glenn and the softness gone rotten.

It all lined up.

Motive.

He's a cheating bastard.

He swoons and makes promises.
She deserves better and knows it.
He stalls so she presses.
He squirms. He panics.
He needs to *shut. It. Down.*
He clocks the press.
He needs a piece of the puzzle: a stolen car.
He finds a hot ride. Woos her into the back seat. Smothers the problem and takes off to make it look like the killer was the Glendale Grabber.

I was rapt with direction.
I needed to test my put-together on the *professionals*.
Those drunk slugs at The Damned Lovely.

Tuesday, July 28th, 4:19 p.m.

I burst through the cage, happy to announce my victorious return.

"What's got you so charged?" Pa had to ask.

I laid out the case. The photo. My lusty loin theory.

The drunk buzzards poked holes: *You think she was banging him based on a picture? You don't even know who took it. Or who it belonged to. That's not investigating...that's just a guessing game.*

Lily cooed from the corner. "Conjecture, conjecture, conj—"

Now Jiles chipped in his two cents. "It's not evidence, kid. Haven't we taught you anything?"

"She had scratches on her arm and back which, according to the morgue chick at least, happened a few days prior to the murder. She was obviously in a fight with someone. Plus she told her friend there was something about the charity that was rotten. Maybe that 'something' is the founder, the guy who started it all. After she was killed, Glasser said Glenn was *especially* cut up and she couldn't even talk to him. I'm just saying—maybe she wanted more. Maybe she threatened to squeal, expose him for the pig he is...So he dresses it up. Gets his paws on a stolen car. (Not impossible!) Woos her into the back seat and terminates the problem by mocking it up like the Glendale Grabber."

It got quiet. They just looked at me. Unimpressed, like all their hard work, those many stories, those lessons of police work thrust upon their apprentice, had been wasted.

"It's thin, Sammy," Slice said.

"Slice, didn't you always say the best piece of evidence is smarts and instinct?"

"Was that me?" He chuckled ugly. "Maybe, kid. Maybe."

They all shrugged and went back to sippin' their bliss.

But I couldn't shake the feeling I'd stumbled onto some version of the truth. Now, I needed to prove them all wrong.

I needed evidence.

I needed a confession.

I slipped off the stool and made for the exit. It was only Pa, perched in the corner with his icy gin and glassy stare, who offered a sly grin, like he might just believe me. Like he wanted to, anyway.

Tuesday, July 28th, 5:55 p.m.

Glenn Royce lived in a huge white house at the corner of Hesby and Laurelgrove in Studio City. Pinner texted me his address, no questions asked. God bless that immoral cop.

I hit the Volt and drove by, hoping to get to his home before the lawyer did.

I figured I'd sit and watch the house. Found a shady spot under an oak tree with a decent view. I perched, happy to wait and watch, like a bona fide stakeout, sipping coffee from the shadows...

The bona fide stakeout sucked.

I had no coffee.

The booze was wearing off and I needed to piss. A time-sensitive issue that crept up against me, so I drove to a park and found a dark corner. Felt pretty rotten on the inside. I was *that guy*: the boozer pissing in a park beside a playground. I couched my dilemma in the strength of my mission. Doing right by Josie. At least I tried anyway.

I hit a Starbucks on Ventura and drank some burnt swill. It gave me a second charge and I circled back to Glenn's, parking across the street under my oak tree. Pretty soon a sparkling black Land Rover pulled into the driveway. But it wasn't Glenn Royce behind the wheel. It was his wife. I recognized her from his family pictures on the desk. She skipped out of the driver's seat wearing tight green yoga pants and a sweatshirt that hung off her body, exposing her shoulders.

She looked rich.

Better than.

Like she belonged to some higher class of people.

She grabbed a couple of Whole Foods paper bags from the trunk then bounced inside the massive house. I couldn't help but wonder if she was the kind of woman who didn't care about bringing her own bags to Whole Foods. Or maybe she just plain forgot her them. Happens to us all, right? Or maybe not. And that's why Glenn was cheating on her. Because she was the kind of woman who refused to bring her own bags or even pack her own groceries. *That kind.*

I could see pieces of the kitchen from my car and watched her unpack the food.

I felt pretty dirty about it, too. Watching her like some kind of peeping tom. Probably on account that I was.

Forty-seven minutes later a white Land Rover pulled into the driveway. Wait. Matching cars? His and hers. Now, that's some stinky cheese right there.

Glenn got out of the driver's side and came around to the back passenger door. He opened it, unclipped a child's seat, and let his daughter out. The little girl hustled to the house, clasping a worn-out lunch bag and water bottle, waiting for her dad to unlock the door. Glenn grabbed a computer bag from the back seat and then disappeared inside the house.

Kids.

Why did he have to have kids?

That cheating prick. It was one thing to cross the line with a wife you've grown to hate but kids messed it all up. Kids made cheating sad and ugly.

Inside he kissed his wife hello. They spoke with each other, cordially. Emotionless. Paint by numbers how-was-your-day drivel with their daughter circling round for attention and food.

This continued for an agonizing stretch of time. I was about to call the mission a resounding failure until Glenn emerged in a fresh shirt with some skip in his step looking like he was about to escape his domestic jail. Sure enough he sprung out of the

house and sped away in his car.
    I stayed on him.

Tuesday, July 28th, 7:29 p.m.

Of course he went to Firefly.

That honeypot of wannabe actresses, divorced men, and flaky souls with a spirit of opportunity. I'd seen Denzel there years ago. He was surrounded by a gaggle of long-legged blonde women. They looked ill intentioned. They looked hungry for something *better*. Basking in that glow of Oscar attention.

Glenn valeted his ride and hit the bar. I circled the blocks looking for a free street spot and finally found one on Ventura in a different damn time zone. The fundamentals of the LA struggle.

I pulled that picture of Josie from my pocket. Stared at her face and tried to focus on my plan. Namely that I didn't have one. How do you ask someone if they committed murder? I hadn't a clue. But. I had spent well over a thousand hours boozing with ex-cops pulling stories and figured I'd wing it.

As I stepped inside, I was hit with those curious disappointed faces. The LA twist. *Who's that walking in and how can they help?* Like a bunch of bleeding soldiers looking for a medic. That red cross of possibility and hope dashed with a sad realization that I was nobody famous.

But I'll give it this: the place was packed with pretty faces. Maybe it was the dim lighting bouncing off the caked-on makeup, or maybe I'd been spending too much time at Glendale's finest Damned Lovely surrounded by weathered, broken souls. No wonder Denzel came here. These people sparkled beautiful. I looked around, wondered if he might be around, joining the rest of the crowd looking for someone more glossy, more interesting, more powerful than myself.

Stay on target, you dolt.

Justice for Denim.

I saw Glenn yucking it up at the bar with a forty-something shlub in a heavy polyester suit. They were drinking Bud Lights. Of course they were.

There was a barstool beside Shlub. I plugged the gap—waving at the bartender for attention as I hit the stool.

I was close. Within range and buzzing inside now.

I could hear them yappin' about some Republican victory in the state senate. Respectable first round Bud Light talk.

I went all in and ordered an old fashioned. It was a spectacular tragedy. Crushed ice with some citrus sweetener. I wanted to scream and teach this twenty-one-year-old out-of-work-actor-excuse for a bartender how to mix a proper drink but stifled my rage, careful not draw too much attention to myself.

So I lay in wait. Sipping the watered-down muck with disdainful swallows. Glenn and Shlub ordered a second round. Shlub said he saw someone named Teddy and moved off like he was eager to score a bump of coke. Glenn pulled out his phone and hit Twitter.

It was time.

My heart pounded.

I activated the voice recorder on my phone, hoping the ambient noise wouldn't drown out my premiere interrogation.

I shot a glance at Glenn. He looked older in person compared to all those beach pictures in his office. Cracked skin around his eyes. In need of a shave this Tuesday *soir*.

He felt my eyes and nodded courteously.

I feigned surprise.

He clocked it.

I jumped.

"Are you...are you Glenn Royce?"

He looked at me, uneasy. Racking sense and coming up empty,

almost on guard now.

"That's so weird. I've been volunteering at Backyard Dreams recently."

Glenn lit up, genuinely impressed. "Oh, thanks."

"Crazy running into you like this. My name's Sam. I've been helping Susan at the new office in North Hollywood. Hanging pictures. Paintin' the kitchen. Navy midnight blue…"

"Wow. Thanks for putting in some time and helping out. Nice to meet you, Sam."

"You're welcome."

I sat quiet. Let him feel in control.

Glenn saw my glass running low. He signaled the bartender and offered to buy me another drink. I graciously accepted.

He glanced at the Dodger game shining on screen in the corner and I figured to keep things smooth to open, the way Jiles preached.

"You a fan?" I nudged.

"For sure. You?"

"More like an addict."

"Great, then maybe you can tell me what the hell is goin' on with Bellinger? Kid is looking OFF."

"Three games without a hit and four unforced errors this last week."

So we yapped Dodgers and the game. I wasn't supposed to like this guy but he wasn't making it easy.

Nearby a customer, some fat guy in a tight T-shirt, was cursing at a waitress. We scoffed and found common ground in the unspoken laws of civility. Now's about the time I started hearing Jiles scream in my ear:

You gotta warm him up.

Let him in.

Gain some trust.

Then pivot.

Catch his ass off guard. Flat-footed.

Once you've got him on your side, smash him with a couple

of hard-hitting accusations.

Pow! Pow! A one-two shot of I know the truth and you're going to squeal, son.

"It's actually kind of sad how I heard about your charity." He looked at me, curious. "Josie Pendleton was a friend."

Glenn shifted uneasily.

Glenn got cold.

Glenn glared like he was searching for something, but I iced him with naivety.

"You must've known her, right?"

"Oh, yeah," he muttered.

"Sad what happened."

"Really sad, Sam."

I let it all sit there in the open. He stared at that floor with a steel-shut gaze. Sucking back some hard feelings.

"Susan said you hosted a nice brunch for her."

"About the least I could do. She was a very special...very...beautiful person."

"Were you having an affair with her?"

Pow!

His jaw clenched down tight. "Excuse me?"

"I saw the picture."

"What picture?"

"The one of her half naked in bed. The one inside that Tom Clancy novel I found in your desk. You know, the one next to the pictures of you and your wife and your kid all smiling together in Hawaii."

The man squared up. Looked cold now.

"Who are you?"

"I'm just a guy who knew Josie Pendleton. Who saw her murdered body on a steel shelf at the morgue. Who doesn't believe she was killed by some random rapist, so I'm doing something about it."

"Are you a cop?"

"I'm flattered you think so. But no. "

"You think I killed her?

"Did you?"

He looked about ready to slug me but instead gave into something sad and darker somewhere inside him. "I was in Buffalo that night, you asshole."

"But you *were* having an affair with her?"

"No."

"Then how do you explain that picture, Glenn?"

And it was like that stain inside him bubbled out again. "Because I wanted to. For Josie? I was willing to throw it all in for that girl. But she refused. So I pinched her phone one day, found that picture and sent it to myself. Kept it hidden at work."

He took a long sip and looked like he got sucked into some more memories. "She said she wouldn't let me destroy my family like that. My life..."

We sat there for a while, and I was afraid he was gonna shake off, so I kept pressing, just hard enough.

"Josie said there was something rotten about your charity."

"You're looking at it, buddy. She hated what I was willing to do to my wife and daughter. Said I was rotten for it. Despite all that I stood for. What Backyard stood for." He sized me up. "Why don't you think Josie was killed the way they're saying?"

I told him about the scratches on her arm and all over her back. He looked angry. Jealous, almost. "Wasn't me. I would never scratch Josie. She was too damn beautiful. I mean who would want to mess that girl up with scratches? Right, Sam? She obviously set the hook in you, too, pal, didn't she?"

I nodded. Not that I owed the man an explanation but that we understood one another.

"I'm not surprised, though," he carried on. "I could tell there was someone else in her life. Someone she was probably seeing. She kept getting calls and texts but wouldn't tell me who it was. I pressed her but, who am I to tell her to be honest. She deserved whatever privacy she wanted so I left it all alone. Until I didn't and stole her phone but there weren't any texts I could find.

Either I was dreaming it or she was using those snap messages that disappear…But if you ask me, she was involved with someone else out there. Maybe he scratched her up."

"Maybe he killed her, too."

"Either way, she's gone. Nothing we can do about it." He sucked back his beer facing that fact, then turned to me, curious. "You went to all this trouble—volunteering at my charity and following me here tonight all because of some scratches?"

I nodded, all pitiful.

"Yeah, Josie had a way of doing that to people."

"I didn't even really know her all that well."

"Case in point, my friend." He went back to watching the baseball game. "I've never told anybody about her. About how I fell for her. Not one person…feels kinda good." He slammed back the rest of his drink, dropped a fifty, and left without saying goodbye to his friend.

Tuesday, July 28th, 8:55 p.m.

I walked back to my car, enjoying the dank cold air. But that was about it.

I'd gotten it all wrong.

The man was bereft. She wasn't the one putting on the pressure.

She was pushing him away. And the man had a solid alibi. He was in Buffalo. I would find out for sure if he was truthfully in Buffalo somehow, but I mean who lies about being in Buffalo?

Still someone laid a hand on her.

I needed to reset.

I needed sleep and a good meal. Protein and kale.

So I decided to grab a burst at The Damned Lovely instead.

This, my chorus.

Tuesday, July 28th, 9:44 p.m.

I crossed the tracks and rattled in hard.

I smiled and flexed my failure with pride. *Yeah, yeah. I was off the mark. You win.* I faltered and flailed and my monster's still at large. Bottoms up. But I'm still one step closer to the truth, ya jackals.

The Rooster stopped clicking and looked up.

Lily raised her glass.

Jewels flashed a smile.

The denim wailed.

And Slice bought me a round. "Stay on him, Sammy. Stay on your monster."

You're damn right, Slice. Imma stay on that monster...

Wednesday, July 29th, 12:49 a.m.

When the buzz wore off I drove back home, officially flattened, wanting nothing more than to bury my face in a pillow for a week. But that wasn't going to happen any time soon.

A black Range Rover was parked in my spot. And a yellow BMW right behind it. Who buys a yellow Beamer? I already knew the answer. A douchebag. Aka my roommate's friends. The reason my night was not about to end any time soon. It was coming up on one a.m. and I had to circle the block for eleven minutes until I found a spot two and a half blocks down with my bumper flirting in the red. I sucked up that fury and flashed a meek grin when I walked in to find some frat boys and two girls in tank tops and jean shorts smoking cigarettes in my kitchen. The girls looked young, on the wrong side of twenty-one. They had wary eyes and tanned skin like they'd been stuck in Florida too long.

Nick introduced me.

It was flat. No courteous spice. No flattery. Which meant he wanted me gone.

The frat boys pushed their chins up a little, as if this was well enough to greet me, obviously unimpressed with another penis in the room. If only I could just tell them I wasn't a threat, I would. But no, they threw the first punch with their cocky glint. Maybe I did have some fuel in the tank for a joust. We're in my house now, you workout-pants-wearing chump. Goes for you, too, Penis Boy, who probably parked in my spot and made me walk two and a half blocks to my own front door at one in the morning, so maybe I *will* try and woo one of these Floridian beauties out from under your punishing excuse of an intellect.

"Whaddya drinking?" I asked the brunette closest to me.

"Rum and Coke. Want one?"

"Thanks." I helped myself, skipped the Coke and double-downed on the lime. I hadn't had rum in a while. It tasted ruddy and sweet. It tasted like I was gonna feel the sugar in the a.m.

It needed ice and I cracked the freezer—

"We're out of ice." Nick helpfully pointed out.

"How are we out of ice, Nick?" I poked. But we both knew he forgot to fill the ice trays. Nick shrugged, almost surprised at the breach of kitchen protocol.

I sucked back the rum and one of the girls shot me a look.

I fired back. "You've got some...fluff on your..." I pointed to a grey swirl lodged on her tank top below her collarbone. She dusted off the little yarn and ignored me. Pretended not to care.

Penis Boy looked angry.

Tic tac yo, bro, game on.

I joined the rest of the boring conversation. They were talking about some sound bite from a guy named Magnet Max that had gone viral lately. Max sounded like a blowhard, right-wing, Capital A-rrogant white boy steeped in extremism convinced the world would be a better place with outdated *traditional* American values.

But I was more interested in that collarbone.

I reached out and nudged her elbow.

"What's your name?"

She looked surprised at the approach. Even more surprised at the nudge.

"Margaret."

"Where you from, Margaret?"

"Tampa."

I feigned shock. "No way, I love Florida. Parts of it, any-way...the Keys."

She smiled, not sure what to do with that. I kept looking at her eyes until she must've felt uncomfortable and looked down at the dirty kitchen floor. Then squeezed her attention at the rest of the flock who were engaged in a semi-heated argument lead by Workout Pants. "How can they be racist if one their leaders is black?"

"Black guys can't be racist?"

"They're not racist. It's not about race."

Margaret asked, probably eager to escape me, "What are you guys talking about?"

"Patriot Strong."

"What's that?" I asked.

Penis Boy piped up. "Some call it a movement. Some call it an ideal. But basically it's a bunch of guys standing up against feminism and—"

I couldn't resist. Nick had talked about this radical outfit over coffee some mornings. "Wait. Patriot Strong? A bunch of guys are calling themselves strong patriots by cutting down *feminism*?"

Nick chimed in, eager to keep the peace. "No, man. It's just this fraternity that embraces traditional male/female roles."

"What the hell does that mean?"

Penis Boy was into this show now. "It means we're about values that made this country great. Values that protect our country."

"What values?"

"For one that men should provide for the wives. For their family. Like it was."

I sized this little man up, eager to prod. "So, you're a member?"

"I ascribe to some of their values."

The girls watched, almost uneasy now.

"What values? That women should be subservient to the husband's career? Just stay home. Do the laundry and cooking. That kinda fifties shit? Ladies, are you hearing this? Does this sound okay to you?"

But Penis Boy straightened his spine and interjected before

they could even speak. "It's limiting to reduce a woman's role of caring for her family to simply cooking and laundry. It's about nurturing, love, attention—"

"Like attention to the dishes while Daddio's out on the town, taking late night martini meetings," I cracked.

"See, you're insinuating he's cheating, which stems from distrust. That's not what we're talking about. We're talking about traditional values, steeped in love and honor. And those defy cheating."

"People cheat," I pointed out. "Always have, always will."

"People cheat for a reason. It could be argued that the man whose wife is out working, instead of caring for his familial needs, cheats because he actually feels *threatened* by her work, making more money than he does. So he betrays her by cheating..."

"Men are scum. Trust me, I am one so I know. We get horny and cheat."

Margaret interjected, "We get horny and cheat, too."

"And thank god we're not the only sinners." The young woman finally cracked a likeable smile so I continued. "But don't you find there's usually more of a loaded emotional component when a woman—a wife, no less—cheats on her man?"

They all shrugged like it made sense but preferred not to engage, except for Penis Boy who couldn't resist. "In prehistoric times, it was the man's job to provide safety, shelter, and food. We've lost that now."

"Yeah, yeah. Hunter gatherer shit. Very profound," I said. "But we're not cavemen anymore. We've evolved. You don't think women should work. What's next? Oh and while we're at it, they probably shouldn't vote either, right?"

"You'd be surprised at how many women actually want to be liberated from the burden of having to generate income for their family."

"Liberated?" I turned to the wiser sex. "Ladies, I offer you the floor."

Margaret kept her mouth shut but the blonde laughed like

this was all very entertaining. "You wanna buy my house, pay off my car, and medical insurance. Fine with me but don't cheat on me. And I ain't *ever* havin' kids..."

She clinked glasses with Margaret and eyeballed Workout Pants like she wanted iiiin. Margaret looked down, awkward and uncomfortable, agreeing to go along.

I pressed her. "I'm on your side here. This doesn't offend you?"

Margaret grabbed the smoke from her friend's fingers. She took a puff and blew it in my face like some kinda tease.

Nick was laughing. Happy to stir the pot. "They don't jerk off either. Gotta strict no jerks policy. Right?"

Penis Boy nodded proudly. "Absolutely. No jerks."

"No jerks?"

"Figuratively and literally. We believe that kind of energy is better used for meeting women and starting a family."

"I see. But then when you do meet that woman, you're all...pent up and probably won't last more than a minute."

The boys shifted uncomfortably. The women shifted uncomfortably. Like maybe they hadn't thought that part through.

Penis Boy chirped fast. "That's never been a problem for me."

"So ladies, lemme ask you, please—do you find that chivalrous, that these guys have been holding out for you...?"

Brunette chimed in, "Hey as long as I get *attended* to, I think it's kinda cool. Ain't nothin' sexy about a guy jerkin' off." She puckered her lips and twisted her mouth, looking to Margaret for back up, but Margaret kept her eyes to the floor at the ugly talk. I was dying to know what she really felt but not at the cost of her embarrassment.

"Well, I guess I'm in the minority. Here's to no jerks all around."

I swallowed the last of my rum and shipped out. I looked at Margaret for a long beat. She looked back at me, as if waiting for something. I smiled and said I was going to bed and that it was nice meeting her. Just her. She looked surprised I said that.

The flock mumbled goodbye. Happy to see me go. With my back to them I bellowed out, "Whose yellow car is that? You're in my spot."

"Oh, sorry," Margaret chirped. "That's mine, should I move it?"

Wednesday, July 29th, 8:08 a.m.

The next morning was rowdy. My brain rattled rough. Bruised off the booze and sugar. Goddamn Rum.

I checked my bank account.

I needed cash in a big way.

I hit the Volt.

I picked up an Armenian guy wearing way too much cologne who didn't wanna talk and drove him to Altadena.

I picked up an old woman going to the movies who did nothing but talk about her granddaughter's accomplishments. I smiled right.

The sun smashed through my windshield and my brain wailed.

It was hot out.

It was an ugly yellow concrete hot that insisted on shining a light into my life's failure.

I knew today was gonna be tough, one of those pinpricks reminding me of how little I had in my life. How I would probably never find out who scratched Josie. How I failed her. How I was closing in on forty, that ugly fulcrum of young vs. old. Soon to be, not just approaching middle age, but forced to embrace that slippery squid.

A creative failure with a bleeding bank account.

My phone rang. It was my father. It was like the man could sense and tug at the shame. He worked commercial real estate and owned a boat. The man never understood the chase. Chasing some vision. Something that might define you as more than just another creative soul in LA. I declined the call, desperate to feel in control of something.

The lick about being a writer is that you always have homework. Any time spent away from the keys is time you're spending away from your success. Away from a potential moment of inspiration that just might push good to great.

Might.

You should try volunteering. You *might* like it.

You should exercise more. You *might* find it helps.

You should meditate. You *might* enjoy it.

I wanted to strangle might and screw those shoulds sideways.

I picked up an old coot named Devon Holmes. Devon was black. Devon wore a suit and tie on a scorching day. Devon had chunky gold rings on his fingers that looked proudly polished. He had lines on his face like a windswept desert, like the sands of time had etched their—whatever he looked cool and I instantly liked him which was rare for a passenger. Even rarer was me starting up the conversation. Retired from a life of working for a rail company. Started in the machine room. Workin' parts. He said he was lucky to still have all his fingers. Not so lucky he could hardly hear now. But wouldn't you know it—they got these hearing aids now. Tiny little nuggets you can hardly see.

"I can tune up or drown out the world as I please..."

Devon was married. Devon grew up in Philly. Moved west with his wife when her mom got sick. Started working in the front office outta Irvine. Yeah. The front office. He got clean. Literally, took him two years to get the dirt out from under his nails. Devon became a father. Devon has two girls. He prayed for a boy back then. Devon had three girls and called it. Devon liked to talk about his girls. They were married, all three of them. Graduated college. I got the feeling life played out nice for the man.

He vibed content.

He glossed over the race card. He glossed over the stain this country musta thrown at him back in the day. When that day was rougher than any rum hangover and a dwindling back account. He glossed over it all. Like he'd battled the storm and came out wearing a smile and a suit in the sun with three girls, ten clean fingernails, a wife he loved, and some little nugget hearing aids he could tune out the world with his fingertips. I dropped Devon at a medical building on Brand. He didn't say goodbye as he stepped out the door.

I kinda wished he had.

Sunday, August 2nd, 12:13 p.m.

I played out the rest of the week in the Volt. Kept thinking about Devon. The smile and that suit warmed my heart. A life lived right. Like some kinda soldier.

He reminded me of Slice...without the disgraced cop part. And the whole drunk thing. But Slice had the same look behind his eye. Jiles would always wedge into conversation what a remarkable cop he used to be. *Remarkable.* That was the word he would start with then talk up how badass Slice could be when a 246 radio call went wide. The first one in through the door.

"A bona fide warrior back when," Jiles would say with a loaded smile.

I always wondered what the hell happened to Slice. How he fell from grace. The demon in his past. I knew he had a story under his skin and I'd always wanted to know more.

Call it inspiration, call it desperation but I decided my next piece would be a write up on Slice. I needed to step back from Josie. I needed to write about something...alive. Something that fascinated me.

A disgraced ex-hero we all called Slice.

I turned off my phone and made a U-turn.

Sunday, August 2nd, 1:19 p.m.

I rolled in and found Slice on his regular perch. His silhouette was all I needed. Most drunks by the age of sixty-five had a spine that rounded over at the top. Arched and damaged. But Slice was different. He managed to keep his back straight which amazed me given how many hours he filled sitting on that barstool with no back support. A committed drunk with a front row seat.

He was watching the Rooster with a crooked smile. Didn't pay me a lick of attention as I saddled up next to him.

"These guys and their computers. Staring at screens all day. With their headphones..."

"I stare at a screen all day."

"You do it in private. At a desk. Like it should be. This guy sits at a table in a bar, surrounded by people, glancing at us if we're too loud. Those glances...like it's a library. Like we're bothering him. It's a bar. He glances like it's a library. What is that?"

"Way the world rolls now, Slice."

"People should go to a bar to drink. To talk to people. To get away from work. Or to hide. Not stare at a screen like the Rooster does."

"He's okay."

Slice was digging in. He had a habit of pinching folks that made him feel old and out of touch. Reminding him that the world was gonna be just fine without him someday. Most of all, I'm guessing he was jealous that a man could make a decent living, sitting in the same room as him staring at a computer when all he does is stare at the box scores and drain his savings.

I shrugged and rolled with it. The Rooster *was* okay but I'd seen those glances—those flits of judgment like he was better and smarter than all of us, getting rich behind a shiny MacBook Pro. Maybe I oughta run the numbers like he was. Probably beats driving LA most days. Still, there were weeks I didn't see him talk to a soul. Not Jewels. Not Jiles. Not even when I crossed him at the urinal. Not so much as a nod hello. I just hoped the stray dog had some badass playlists to keep his mind from going crazy lonely or worse coming in here and shooting us all one day. If anyone was gonna do it, it would be the Rooster.

I didn't say much to Slice up front. I didn't want to rattle him. I settled in and sipped on my drink like any other Sunday.

We waxed Dodgers.

We pushed opinions.

We silently marveled at the woman's curves sitting at table nine, pretending to be gentlemen.

We wished together and drank like old friends. I felt like a spy.

Then strangely, when it came time, I felt all nervous, like how I felt just before asking Sarah Croftan out on a date in eighth grade: "So...I need to write a profile piece to bolster my portfolio. How'd you feel if I wrote somethin' on you?"

Slice laughed like I'd hit him with a backhanded compliment. Like I was diggin' into the old drunk. But I left the laugh alone, letting it sink in long enough for him to realize I was for real. Eventually he looked at me. Baffled.

"You wanna write about me?"

I couldn't tell if he was angry or about to cry.

"Yeah, just a profile. Couple thousand words."

Those soppy wet eyes trying to make sense of it all.

"Why?"

Because the rest of the slugs I had pegged. But Slice was different. He wasn't like the other cop-o's at the Lovely. You don't quit the force three months shy of a pension. Something went down. Something ugly. There was a story there, probably one he was ashamed of. Full with skeletons and victims and people he'd betrayed. The people who made him come in here and drown out the sunshine with whiskey. So, hell yeah, I wanted the scoop. And I was desperate for something to get my mind off Josie.

So I lied my ass off.

"Why not? You got somethin' better to do?" I smiled. "Call it a puff piece."

"You wanna write a puff piece about me? I'm just a guy on a stool. What about your monster?"

"Gotta flush the line. C'mon, I'll buy you a round."

I flagged Jiles, and plied Slice with the promise of some iced Walker Black, not the well crap he'd been slamming all day. He grinned like a toddler, and I knew I'd set the hook.

"Hang on, let me get my computer."

THE SLICE YARN

His real name was Gregory Baskin.

He was born in Naperville, a small town just outside of Chicago, in 1948.

His mother died when he was eleven.

His dad was a mechanic. A wizard with an engine and dirty fingers by nine a.m.

They ate chicken and tomatoes most nights.

They listened to the fights on the radio.

Dad played cards and chewed tobacco on the porch with his friends. They talked dirty, and dreamed of bigger things.

Those dirty fingers. Spiking a dip.

There was never money. Never.

Slice showed up to school but it didn't take. Too many numbers and verbs and distracting short skirts. He posted bail with a C average.

He cleaned cars at the garage for cake.

He smoked cigarettes and hated the winter.

He smoked cigarettes and knew a girl named Betty with legs. She was driving to California and going to be a star.

He pinched his dad's Buick and followed that tail west.

It was the summer of 1965. The world was blowing up.

LA was lit. Watts was blazing.

Betty split.

Gregory Baskin was all alone. The kid was only seventeen and lost in a big smoke.

One night, he watched a man step out of a Cadillac on Normandie with a .38. He shoulda laid low. He shoulda walked away. The man pointed the .38 at a redhead with painted fingernails and wicked cleavage.

But Gregory Baskin got there first. Gregory Baskin remembered those Floyd Patterson uppercuts and Benny "Kid" Paret hooks. He was ferocious. Unleashed like never before. *Crack! Bang! Crunch!*

The .38 went wide and the man hit the pavement.

Gregory Baskin was a hero.

The redhead talked him up for the police report. Word got out on the wire. They sent a reporter. Photographer, even. He popped a winning smile for the flash bulb.

The night was a spike.

He was a high and mighty hero in his heart. He woke up early and cracked the *Times*. They buried it on page eight. Nothing more than a stick-up gone wrong. No one shot. Just a good-willed stranger. It burned deep but he buried it. He couldn't wait to tell his old man when the moment was right. But time dragged on and the right moment fizzled out. Pops died a few months after.

He caught work in a garage on Western. Cleaning carburetors and greasing axles. He looked at his fingers on a Monday afternoon in May. He couldn't get them clean.

He was gonna die one day, and wondered if they'd be able to get his hands clean.

He thought about his old man.

He thought about the spike.

He thought about helping red again. About helping all those many reds out there. He wanted to be a hero in his heart again.

He signed up to be a cop that Tuesday.

Gregory Baskin found his angle. Most kids hated the academy, but he soaked it up and cleaned those fingernails till three a.m. some nights. Till they looked bright.

He looked good in a uniform and he knew it. He *felt* good. Felt good the way girls looked at him. A swirl of admiration and contempt and *you'll protect me, right?* He worked Studio City. Close to the Warner Bros. lot and the glossy homes of Toluca Lake. He steered clear of the downtown grime and hatred.

He married a girl from Encino. Her name was Jane. She wore sundresses in December and they bought a house in Burbank near the stables.

They tried for kids. They tried and tried but still only had each other after a good three years. It wasn't always rosy, staring at that empty second bedroom. Maybe they'd adopt a little girl someday. *Wouldn't that be sweet?*

For nine years he never pulled his gun.

Life tasted sweeter than a goddamn cherry.

And then Julian died.

Julian Chavez was his partner. They were brothers by then. Brothers by *I got your back, you got mine. To the death, amigo.* Not fate or blood or the genetic strain.

On September 25th, 1987, Julian went to Norms on Riverside Drive for eggs over easy.

A coked-up crackhead ordered fries to go and pulled a shotgun.

Julian stepped in.

Julian went down.

The crackhead split.

Gregory Baskin got the call at VideoPlus where he'd gone to rent *Romancing the Stone*.

The body was gone when he crossed the yellow tape.

Too late, amigo. He stared at Julian's blood pooling thick on the linoleum. Gregory bent down and touched his brother's red blood and something broke inside him.

He didn't feel guilty, he felt betrayed. Like by God or some stupid shit like that. There was nothing he could have done to save the man.

Or was there? He stewed nights. He stared at the clock on his bedside table, night after night. Those red numbers.

He thought about the spike.

He thought about the bigger picture.

He wanted to get his hands dirty again and work something like Vice on Central.

He'd lost the spike.

He coulda ordered eggs that night.

He smashed three whiskeys and called for a transfer. Downtown proper.

He never told his wife.

They dealt him a rookie's hand. Made the poor bastard search down the junkie's wet pockets. Dig fingers into wet scary holes like a grunt.

On a rainy Tuesday in K-town, he was the first boot through the door. A switchblade lunged from out of a closet. He broke the bastard's jaw and saved a seventeen-year-old girl bound to a rusty cot. He was shaking fierce when the dust settled. His shoulder was all sliced up. But the girl was safe.

They called him a hero that night.

They called him Slice.

He earned his cred and loved every moment.

He loved the danger, the fear, the win, the pounce.

He thought about the redhead.

He plugged overtime. He'd roll in late and wouldn't want to wake up his wife.

He started sleeping in that spare bedroom. Jane missed her husband. Missed the way he looked at her. Missed those soft Studio City eyes.

Slice's eyes were different now. Were they haunted? She wasn't trying to be dramatic but that seemed to be the word that best fit.

He was burning bright and pinched a bump here and there. Just to keep the lights on. Keep the guard on straight and the blood flowin'. He was all *crack smack boom!* Tight. Slice was punching overtime and making a difference. Red woulda been proud.

Then he found Mario.

Mario was four. Mario was pulled from a crack den in Boyle Heights with scars on his stomach, and up his back. Not that he'd let you see 'em. The kid had been kicked around something fierce and wasn't the least bit shocked when seven armed cops busted through the front door. The kid leaned on Slice for some change. He wanted a pink lady apple because he loved pink lady apples this time of year, and the Chinese man on the corner was good about giving them out on the cheap. The kid knew the routine, and he'd be hungry until his daddy came back from the station. The kid was relentless and beautiful and had been dealt a rough hand. It wasn't the first time Slice had come across runoff like this, but something about Mario wracked him. Something about that kid's damn spirit, that no matter how much filth and evil surrounded him, he weathered the storm and just wanted a pink lady apple.

Slice knew the system would lay in. He knew the kid was in for a rough ride and knew better than to make any of it personal. But for some reason he couldn't square, Slice wanted to give *that* kid all the apples in LA and decided then and there he might try. I mean, that spare bedroom after all. He scribbled some words on the report that young Mario had an angle on the case and needed to be in police custody.

It was 1989.

No one would care what happened to this little crack baby from Boyle Heights so long as it didn't cost the city any more nickels. He'd make right with Mario's folks when the time was fit. Part of him felt right guilty ripping him away from his father but a bigger part didn't care after eyeing those scars on the boy's soft skin.

The sun was coming up and Slice rolled into his driveway with a bag of pink lady apples and a kid in the back of his unmarked. He stared at the window of his wife's bedroom.

He knew how unfair this was to her.

He knew this would be ugly.

They opened the door and the kid took in the place, wary, but you could tell he almost felt safe. Jane emerged in her nighty and didn't understand. *How could he just take a kid?* Then she saw the scars. It still didn't make sense, but it made it easier and she got the boy some toast and a glass of milk. She stared at her husband with contempt and admiration while little Mario lapped up the milk and shoveled crunchy toast into his face.

Of course, she was furious.

Of course, she disagreed on a fundamental level that what her husband did—ripping this kid away from his parents—was anything but okay. Not to mention illegal. How was this part of the oath, Gregory? (Slice told me he liked that she still called him Gregory. That his name lived on, inside the walls of his home.)

Of course, she was in a tight spot. A no-win situation cuz in her heart she knew this was best for the kid. But God's standard practice gives you nine months to get ready and think and prepare and paint the spare bedroom the *right* shade of yellow and buy clothes and absorb the fact your life is gonna be forever different. Not when you come out of the shower on a Wednesday morning before work.

Of course, she came around. The kid was sweet and beautiful and full of scars that needed healing. *Why not them? Why not her? What else had she to do that was so important? Brunch with Ellen? A date with her husband who she saw everyday anyway?* The kid was beautiful and she knew it...

The first three years were tough. Mario was a boy confused.

Mario would lash out. Mario would rail on the people who said they were there to help and protect and make his life better. Who *loved* him, or so they claimed. But Slice knew he had every right to be pissed. Mario was mad inside. But Mario came round. Slice felt that down deep deep deeeeep the kid knew in his bones he was one lucky bastard to get saved by a Vice cop looking for a dealer that night.

They went to ball games together. Mario played basketball. Slice even offered to coach. The man hated basketball but he knew the desk sarg' would ease up on his hours and let him break off to see his kid on the court.

It was after one of those practices when Jane turned up with some roast chicken and a Greek salad that they ate dinner on a park bench. A night they both realized Mario was the best thing that ever happened to them.

Then after that Greek salad, it all just crashed.

Jane got sick. Diagnosed with some rare liver cancer and just up and died four months, two weeks, and six days from the day she called the doc complaining of back pains.

It was February.

It happened faaasst.

They buried her body in Forest Lawn.

Mario and Slice were solo, now. Adrift. Like the glue of good reason and fairness and discipline had melted away, leaving these two men of oh so few words to wrestle down life.

They lost their compass.

They didn't talk at the dinner table.

Slice buried himself at work. He hit Vice hard. He filled the pain by hitting the streets and crackin' faces.

Mario started hanging out with chumps. Teenagers with bad skin, heavy backpacks, and sneaky smiles. Stealing cars and robbing homes.

They were father and son proper—butting heads and nodding on Sundays some. Slice liked to call it respecting privacy, but it sounded like the kid needed to feel okay and loved, you ask me.

Eventually the boy straightened out. Hit up a community college in Chatsworth. And got some science skills. Chemical biology. Slice was proud. The kid's hands were clean. The real clean. He had prospects and a pretty girlfriend.

But Slice didn't slow down. He didn't have a woman to tell him he should. The older he got, the less he cared. Cleaning up the streets still felt like the best play on Monday morning.

His fellow officers reminded him he was eligible for a transfer— roll to some cushy transit detail. Go back to the Valley and sit on a curb directing traffic on a movie set. Hell, work the lot. Let those tourists click and smile. Let the LA sun shine on your badge and pretend everything's smooth-y-smooth. But he shrugged them off and kept crackin' faces.

By 1999, he was the big dog in Vice. Knew all the players south of the 110. Knew the routes. Knew when those Shanghai cans were pullin' into San Pedro. Knew all the crooked truck drivers with too many kids to feed, happy to reroute. Knew the booby traps set up in crack dens lookin' to maim pigs like him.

Back home, Mario moved out.

The house got cold.

Slice was putting in overtime. Nights and days. His LT let it slide. Figured Slice could handle it, right? He was unflappable.

Slice tapered off and stopped talking, polishing off drink number three. He wanted to call it quits. For now. I was gonna press for the goods but figured best to let lie. Not like he was going anywhere.

I could tell he liked flipping the pages on his past. Digging up those lost memories. Maybe there was some ugliness to come out soon, but so far his tale was pretty clean. And kinda heartwarming.

I'd dig deeper on his skeletons but so far it didn't feel like he was pullin' any bio punches. If I was gonna run with it, I'd have to fact check it soon enough but felt I had at least enough for a start. Something to show my contact at the *Glendale News-Press* who I could push for a few bucks. *A local hero?* Man, was that telling of these times. We gotta settle for Slice. And I hadn't even reached the disgraced part yet...

He slipped off his stool and rattled across the floor to the bathroom. Jiles angled over, sniffing something off.

"What's with the charity? Why the hell d'you buy Slice three drinks?"

I let him in on my editorial dreams and he actually liked the idea of a write-up on Slice, even though he was wary of some truths going wide. I wanted to ask Jiles what he meant when the door burst open with an ugly pang.

We could all make out Detective Pinner's girth parked in silhouette over the threshold, purposely holding open the door and letting in that stuffy, piss-off-heat inside.

"Close the goddamn door, Pinner!" Jiles barked.

Pinner lumbered up to the rail right next to me. The man smelled ripe, likely at the tail end of a long ass shift. Yeah, one whiff and you could smell the streets on him.

"What the hell happened, Sammy? Writin' not payin' the bills? You tryin' to be a cop now?"

I knew what he was talking about. "What are you talking about?"

"Your little undercover job. The fellas told me you turned over some pretty nice cards snooping around that charity."

I shoulda known the fellas woulda leaked my intel but shrugged it off. "I was just curious."

"Just curious doesn't go out and volunteer at some charity for days on end. Just curious doesn't stake out the owner and confront him at a bar accusing him of murder, kid."

I looked around the room, pointedly eyeing the slugs: *Just who the hell's been feeding this man my dirt?* But they all maintained their dubious glaze.

"I'm not a kid, Pinner."

"Oh, sorry, your little baby face was getting in the way."

I wound up but kept my eyes straight. "All I do is listen to you chumps line up a case day after day, how to work the evidence, 'Look at the facts, Sammy.' So I looked at the facts and to me it still doesn't add up. So I asked around some...that's all. I was curious."

Pinner grinned and his front tooth edged out over his top lip like a weasel. "Boy, I shoulda known better than to show you those cold tits on the slab. I'll bet you still got that image burned bright in your brain, don't ya?"

I straight-faced.

"Jesus, I really set the hook, didn't I?" He laughed like it was funny, and a piece of his spit hit the bar.

I felt like punching him in his fat bastard nose and hitting his fat bastard face, but he was right about the hook.

"Relax, I'm proud of ya. Wish I still cared that much. Besides, I'll take all the help I can get if it brings down my numbers."

He whistled at Jiles. "Hit me up with a Jack and Coke, Jiles. And put some limes in it. Big fat ones." Then, putting on the good cop, he turned to me. "Skinny limes are the worst, right Sammy? The ones that just mash but no juice comes out. The worst."

"She was seeing someone. Did you even know about it?"

"No, cuz I wasn't looking. You're wasting your time sniffing around all that personal crap. It's the Glendale Grabber."

"How do you know? Are you any closer to finding him?"

"Of course we're closer."

"How?"

"Na, na, na... I've shared enough meat on this one."

"Afraid I'm gonna scoop your collar?"

"I'm not afraid of anything but I don't want you getting in the way of my job, kid."

I alcoholic-shrugged. The *who cares anyway* that we regulars had perfected. "Don't worry, Pinner, I'm over it. Was a stupid waste of time. I didn't even know her and I almost got my ass kicked."

Pinner laughed like a frat boy envying some rite of passage. But the minute the words came out I knew it was all a lie. Josie Pendleton's murder wasn't a waste of time. I wasn't over it. I wasn't over her, I wasn't over the slab, the scratches, her skin, the wonder, the burn, the loose ends and the Glendale Grabber line. Any of it. I wanted more. I wanted concrete truths and indefensible logic on when where why and whothefuck dunnit. Talking to Pinner only fueled my fire.

"You afraid my little kid face can beat you to it? Whaddya got?"

Pinner chomped the bait. "We're into the rape kit. But nothing's comin' up on the swabs. No juice. No DNA in the system. No prints. The bastard runs a tight kill ship."

"What about the boyfriend? Who scratched her up? What'd you get off her phone?"

Pinner sucked back his rum and Coke and fat limes and looked me in the eye as he wiped off his upper lip. "Wouldn't you like to know." He looked around the bar. He was losing interest and folding fast. I needed a fresh angle.

"What about the car?"

"The car?"

"He stole a car, right? Whose car was it?"

"There's no traction with the car."

"Okay, but I mean, if I was gonna steal a car, I might do a little research or have a connection or know something about—"

"Jesus, I told you, it was *random*."

"Then who owned the car?"

"Some woman named Sally Harnell. It was a clean 2006 beige Camry. Little old Sally lived in Eagle Rock. She was seventy-two years old. Rented a small two-bedroom apartment off Mount Royal with a cat, and a live-in nurse. Old woman's suffering from early onset Alzheimer's—hardly left her house 'cept to go to the doctor, or get cat food at Trader Joe's on Colorado. Trust me. We dug in—there was no connection to Josie Pendleton."

I pretended to be disappointed but felt pretty glorious for

squeezing out some facts.

Pinner continued to steam, "We know what we're doing. So just back off and leave it to the professionals, all right?" He dug his pudgy fingers into his icy drink and pulled out another lime. Sucked back the fleshy pulp. His phone squawked and he lumbered over towards the men's room.

"Can I see her emails?"

He handed me a middle finger and disappeared into the john as he accepted the call. You just knew he'd keep talking to some poor soul while holding his dick at the urinal like it was no big thing.

Seeing Pinner rolled me up.

Seeing Pinner reminded me of her denim shirt on my desk. That I couldn't just sidestep this itch with a write-up on Slice or an afternoon sharing rides in the Valley.

I looked up Sally Harnell on my phone. No Facebook. Twitter. Or any social media. There were some faces that popped up on an image search, but I couldn't square them. I circled the drain of a fruitless Google search six clicks deep desperate for some actionable intel. Twenty-six minutes later, I threw in the towel.

I needed a fresh angle.

I'd run aground playing it safe. Noodling her friend Allison Hager. Dancing undercover at the charity and sniffing around Glenn's dirty laundry. This ghost was gonna keep haunting me, and I couldn't afford rudderless sidestepping anymore. I needed to strike deep. I needed to go personal.

Phone. Texts. Emails.

It was time to pop the hood.

I needed to hack into Josie Pendleton's life.

And I knew the just the right slug for the job.

Friday, August 7th, 11:01 a.m.

The Rooster.

The man in the back corner booth facing east and away from the door. Away from the action. Away from our faces and lives and struggles. I wasn't sure if that was because he was too busy wrestling his own or just plain hated us.

He was an ODD swallow.

We didn't know if he had a wife, boyfriend, dog, any friends, family, or foe.

We didn't even know his name cuz he paid cash every day.

He kept to himself, buried behind a screen for a loaded eight to ten hours, six days a week save for most Sundays. So what the hell did he do on Sundays? That was the going bet. I laid odds on church. Slice called the track. I reminded him it ain't the forties anymore. Jiles figured out he worked the markets but couldn't squeeze details. He had a notepad next to his computer filled with rantings and numbers like some kinda math professor. Then, back one April, I was barking about a phishing scam that had their hooks in my data. Jiles said I oughta talk to the Rooster. The man had to know a thing or two about computers given he stared at one every day of his life. I countered at first but then came around and realized screw it, why not. Not surprisingly, he was pretty goddamn indifferent about helping me. Kinda indignant, actually.

But then on his way out one day the Rooster tapped my shoulder and said he knew a guy who might be able to help. I pressed for details but the Rooster went mum. *He just knew a guy*...I laid out the issue and he told me to leave my computer with him for a night. Now, that felt fishy as hell, but in the end, I figured I came to *him,* right? He offered to help. For free. And if he messed with me, I knew where to find him. So I gave it a whirl.

The next morning he handed off Benny and said I was good to go.

The sonofabitch worked magic right. Whatever his bent, the man knew the grid and how to work behind the firewalls.

So I ambled up to the Rooster. I started up but he didn't need the *Reader's Digest* version. For all his apparent isolation, the man was pretty dialed in. He knew all about Josie. The chatter. My obsession like it was the Lovely's tabloid.

Still, I pressed the point home: I needed to get into Josie life. In a most digital way. I wanted emails, texts. I wanted *private communiqué.* I wanted her data all up close and personal in my face. I wanted to know what kinda music she listened to. Movies she watched. Songs she liked. The bad gym mix. Her Counting Crows ugly secret. Her favorite stupid emoji. All of it.

And *pictures.*

I wanted pictures. Not the Instacrap. The ones she *didn't* want people see. Images of her hands. Discarded shots of her cheeks and legs. Those private mistakes.

I told him I didn't I have a lot of throwin' around money. But he waved me off. Said he had a favor in mind that would come up soon I could help him with. It sounded super shady, so I joked so long as I didn't have to kill anyone.

The Rooster blinked twice.

"Nothing like that," he muttered evenly, all creepy.

Oh-kay man. "Well, thank you. And yeah, whatever I can do to help in return." I told him I'd put together my intel and ship it off soon. He nodded, like he didn't really care and plugged his headphones back into his world of whatever the hell the Rooster does...

* * *

Guess you'd call it a success but I was pretty skeptical. I mean, I still didn't even know the guy's name. But if he could dig up some dirt on her personal life, that was good enough for me.

Yeah.

It soon crossed my mind that this was a severe invasion of Josie Pendleton's privacy. But that eroded fast. She was dead. And I was in love with her. There had to be something noble about it. That's what I told myself, anyway.

Then I ordered a Bulleit and killed the afternoon watching baseball with Pa.

Tuesday, August 11th, 7:10 p.m.

I was back in the Volt.

"Hi *Robert*."

"Hi *Bella*."

Hi *whoever you are just don't barf in my back seat.*

I rocked a twelve-hour shift.

I was bagged and bug-eyed by the end of it but earned some decent smack on account of a run out to LAX. The fare landed me out west, so I parked just off Main Street in South Santa Monica. I walked out to the beach and pretended not to care about sand getting into my shoes.

It was surprisingly beautiful.

It was California proper.

One of those sappy postcard moments where the sun was setting and made me appreciate my life.

And that I should really exercise more. (And kale, buddy, kale...)

Anyway, all these people in good shape with tight bums and tanned arms and perfect smiles drifting by on road bikes with kids and mortgages and things all working out in their lives...

No wonder so many people moved to California. When you stripped away the circus and concrete, she was pretty lovely all by herself.

For whatever reason Allison Hager's face burned into my memory. I really messed that hand up something fierce.

I wanted to make it right with her. Figured I'd go old school and drop off some flowers at her place. Like an orchid. *Who doesn't love an orchid?*

And they were only like ten bucks at TJs. The small ones, anyway.

Or maybe I should impress her with a big one. Or would she find it overwhelming?

Maybe I could buy it all back. It was worth a shot.

I bought a purple and white orchid for Allison at a Trader Joe's off Lincoln. Drove home once traffic died down smiling on the inside like I'd finally done something kind and pure.

Tuesday, August 11th, 9:00 p.m.

I got home and took some crap from Nick about the orchid. He pegged that it was for a girl I wanted to bang. His words, not mine.

"Nice pussy flower."

Fuckin' Nick.

I hadn't talked to him since the delightful white supremacist event in the kitchen and in no way wanted to revisit the events, but he brought it all up and apologized for his guests smoking in our house. I marveled how this human being apologized for the smoking instead of the white supremacy part.

He laughed it all off and eventually copped to, "Sure, they're a bunch of idiots. But man are they entertaining."

"It's sad and disgusting to me that you find radicalized racism entertaining."

Nick shrugged, careful to keep things level. He steered out of the way. "Kinda fascinating about the no jerks thing, though, right?"

"Not really. It's just an excuse for guys to feel empowered. Who cares? Jerking off is like anything else—you do it too much, it'll turn ya rotten. I mean, you drink enough water and it will kill you."

He looked at me with a peculiar face.

"I'm just saying, there's a time and a place."

"Fair enough. But you listen to that guy Max yet?"

"Why would I listen to that garbage? No. Of course not. And I don't ever want to."

"See *that* I don't get. You're a writer. You spend all your time drinking and moaning about how hard it is to drum up cool, inventive, unique characters. And here you have a genuinely fascinating man, a real life 'villain' to you, right? And you're too stupid to invest. Sammy, you gotta listen to him speak. For research if nothing else."

"That stuff makes me physically angry. That's not gonna help my writing. It's only gonna make me furious at how stupid you people are and then make me drink *more*."

"Your loss, man."

"It's really not. And please don't bring those types of people home again."

He shrugged, knowing full well he had every right to ignore my request as I picked up my orchid and marched off to my room.

"By the way, most girls don't actually like orchids. They say they do, but they don't." I kept walking. "No, man, it's true! I read an online Nordic research paper that said eighty percent of women find the petals remind them of their own labia. And that most girls don't like looking at flowers that remind them of their own pussy. So...You bought a pussy flower."

I closed the door.

Nordic Research. Orchid. Petals. Women. Labia.

I dug four Google pages deep. No such article. Only reprehensible but hard-not-to-stare-at images of orchids matching women's genitalia.

Nick had a special way of punishing me. *What if he's right?* I even said it out loud. But then I shrugged it off and got back to business:

Allison Hager's address.

I couldn't track it down. Kept hammering away with only negligible leads

I needed to get my mind off it.

I thought about jerking off.

111

I thought better of it.

Thought about Magnet Max.

Wait. Was Nick right? Did I do a lot moaning?

Maybe I should just listen—*for research*.

I found a YouTube channel with Magnet Max spouting fury and hate about the status of white males in American society. How in his view we've become relegated to second-class citizens. How we've been demoralized by liberal values and relegated to pandering yes-men who are engineered to mend and fix an unwavering, festering guilt bestowed upon us by feminism and pear-shaped civil rights dogma. I wanted to strangle the bastard.

All said, the man was one righteous orator. He was like a modern-day young Hitler with a hipster haircut and tailored beard wowing his swooning cronies with deliberate pregnant pauses and punctured emphasis. How minimized the white male in modern America has become. How feminism and civil rights have eclipsed all that was great and powerful about what this country stood for but is day in, day out like some pulling tide eroding our true Western values down into dust.

I couldn't take much more and texted Allison, hoping she'd be cool enough to send me her address.

The dots flared success: *1146 Yale St. 90404*

I was exhausted and passed out.

But I jerked off first.

Fuckin' *Nick*.

Thursday, August 13th, 12:12 p.m.

I stuck to my guns and kept the orchid. Then spent thirty-nine minutes trying to figure out the perfect, sweet, most Oscar Wilde quip to signify the swirling feelings twisted up in Allison and, well, landed on: *For you.*—S.

I drove over and quietly inched up to her door, leaving the pot on her front step. I glanced inside and the place felt empty. Like hardly lived in. Or she was uncomfortably clean. I edged away, free and clear.

Maybe she'd call. So many stupid maybes...

I didn't feel like hustling strangers through traffic.

I felt like drinking a Bulleit but it was too early.

I needed to write something.

I didn't know what.

I didn't care. Sometimes I'd just sip coffee in the box and feed drivel through my keys. It gave me a feeling of purpose, that I didn't just burn an afternoon with nothing to show.

I'd have pages. Pages of nonsense, but I'd have 'em all right.

Friday, August 14th, 1:55 p.m.

When I walked inside the bar, I caught Slice at his perch. Grinning.

"What's got you so teed up, Slice?"

"I'm happy to see you."

"Right back at ya, amigo."

And I *was* happy to see Slice. I joined him at the bar, ordered a Bulleit and promised myself I'd sip slow. I was only three sips deep when the Rooster tapped my shoulder and grinned something creepy.

"I got it," was all he said before walking back to his computer, waving me over.

It was a loaded walk. Cuz whatever he found wasn't meant to be seen by some dude in a bar with a helpless crush. Which meant I was on the cusp of invading some pretty serious illegal private territory of a dead girl. And, yeah, I felt guilty. But I was doing it *for* her, right?

I actually said, "Yeah" out loud as if to assure myself stepping back to the Rooster's corner.

"Before I show you this, I need you to do to me a favor."

"What kinda favor?"

He clammed up and looked like a cocker spaniel in trouble.

"Just...well, an introduction."

He nodded his head across the room at Jewels, who was serving a couple of lush lookin' frat yuks.

"...to Jewels?"

He nodded and kinda shook all over.

"But it's Jewels. You *know* her. You're here every day."

He squirmed. Shook his head. Twisted up his face like no, no, no, you don't get it. And I truly didn't.

"Well, she knows you."

His eyes drilled into me. "What do you mean? What does she know?"

"I mean, she knows who you are. She waits on you, right?"

More twisting and squirming like no, no, no, you *don't* get it. Then he stared at her with loaded eyes. Sitting there in his seat. Locked in.

"...Okay. Okay...I get it. You wanna talk to her. Get to know her. More than just, I'll have another Coke?"

"Yeah." He nodded uncomfortably. Then mumbled more under his breath.

The poor bastard.

"Of course, man, no problem. Leave it with me."

Assured, he saddled back in behind his computer and twisted the screen for me to see. He twisted it like it was no big thing, like I was checking out some stupid selfie or humdrum email but there in front of me was a picture of Josie Pendleton, completely naked in front of a mirror taking a picture of herself in a most private, most intimate, most unflattering, most raw moment.

I shut my eyes and started barking. "No. NO. No." The Rooster buckled, confused. "No—that's not what I want."

He shrugged, confused and nonchalantly minimized the picture. "You said you wanted pictures."

"You're right, I did. I just...wasn't expecting that. But thank you, I guess. Were you able to access any of her emails? Or texts?"

He opened a new window and a stack of her emails filled the screen. My mouth slung open. This was my treasure. My inside Josie Pendleton track.

"Yes. *This.* Thank you. This is more...my speed."

He nodded. Like he only half understood.

I started scouring the messages, but this was all too much

and all too overwhelmingly wonderful. I wanted to savor it all alone, in my own time.

"Can you send this to me?"

He pulled out a thumb drive and dumped all the files onto it. Then asked curiously, "You don't want any of the pictures?"

Of course I wanted them. I wanted to devour and inspect every last one. But I just wanted them on my terms.

"Sure, I'll take 'em."

After all, I was running an investigation. Highly illegally. Morally dubiously. But for all the right reasons, right?

Justice for the denim.

It filled my guts with a buzz.

I had reading to do.

I was back.

I ordered another drink and hustled into the box.

I locked the door and slammed on headphones. I needed quiet. I plugged in the thumb drive, keyed up, ready to take the plunge into the illegal rich digital details of Josie's life.

And with one easy *click!* there she was.

Josie Pendleton.

Alive.

Definitively unaware of her own mortality.

It all hit me off guard. The sparkle in her eye made my guts roll. The first shot I saw was Josie on a mountain hiking somewhere. Taking a selfie next to a dusty trail with the sun blanching out most of the frame. But she was there. Smiling. Happy. Alive. And I kept thinking about those final moments of that sonofabitch choking the life out of her. I tried not to wallow and smashed some booze but it only stirred the punch. I carried on, scrolling through the shots. Hoping like with some kinda roulette spin I'd land on a picture of her that didn't stir up all the ugliness. The winner was a shot of her behind the wheel of a convertible. It was a simple picture—looked like she'd found a sliver of good light at magic hour and hey, why not take another picture? She looked plain and normal and nothing like the sacred image burned into my memory of her slender form straddling the bar seat buried behind a book. She was just a girl in a tank top stuck in traffic.

Far from the slab. Naked and blue.

After an hour of watching snippets of her life, my desire to find her killer only grew so I pivoted and pulled up her emails.

I scanned the names and subjects and first couple lines of content. Reading wasn't as tough as the pictures. But it was weird to see so many emails come in after she was killed. Like Rachel Schow who was furious at Josie for not getting back to her over some essay on the *Art of Being a Woman in 2016* Josie'd evidently promised to forward. Most of the emails stopped piling up six days after her death, at which point Rachel musta heard and probably felt right bad.

I sifted through weeks of messages. Most were pretty generic. She had a brother in Pasadena. Parents in Brentwood. Friends who liked her. Companies who wanted her money. Art projects she was working on. Charities she loved and wanted to do more for. Susan Glasser talking about her bird Montgomery. I coulda looked at these messages for hours but what stung was how that outbox stopped cold.

I thought I'd glean more intimate intel from her emails but realized like most millennials she probably relied on texts or private message apps for anything super personal. I was getting near the end of my drink when I caught a message to her brother with a single line at the bottom that shot electricity up my spine.

————————Original message————————
From: rusticcat@gmail.com
Date: Thu, Jun 25, 2018 at 7:02 p.m.
Subject: Liza's birthday
To: jjpendleton98@gmail.com

You comin this Sunday for Liza's birthday? She'd love to see ya. And you know we have a bounce house so...you kinda can't say no.

—————————Reply message—————————
From: jjpendleton98@gmail.com
Date: Thu, Jun 25, 2018 at 7:39 p.m.
Subject: Re: Liza's birthday
To: rusticcat@gmail.com

hey bro sorry. I've been slammed with school and a little project I'm working on the side. super crazy stuff. I'll tell you all about it when I see you. but yes! I'll be there on sunday.

—————————Reply message—————————
From: rusticcat@gmail.com
Date: Thu, Jun 25, 2018 at 7:39 p.m.
Subject: Re: Liza's birthday
To: jjpendleton98@gmail.com

Cool. Wait what kinda project? At Backyard Dreams? Or school.

—————————Reply message—————————
From: jjpendleton98@gmail.com
Date: Thu, Jun 25, 2018 at 7:40 p.m.
Subject: Re: Liza's birthday
To: rusticcat@gmail.com

Backyard. kinda too early to talk about but I'm getting my robin hood on. Striking down the almighty...doin' what i do.

and don't worry big bro. I'll be fine :)

————————Reply message————————
From: jjpendleton98@gmail.com
Date: Thu, Jun 25, 2018 at 7:41 p.m.
Subject: Re: Liza's birthday
To: rusticcat@gmail.com

Oooookay Robin Hood. Just don't do anything stupid.

Robin Hood. I stared at the words.

Robin Hood how? *Stealing from the rich and giving to the poor?* Josie Pendleton was a student with loans who volunteered at a charity in her spare time. Glenn might be a wannabe cheating loser but stealing from his charity meant she was stealing from disabled kids. I just didn't buy it.

Before long I found this:

————————Original message————————
From: jjpendleton98@gmail.com
Date: Wed, July 01, 2018 at 11:11 p.m.
Subject: story
To: jimmyface999@gmail.com

You in town? I'm working on something you're gonna like.

————————Reply message————————
From: jjpendleton98@gmail.com
Date: Wed, July 01, 2018 at 11:11 p.m.
Subject: Re: story
To: jimmyface999@gmail.com

Yeah I'm around. Can you give me a bite? Big or small?

————————Reply message————————
From: jjpendleton98@gmail.com
Date: Wed, July 01, 2018 at 11:11 p.m.

Subject: Re: story
To: jimmyface999@gmail.com

I'm gonna blow the lid off a very powerful organization…and I'm gonna need your help once I got the goods.

—————Reply message—————
From: jjpendleton98@gmail.com
Date: Wed, July 01, 2018 at 11:12 p.m.
Subject: Re: story
To: jimmyface999@gmail.com

C'mon at least give me a taste? Corporate? Local?

—————Reply message—————
From: jjpendleton98@gmail.com
Date: Wed, July 01, 2018 at 11:12 p.m.
Subject: Re: story
To: jimmyface999@gmail.com

☺

That was it. A smiley face.
Like a ghost with a grin.
But I was buzzing. This was six days before Josie was killed. Who was jimmyface999@gmail.com? Did the cops know about this? He sounded like a reporter. Best I could tell this was the only time she'd emailed him. So I figured I'd search the word *organization* but whatever dark net program the Rooster used turned my results into a barrage of ugly illegible computer speak. With no better choice, I started going through one and by one, looking up *organization* for the last month. I went deeper and deeper and realized I'd burned close to three hours looking for some nugget of some clue I had no bearing on.
I changed gears. Who the hell was jimmyface999? I couldn't

approach them directly, given my way in was through Josie's illegally hacked email. But maybe I could find out by at least knocking on their door anonymously. I pulled up one of my fake email accounts and wrote a message:

—————————Original message—————————
From: Thepistongame@gmail.com
Date: Fri, August 14, 2018 at 8:08 p.m.
Subject: ASAP
To: jimmyface999@gmail.com

Hey Darren,

I can't come to the event so PLEASE tell me asap where I should send the package.
Thanks—AP.

Within seventeen seconds I got a message back:

—————————Reply message—————————
From: jimmyface999@gmail.com
Date: Fri, August 14, 2018 at 8:08 p.m.
Subject: Re: ASAP
To: Thepistongame@gmail.com

This is not Darren. You have the wrong email.

—————————Reply message—————————
From: Thepistongame@gmail.com
Date: Fri, August 14, 2018 at 8:08 p.m.
Subject: Re: Liza's birthday
To: jimmyface999@gmail.com

Sorry. Who is this?

I sat back and waited. Seventeen seconds came and went. Seventeen minutes came and went. No dice.

It was long shot at best. Still, it confirmed that whoever this person was, was out there, alive and well and might have the goods on who killed Josie. So how the hell could I get to them?

I needed to think…

I needed to piss.

I needed another drink.

When I emerged from the box most of the place was practically empty. Lily was yuckin' it up with some buttoned up lawyers. Then, I caught the Rooster eyeing me as I walked out. I lobbed back a gracious nod but his eyes moved off and landed on Jewels then back to me as if to say *your turn, friend.*

My turn, indeed, but the guy was gonna have to wait. How the hell was I gonna get Jewels to take an interest in the Rooster? That was gonna take an angle.

And right now I needed a drink.

I hopped up on a stool next to Slice and filled him in over a fresh Bulleit. I didn't expose the Rooster's end but I had a feeling Slice was wise on the angle. I knew he'd seen me talking to him in the corner. Anyway, Slice called the ball and agreed jimmyface999 sounded like a reporter. He figured Josie had the scoop on something and needed his help to spread the word. I liked the theory but the chances of jimmyface999 getting back to me anytime soon were getting worse and worse, which meant I needed a new road. I didn't have enough intel to be valuable. It was time to strike closer to the source. And I knew exactly where to start.

Her kin.

Saturday, August 15th, 11:01 a.m.

David Pendleton lived not far from the Orange Grove exit off the 134. He had a wife named Ruby and a pretty little girl named Liza. Seeing those faces smashed me back to Josie's funeral reception and talking to her crazy aunt. I remembered seeing pictures of David and his family around the house. He seemed like a decent guy based on some generic online recon: worked for a corporate law firm downtown. Went to UCLA. Sports fan. Traveled to Costa Rica for a surf trip. Married his college sweetheart. Kinda all around. I knew digging around Josie's death wasn't gonna exactly butter her brother up with joy and figured I'd need to sidestep the truth to get him to open up. Aka lie. Just what the hell kinda Robin Hood stuff was she up to? If my sister was digging up skeletons on powerful organizations, I'd make sure she was safe about it. Hopefully David was the same way.

We met at a Starbucks downtown near his work off Broadway and 6th. He was buried in his phone and looked like he had very little free time this morning.

I'd called him earlier and told him I was part of the Backyard Dreams crew who were doing a write-up on Josie. Of course, we at Backyard Dreams wanted to write a sparkling piece and before I could even finish the fiction he offered to meet up. Guess I shouldn't have been surprised I hit a nerve.

He greeted me with a hard handshake and offered to buy me a coffee. We ordered our brews and mixed conversation. The usual bent: LA traffic and heat. He suggested sitting outside, and we found a spot in the shade of a skyscraper. I thanked him for the coffee and taking the time sit with me as I pulled out my phone and hit record on a voice memo.

I eased in by saying that all of us at Backyard were devastated so…"For the next newsletter I wanted to write a special profile on your sister. I wondered if I could just ask you some questions about her."

He shifted uncomfortably.

"Of course. Sure."

I started off with the usual bio crap. "What was she like as a younger sister? How would you describe her growing up?"

He took some deep breaths and let loose about their child-hood. The more he talked about her, the more decent he seemed and the more I felt like a weasel. Poor bastard just lost his sister and I was frothing for inside dirt: *Was she the kind of girl you hated in high school or the one you wanted to save? Who did she love and why? Who broke her heart?*

But her brother just fired off generic cheese about how *nice* she was, the kind of girl who would pick up litter on a hike or take a spider outside before killing it in the house. *Reader's Digest* drivel sans dirt or soul. But at least the drivel made an easy pivot.

"Probably what led her to working at a charity like Backyard Dreams?"

David took the bait. "Josie worked tirelessly with under-privileged kids. She used to volunteer at the zoo summer camp until they pretty much HAD to start paying her for all the time she put in. And of course her work at Backyard was tremendous. She was instrumental in creating all those fundraising galas and charity walks. But you know all about that…"

I fueled the fire. "Oh, yeah. Glenn was lucky to have her. We all were…but I'm curious, did she ever talk about her involvement at Backyard in detail?"

"No. Not really."

"She was always so busy. She kinda reminded me of a modern-day Robin Hood with all that fundraising."

The ace jarred him. "Well, it's funny you say that...that was one of the last things she wrote to me about. She even said she felt like Robin Hood. She was pretty cagey about it all but I pressed cuz...honestly I was worried about her. She had a habit of being a little too righteous in the faces of wrong people. Standing up for what she believed in regardless of who she pissed off."

"Who was she pissing off?"

"Oh, I don't think it was anyone at Backyard."

"Still, now you got me all curious."

"Well, it was weird. She started hanging out with this guy. I never met him, but I could tell when she was hiding the fact she was seeing someone. Probably someone older, someone her very protective older brother wouldn't approve of..." He smiled like I should've understood.

"You think it was Glenn?"

"Nah, she was smarter than to get mixed up with a married man. And it wasn't like that."

"Whaddya mean?"

"I'm pretty liberal and I got the feeling this guy's values were way right of mine. And by right I mean capital W wrong. That kinda right, if you know what I mean? No offense if you're...you know..."

"None taken. So you think he was pretty right wing?"

"I can't say for sure. But she usually told me about the guys she was seeing in the past, so that was my hunch."

I was spinning inside. The *scratcher*. But I had to play it cool.

"What was his name?"

"Joel, I think."

"Joel...?"

"I don't know, man...Why does it matter? You're not gonna put any of this in your write-up, are you?"

"No, sorry. I get curious sometimes. My dad always told me it was my best and worst trait."

He clocked me a side-eyed look like he knew something

was stinky. I figured this was the end of the line on the Joel questioning so I tried to buy back some faith and steered the conversation toward family stuff...

He spewed more generic copy about how *nice* she was but that was as eloquent and deep as this man was going to dig. And I mean, *nice*? Charles Manson was a charmer but that don't mean he wasn't a monster. Nice gets me nowhere.

After more minutes of babbling I cut the interview short. He looked puzzled but was more than happy to walk away. I knew I'd messed up; tipped my hand by needling questions about her boyfriend.

But I didn't care.

I was buzzing.

I'd finally found a compass towards that gnawing question. What kinda monster laid those scratches into Josie Pendleton's skin?

The scratcher.

And now, I had a man named Joel.

I scurried to my car, hiding in the shade of the LA skyscrapers, scampering along the concrete with an eager flurry.

Like a some kinda weasel.

Saturday, August 15th, 4:09 p.m.

There are times when, even for a functioning alcoholic who soaks their taste buds in delicious poison day in and day out, that a sip of booze strikes some perfect clit at the back of the tongue where for just a few moments the liquid smashes in with an ecstatic bliss that pops goose bumps on your neck and fills your body with a shudder of delight.

Yeah.

This was one of those moments.

Cuz I had Joel.

I scooped up my Bulleit and locked myself into the box. I dragged the net, and searched *Joel* in her emails. Weirdly I didn't find anyone named Joel that she was intimately close with. There were no *hey great seeing you the other night.* No *hey Joel that was a mind-blowing orgasm, wanna do it again* or *go to dinner* or *a hike* or *come over to watch a movie* or *talk* or *meet my family* or anything in her emails for the last three months that seemed to be from a guy named Joel. Still, there were traces of some Joels in her life and I dragged the net to find:

Joel Johnson: an accountant in Century City affiliated with a firm Johnson, Sachs, Overmeyer that Josie was cc'd on an email from some guy named James in regards to a tax receipt she needed. I called over and turns out Joel was now seventy-eight years old and perched in a nursing home in Sacramento. Strike one.

Joel Dawson: a character in a bad play called *Frozen Supper* she saw at a Santa Monica Boulevard hundred-seat theater with a friend named Phoebe in 2017. Joel was fictional. Strike two.

Joelle Segretti: an Italian exchange student in her Perspectives on Modern Art class she took last year. I did some further digging on this cat but according to his Facebook page Segretti, who she shared a bunch of friends with, had been living back in Florence for the last eight months and was out of the country around the time of the murder. Strike three.

Then there was Joel Ames: a client service rep in Woodland Hills doing a follow-up survey on a line of skincare products she purchased. He worked for a marketing firm. I reached out to human resources, determined to track him down but he was based in their Florida office.

Was David Pendleton lying? What kind of woman doesn't write at least one email about a guy she's seeing? To a friend. A cousin. A brother. What the hell was goin' on?

I sucked back the rest of my drink and pushed away from my desk. My inside lead just vanished.

The Pluckin' Strummers were pluckin' to their goddamn hearts' content when I landed at the bar. Jiles was shimmering with happiness so I leaned on Jewels for my drink and realized I still owed the Rooster a lead.

"Jewels...you ever talk to the Rooster?"

She shrugged no and screwed up her mouth, repulsed at the mere thought of engaging with the man.

I definitely needed to bridge the gap.

"Yeah, that's kinda what I thought until I got to know him. But he's super cool. Knows a ton about marketing and starting small businesses. You should talk to him about your jewelry line—maybe he can help puff it up. Drum up some sales."

This time around, she clocked the Rooster an intrigued look. "Really, he knows about that stuff?"

You could see the prospective profit wheels turning. The way out...*Through that guy?* Her mouth relaxed and eyebrows danced up and down like she might consider talking to the man for more than a tip.

One small step for Jewels.

One giant leap for the Rooster.

Now all I needed to do was see if he could talk his way through a bullshit marketing campaign for the world's ugliest line of jewelry.

When she stepped away to put in my order I shuffled over to the Rooster and gave him the heads up. He looked like I'd punched him in the gut. "Relax. You just gotta sell her with a few marketing bullet points—brand transparency, market share, net profits—then just talk to her."

He didn't smile. He didn't say thank you. He was already sweating fierce and hitting up Google for a lifeline.

"You got this, man."

I needed to refuel and stepped up to the bar. Slice angled a look, curious where I'd been, and I told him all about my lead on phantom Joel. He was excited for me but agreed somethin' was funky if she never even mentioned him in one stupid email.

We spewed Dodgers.

We smiled and felt like friends with history. I got hit with that wonder of just what the hell did this man do to get fired from the force. Who did he betray?

The Strummers were howling something fierce and Slice couldn't take it. He waved a hand and made for the door. And like some teenager with a hope-boner on a date, I downed my drink and caught up with him.

"Lemme drive ya."

He clocked me the look.

"I've been in there for three hours and had the two drinks...I'm fine."

"You're not gonna charge me, are ya?"

"I don't charge friends for rides, Slice."

He looked at the ground, like he was caught off guard.

"You wanna ride or not?"

His old lips pushed out an awkward *okay*. Like we were entering some new phase of our bromance outside of the bar. God forbid we actually regard each other like human beings. Or, like friends.

Then we walked to the car in silence.

Saturday, August 15th, 9:16 p.m.

The inside of Slice's apartment made me wanna cry.

The walls were covered in old black and white, and fading red, eight-by-eleven pictures of cops in every setting you could imagine.

Squad cars.

Precincts.

Squash courts.

Diners. Charity fundraisers. Homes. Streets. Beaches...the wall was covered in dudes wearing tight eighties' shorts with mustaches. Real mustaches, none of this thin tailored, waxed, Silverlake crap. At first glance I thought I was staring at one of those murder boards you see on network television cuz a lot of them were pinned with tacks or just pasted against the wall.

But it was Slice's life.

It was Slice trying to hang onto his life.

The memories of a man once proud.

He looked good as a young cop. His eyes were different. They looked sharp. Strong. Like they were hunting or something. Not the glazy stare he rocked now.

Slice poured me a cheap scotch and said it was the best he could do cuz he didn't like to keep booze in the house, but his son had left a bottle the other week.

I accepted and stared at the wall. Rapt.

I mean, I knew was Slice was a cop back in the day but seeing all these pictures made it real. Not just some tall tale an alcoholic was cooking up for sympathy and an extra round.

He really *was* a cop. And a decorated one by the looks of some of the medals and those smiling handshakes in front of oversized LAPD emblems.

"Wow. This is impressive."

He shrugged like he agreed but was too proud to admit it.

The room got quiet and, surrounded by that all that bravado and valor, I couldn't stop myself. The loaded question just erupted from my mouth.

"What happened?"

Slice took a deep breath, then let out the air like it had been in there a month and finally just shrugged.

"I shot a guy. His name was Marcus Yates. He was rotten. Everybody knew it. No one could prove it. But I couldn't stand by and watch Marcus hurt people. *Kids*, you know...so...

"I shot him on a Wednesday afternoon behind a Staples on Vermont. Shouldn't have done that. The department found out. And when word started to get around, my brethren in blue protected me. They buried it but said I had to walk. No questions. No pension. 'Just walk away, Slice.'"

And on that ugly note he turned and disappeared to take a piss.

I don't know what I was expecting, but the way he just burped it out like it was some mishap on Wednesday afternoon, like some street cleaning parking ticket snafu, rocked the hell out of me. I tried not to get all poetic and shit but it was hard not to, surrounded by his glory days on the wall. No wonder Jiles, Pinner, or any of those guys never leaked the story. Maybe they were the ones who helped bury the truth.

I probably shoulda known better or had more decency but I pulled out my phone and started snapping pictures of Slice's history wall. When he came back I played it off and pretended to be on my phone. He poured himself a glass of tap water and I realized I'd never seen this man actually drink water before. It was like seeing a coyote on Sunset Boulevard. Kinda odd and out of place but I guess it made sense. He started up about the

Dodgers and obviously didn't wanna dwell on his past. It wasn't until after we'd gone over the bullpen roster that I caught a curled-up photo beside the couch. It was Slice with his arm around a young boy and a pretty woman in a yellow sundress.

The faces sparkled.

Soaked in sunshine and love.

He kept blabbering about baseball but all I could take in was that image of Slice—glowing as a husband and a father instead of some broken-down, disgraced ex-cop at a bar. I had a million questions but I sipped my bad scotch, yapped ball, buzzing inside cuz I'd finally unlocked the mystery to my hero's demise. And I knew this was the key ending for my article. Now, I needed to get it on the page.

So I downed my drink, thanked Slice for the burst, and weaved home.

Saturday, August 15th, 11:49 p.m.

Slice was a murderer.

A cop who killed a kiddie raper.

Jesus.

I couldn't rat him out.

I had to throw some shade on the truth.

I laid out his past. His present. His damned future. It all lined up nice. The disdain of it all. Disdain, that gem...

I sipped bourbon in my room till my head swirled and my hands couldn't type.

Sunday, August 16th, 3:09 p.m.

I woke up in my clothes with sweaters on my teeth. A cracking pain in my skull I most certainly blamed on Slice's scotch. But after taking a piss and five ibuprofens, I was back in the game. I stirred my boy Benny from his standby slumber and more words kept pouring out of me. I wanted to scream and skip like a child cuz the words oozed out right instead of having to pull them out with white knuckled claws.

I found a bagel in the kitchen and it was enough to keep me going for another four hours until I finished. I called it, "Disdain, That Gem."

It was 4,122 words.

They were my words.

They were truthful and beautiful and nobody could take them away.

For now, anyway. While they slept on my hard drive hibernating like a diamond waiting to be appraised. Aka until my agent read it and asked what ELSE I've been working on...

I wasn't ready to ship it out. I wanted to hang onto the feeling of success in my stomach and fill it with food and maybe even the company of people while I glowed with confidence.

I took a shower.

I did some push-ups.

I shaved and felt like a miracle.

When I walked into the kitchen Nick was sipping Diet Coke next to a memorable and still quite beautiful face. Margaret with the collarbone. *Was Nick sleeping with Margaret?* I couldn't imagine them together but hey, I was probably just jealous. She was even more beautiful in the daylight.

We waxed pleasant, preferring not to stir up our previous chat about local Nazis or as they likened, the Patriot Strong.

"Margaret was just telling me about an event you should come check out, Sam. A fun meet and greet."

"Lemme guess—a delightful, racist-enthused, unite the right scream-a-thon where people get harassed and possibly even killed?"

"C'mon. Don't get all uppity. More like Unite the Pasadena City College kids. Educate these fine youths on deeper wholesome American values as exemplified by Patriot Strong."

The mention of Josie's college made me even consider the idea of going. An excuse to hit the campus she walked. See the doors she crossed. The faces and places in her world. But then the *Triumph of the Will* homage rallying innocent impressionable youths made me write off the idea immediately.

"Thanks, I'm good." But I couldn't resist Margaret's face. "Why don't you skip it, Margaret, and hang out here?"

Nick got stiff and Margaret flashed that embarrassed smile. "That's sweet but I actually get a kick out of these things. They've got some pretty far-out ideas. Magnet Max is speaking."

Nick lit up. "Max will be there?"

Margaret confirmed with a shrug. "That's what he said on Twitter. You really gotta check this guy out, Sam."

"Magnet Max?"

"He's an incredible human being."

But I'd already checked him out. That night with Margaret and the alpha douches with the yellow Beamer. I looked him up online. He was their de facto leader. An Aryan cross between a young JFK and Lenny Bruce with deplorable values against women, minorities, and anyone from a country without 'Western values.' "Yeah, thanks but no thanks. I saw the guy's rants online. He puffs a pretty big game."

Nick said, "I've never seen him in the flesh but you can tell he has a way with people. Young kids, too. It's incredible the way he lures them in, gets their minds all warped."

"See, Margaret? Don't warp your beautiful young mind. Hang back here with Magnet Sammy. We'll smash a latté and vibe about rainbows and Jackie Wilson."

"Who's Jackie Wilson?"

"The singer?"

Margaret looked on blankly.

"Seriously? You gotta let me play you some Jackie Wilson. It might just change your life."

I got a genuine smile but she wasn't ready to defect.

"Suit yourself. Go warp your values with a man named Magnet Max."

"It's just a moniker," Margaret pointed out.

Nick was curious, "What's his real name?"

"Joel Brighton," she said.

He crunched up his face, "Joel Brighton? Really? His name's Joel?" The truth seemed to deflate my beloved roommate. But all I could focus on was that word she had uttered so nonchalantly.

Joel.

137

Sunday, August 16th, 4:38 p.m.

I came in hot.

We could always tell when one of our own had braggin'
rights. The skip in the step. The hustle up to the stool. That's
what Jiles called it. *The hustle up*. He knew to top off the booze
just right. To endorse a second round or better yet a round for
the house. A wise barkeep there ever was.

Johnny Cash bellowed in the background about a man coming around and angels singing.

Jiles dished a Bulleit and nudged up his chin, knowing full
well. "Whaddya got, kid?"

I'd hoped Slice would be around for the put together but I
didn't see him so let loose, layin' out the chips for Jiles and
Pa.

1. Josie went to Pasadena City College and said she was
   gonna take down a big powerful organization.
2. Patriot Strong were holding rallies at Pasadena City
   College.
3. The leader of Patriot Strong is Magnet Max. But his
   real name is Joel.
4. Josie's brother said she was seeing a guy named Joel
   with hard-hitting right-wing politics.
5. Maybe Patriot Strong was the powerful organization
   she was talking about, not Backyard Dreams.
6. Maybe Magnet Max is my Joel.

Afterward, Jiles smiled like a proud pappa but was quick to

caution, "Don't get ahead of yourself, Sammy. It's all speculation."

I shook my head like a teenager who understood the world better than his own father. "C'mon, it all lines up, Jiles. I swear, I caught a piece of the wave, just like you and Slice would call it back on the beat."

The wave. Cop talk for a ride in the gut. A flutter of *fuck ya, I've got the answer.* It wasn't like solving a math problem where all the pieces lined up tight and clean. Or a piece of happenstance good luck that lights up your day. No, no this was the wave of intuition, when a case drops and a cop's been working it for nights on nights, sweating it out and a sliver of truth drops in and the whole puzzle catches light and you know you've cracked it cuz that gut flashes with a wave of promise that everything you've worked for suddenly has purpose and promise that helps make sense of your fight against the world's demons.

Jiles went with it and admitted some of the facts looked promising.

"So what's your next move?"

"Time to dig. Find out everything there is to know about one Joel Brighton."

Aka Magnet Max.

Aka the scratcher.

Aka the man who murdered my girl.

Sunday, August 16th, 6:09 p.m.

First thing was to check Josie's email for Magnet Max. The results were cloudy with a chance of promise. To no surprise she never referred to him as Magnet Max. But about two months back I found the word Max in a bunch of emails sent to her friends.

Max.

In a message to a girl in her class named Gelia Harrison on January 6th, Josie admitted she was *fond* of a guy named Max. She literally used the word *fond*. Now, this struck me as odd on a number of levels. 1) a twenty-something college girl living in LA referring to a guy she has the hots for as *fond*? It was too polite. Too untwenties. If Josie *really* dug this guy, I just don't see her describing those tingling-early-crush-feelings with Jane Austen *fond*-ness. 2) I admit I didn't actually know Josie in real life but whatever. Maybe I could at the very least understand her. I'd put in my time on discovery, processing every little shred of information about her. And nothing about her indicated she'd be *fond* for a hard-hitting fanatical alt-right bro nicknamed Magnet Max. It just ran counter to everything she represented.

The rest was nuggets.

Shavings.

All her emails mentioning Max were detached. I'd seen her describe a tulip on campus with more passion and interest than the man she was supposedly having sex with. And there wasn't a single email from the man himself.

It all felt like a runaround.

I changed gears.

I emerged from the box, took a piss, and ordered another drink. I was gonna yap with Pa but he looked pretty gunned so I went back at it and scurried into the box and keyed in a couple of hopeful words to my search engine: *Magnet Max.*

Real name née, Joel Brighton was born in Boston to an Irish Catholic family. He had a slew of brothers and sisters and by all accounts a healthy, educated middle-class white boy upbringing. He studied Political Science at UofB but dropped out after two years. Around then he started a podcast called Patriot Strong with his high school buddy Robert Ross. Just two dudes barking polarizing propaganda in a cramped one-bedroom apartment. But within three months they had a decent following of like-minded morons who agreed the world would be a better place with more white guys in power. The wave of ignorance kept gaining steam and sound bites would get posted on news sites and blogs and any self-serving outlet who'd benefit from a clap on the back. Eventually they went face to face with folks and started talking at universities. Rallying people to their cause. That is until they were physically attacked and asked to leave. Again and again. But eventually they picked up some legit heavyweight sponsors. Private donors who were by all accounts afraid to have their names smeared in public but hell yea they wanted to be in the racist game.

The funding allowed for Joel and Ross to go wide. And go wide they did—they started popping up all over the country. Barking at colleges. Counter-rallying against women's rights marches. Gun control protests. The bully in the schoolyard eggin' for a fight. They grew stronger and stronger, but somewhere along the way Ross threw in his cards and cashed out. Probably on account of Joel's outgoing, rabid fanaticism that constantly put the cofounder in the shadows. So much so that he splintered off to become some kinda political consultant in South Carolina.

This left Joel to carry the torch all by himself. He was reborn as Magnet Max for his impressive ability to pull in soft-minded fools who figured this guy might have some value to add to the planet. Who preyed on weak-minded plebes with no money and no education and lives fueled by fear of the *other*.

The other race.

The other sex.

The other religion.

The other America this country was turning into.

The fear.

Max tapped the fear hard. He wooed them in. Listening to his rhetoric, the man definitely had a way with words, I'd give him that. His swill of promise and potential for a better country we COULD be if only we play the nuclear race card. Think about all the money and resources we waste hating each other. Divide and conquer. Let *them* be. Set them free. Of course, he never answered where *they* should go or if they even wanted to.

Hours flew by and I understood why they called the guy the Magnet Max. Researching the man was like watching terrible pornography. Filthy. Wrong, so wrong, on so many levels and I really needed to stop ingesting the images and thoughts, but damn. Wow. Just look at the ugliness bounce and jiggle.

Until I was tapped. I felt like I needed a shower.

And yeah, another drink.

I emerged and found Lily at the bar. She smelled sweet. I always liked seeing Lily. She was tough. Told it like it was. "How'ya been, Sammy?"

"Aces, Lil. Aces."

We sat in silence, sipping our bliss, listening to Roy Orbison coo. That man could sing a piece of God.

And by the end of the night, I knew what I had to do.

It wasn't gonna be pretty.

But I needed to square the lead.

I needed to find out, no *rule* out, the possibility that Josie was involved with Max. Maybe I was way off base but if he was the scratcher, if Josie was tangling with their organization, it was more than possible someone might have killed her.

I needed to infiltrate Patriot Strong. Pay Magnet Max a visit and shake hands with the devil himself.

Friday, August 21st, 3:23 p.m.

When I finally heard back from Nick and told him I'd consider checking out his friends' beloved fraternity of Nazis (though not in so many words), he wondered what the hell had changed my mind. I told him a shade of the truth: *research.* The line was enough to buy his trust and he said the best way was to take a trip to a weekly meet and greet at their fraternity headquarters in Long Beach.

The next few days I spent scraping together cash sharing my ride around town and contemplating my angle. When the day finally arrived, Nick and I drove down together but on the way there, he needled the hell out of me.

What kinda research you doin'?

Who's it for?

Why why why's comin' at me all the way driving down the I-5.

I made up some yarn about a character in a new screenplay I was writing, and he was dubious, shooting off side-glances as if trying to make sure I wasn't going to sabotage this beloved tribe. Or his good name.

Fuckin' Nick.

But it felt good going south undercover.

Slice and Jiles would be proud.

Friday, August 21st, 5:01 p.m.

When we finally landed and made our way towards Patriot Strong's headquarters, I was struck by one thing: money. These guys had cash. The HQ wasn't some hand-me-down, decrepit Alpha Omega townhouse. No, sir. These white boys had *dough*. This was a three-story mansion on a hill with a badass view of the ocean. Beautifully manicured grounds. A tight green lawn. Blooming flowers. Pristine.

My stomach tightened as we crossed inside the main foyer cuz I remembered the real reason I was there.

The Scratcher.

We were greeted with three smiling faces, none of which were Magnet Max but one that was black. It caught me off guard. *Why's a black guy hanging with a bunch of alt right fascists?*

Nick introduced me and I shook hands, playing it cool. I forgot their names immediately except for Oliver, the black guy. I kept staring at his face, like I was trying to figure out the angle.

"Welcome to Patriot Strong. I'm Oliver. My friends call me Oli. Come on in, can I get you a drink? Some food?"

Oli sounded like a white black guy.

Oli motioned to an open bar and a huge spread of catered food. I counted seven different salads, breads, cheeses of all colors, wild smoked salmon, fresh shrimp, marinated chicken breasts, fruit platters. Nearby a group of twenty somethings were slamming back chow and sipping drinks looking ripe with guilt as if all this free food was too good to be true.

"Maybe just a beer for now, thanks."

As I followed Oli to the bar Nick stayed back and chatted with the other faces and it seemed like they all knew each other. Oli handed over a cold Corona with a fat slice of lime and a smile.

"So how'd you hear about us, Sam?"

"Nick's my roommate. He talks about you guys all the time. Guess I needed to see if for myself."

"Glad you came out, man."

"Nice place…"

I smiled and took a sip of my beer. Pretending to be happy, glancing at Oliver. He clocked my feeble poker face.

"Yeah, you're not the first to be confused, man. See, a lotta people think this organization is racist but the truth is we're race-forward. We've moved beyond issues of race. We're about *values* here. Values that this country has lost. Values that we want to re-institutionalize on a national level." He smiled, flashing a mouthful of polished white teeth. "But I'm not here to drown you with shop-talk. There's way smarter people here who can do that for you. Just have a drink and hang out. We're good people. You'll see."

He led me out towards the backyard and my mouth literally hung open at the sight of so many tall, white, beautiful bodies and skin and smiles laughing and playing next to a giant infinity pool. They were lounging and listening to music and all happy happy. Drinking. Flirting. As if this entire fraternity weren't based on segregation and hate.

I hung back with Oli and took in the scene. It reminded me how small my life had become. Holed up inside a stuffy bar in Glendale. These people radiated joy like they were high on some kinda California drug. Oli started asking me questions about my family. My religion. My values. He was open and intrigued. And the more we got to talking, the more it pissed me off how nice he was. I didn't want to like Oliver. I didn't want to like anybody here. I had a job to do.

I played nice, pinch-sipping my beer for over an hour, hiding in the shadows until finally the master of ceremonies himself,

Mr. Magnet Max, graced us all with his divine presence. At first I wasn't sure what was going on until a crowd of faces started craning their attention to the back door where a man stepped out into the sunshine with a formidable swagger.

He was a tall beast of a soul, well over six feet, with sprawling shoulders and a square wide jaw attached to an impressively full head of slicked back blonde hair and a tight well-manicured beard. Sleeves of tattoos spilled out from ripped arms under a crisp white T-shirt, and he instantly reminded me of a Viking. A virile, hot-blooded, physically imposing man with a sharp look in his eye wired to a wicked brain.

Just by looking at him, I could tell immediately why people would follow this man. As if he might protect them in whatever battle they were fighting. Boys and girls alike. Hell, if I was backed into a corner I would want him to back me up. *Magnet Max.* A man who actually lived up to his moniker, literally sucking people's attention into his orbit just by walking through the crowd. Looking around, I'd failed to consider how many people this man influenced. How many weak-minded fools wanted his attention? And being here now, I was struck with an ugly fear. *Was Josie one of them? Did she get sucked into all this? Did they pull her down, too?*

I needed to get to Max. But I'd underestimated how hard that was going to be. He was a hero here. Still, I didn't hoof it all the way out here to hang back in the shadows. I looked around for Nick, hoping he might introduce me, but he had his hands full, talking to three stunning blondes at the side of the pool. So I hung back with my buddy Oliver and waited for the flock to thin out before asking if he'd introduce me to Max.

Oli graciously took the bait. "Of course, amigo."

We weaved through the crowd. Oli edged up to Max, who turned and greeted him with a warm hug. Then Max turned and looked me in the eye. Smiled warmly and offered his hand, like a gentleman might.

"Max, I want you to meet Sam," Oli said.

My world got awfully slow and cold, but I froze a placid smile on my mug and accepted his large hand as it dwarfed my palm.

"Nice to meet you, Sam. Welcome to our home."

I hit him with a slice of the truth, "I've been excited to meet you, Max."

I looked at his nails. The nails I suspected had dug into Josie's back. They were short and clean and altogether disappointing. I wanted to accuse the bastard right then and there but buttoned up and greased smooth. Applauded his success and visions for a perfect white future.

Except driving down here I figured if I was too gushy, Max would chalk me up as another plebe without a brain. I'd have to lay in some doubt, some seeds of moral pushback, suspecting this man would stop at nothing to get me on board with his cause.

So I started the dance.

"Some pretty big ideas you guys are backing here. It's intriguing. But don't you think it's limiting to disparage progressive women's perspectives? By turning your back on them, you're really cutting into your potential followers."

Max looked pleased I was here for more than just free booze and skin. He gazed hungry and eager like I was some piece of meat he wanted to chase and devour.

"We're empowering women. Liberating them from having to fight against their God given strengths. Women have been blessed to have children. To nurture families. By returning to traditional roles and allowing men to forge the financial growth of the family, they can flourish in a more wholesome manner."

The man gabbered on his crazy bent. He was incredibly present, unlike any other human being I've ever known. It wasn't just his good looks; it was something bigger, something intangible that when his eyes landed on you, only you mattered.

He saw my empty beer and asked one of his plebes to grab me another.

"I'm driving home soon, so I should probably—"

"Driving home? Don't do that. Look at this place. Look at

these beautiful people. Stay. Stay the night. We got room. Hang out. Eat some food. We're just getting started, Sam."

"Are you staying the night, Max?" I tried to sound like a little lamb he might wanna slaughter.

"Of course."

A beautiful woman slapped a cold beer in my hand. I wavered, stared at it, pretending like I had to contemplate the proper decision.

"Maybe just one more."

Max flashed a grand smile like we were all best friends. I took the beer and walked away.

I'd set the hook.

Now, I needed to eat some morally compromised free chow and strategize how the hell to land the shark.

Friday, August 21st, 8:11 p.m.

I smashed some shaved fennel salad with hints of mint and orange. It was fantastic. Not to mention the nine incredibly perfect spare ribs I ripped off the bone with my jaws. Thankfully I found a little corner in a back room enabling me to shovel the meat down my trough with abandon and sans fear of beautiful girls witnessing the grotesque performance.

But then I saw Margaret.

She was by the pool.

Dangling her legs in the water, makin' a splash.

Laughing, sipping a cocktail.

She couldn't see me. But I could see her.

I watched her.

I watched her yellow bikini stretch and pull against her skin.

I watched her mouth. Smiling. Trying to fathom if she truly understood what this place represented.

I wondered this while smashing a fresh brownie with whipped cream followed by a spoonful of chocolate mousse.

I figured I'd get only one, *maybe* two chances if I got lucky, to speak to Max, so I had to come in ready. But it was too soon since our last tête-à-tête. And currently, he was buried in a heated conversation with some alpha dudes near the pool table.

Nick was nowhere to be seen.

But Margaret was.

And I had time to kill.

I walked up to her expecting a frosty welcome but she sparkled a surprised, quirky smile my way.

"What are *you* doing here?"

"Guess I just had to see it for myself."

"Cool, right? Is Nick here?"

"Yea, why?"

She shrugged like she didn't care. But that was a shrug ripe with care. And disdain. And I knew it well.

"Somethin' happen?"

Another shrug. Nick had obviously pissed her off. *Welcome to my world, Marge.*

"Where's your suit?"

"Didn't get the pool memo. Got an extra one?"

She actually laughed at the terrible joke and took the last sip of her drink.

"Need a refill?"

"Yea. Whaddya drinkin'?"

"Swill. Something they call beer. I need to find a real drink."

"I'll join ya."

She stepped out of the pool and wrapped a towel around her dripping legs. We made our way to the bar and I offered to make her an old fashioned. She said she'd never had one. I told her it might change her life.

"Like Jackie Wilson?" And again there was that laugh.

Say what you want about Patriot Strong's dubious moral compass, but they stacked a bar with fantastic libations. I stirred us up a couple of OF's and we clinked cheers like actual friends. We gabbed the usual bent. But she looked lost, like something was bothering her, so I cut to it.

"Nick piss you off? He's pretty good at that. Trust me, I know. I live with the bastard."

"I don't want to talk about it. What are you really doing here, Sam?"

"I wanted to meet Max."

"Why? I thought you didn't buy into all this."

"I don't...but he interests me."

"He's a beautiful man. A visionary."

"So that's why you're here, Margaret. For Max, too?"

"No, not just Max. These are my people. My tribe." She sucked back her drink like she really enjoyed it. I clocked her an incredulous glare.

"Whaaaat? They are." She felt the need to reassure me.

"Can I tell you something? It's a secret…"

Margaret looked at me, wary of a trap. But I waved her in close and whispered in her ear like a true conspirator:

"I think you're better than this. You're better than ALL of these people."

She pushed me away, like this was some kinda joke.

"These people may be rich and beautiful but they are all…rotten. And on the inside, you might just be better and more beautiful than all of them. Just my two cents."

She laughed like I was crazy. Like maybe she didn't know how to process those words so instead she belted back her booze and stood up, a little wobbly, looking down over me with a smirk.

"I like this old fashioned. Can you bring me another? I'm gonna go upstairs to my room on the third floor to take a shower."

She stepped away, disappearing behind a crowd of chiseled men listening to Max give an impassioned speech.

I shoulda let her go.

I shoulda found Max and lapped up his drivel and stayed the course on why I had come here in the first place.

I shoulda let her cool off and forget about my impassioned plea and never think about her yellow bikini and soft mouth.

But hey. She was thirsty for an old fashioned.

I couldn't let her suffer.

Friday, August 21st, 8:41 p.m.

I wandered upstairs loaded for bear with two brimming cocktails. The hallway was empty. The walls on either side were filled with portraits of American patriots. Soldiers. Leaders. All white dudes in power. And encased behind glass were random artifacts aiming to prop up their cause. A musket from 1876. Or so it claimed to be. An American flag from World War II. A signed Jim Morrison poster scrawled with the slogan: *The West is the Best*.

I didn't know where the hell I was going and meandered into some kinda office filled with filing cabinets and computers and certainly no Margaret in need of a cocktail. I kept on going and discovered most doors were locked until I caught the last one on the left, cracked open, spewing small whispers of steam near the ceiling.

I knocked.

"*Margaret?*"

No answer but I, a man of old-fashioned integrity, a man fulfilling his drink request duty, entered the room and heard a shower running in an adjoining bathroom with the door hanging open.

"Gilda, are you decent?"

My perfect throwback quip was lost in the echoes of hot running water.

"Margaret? I got your drink. Do you want me to—"

"Bring it in here!"

I inched the door open and she was standing under the water, still wearing that yellow bikini. She waved me closer in, so I

153

stepped over and handed her the drink but she stepped back under the water, waving me in closer and closer and closer until the water started splattering my clothes and I was getting wet, all very wet but something about this thrilled her so she crept over and kissed me, pressing her soaking skin against my clothes, and so I kissed her back and almost dropped the drinks but stayed steady until my clothes were soaking through and she laughed and took her drink and we shared a smile and raised a toast, careful not to say anything and ruin this delightful moment happening right then and there so I handed her my drink and took off my clothes and she giggled a little at me and my excitement but she looked excited herself and flattered even and handed me her drink and slipped off that yellow bikini and I marveled at her perfect skin and smile and breasts and godlike folds and so we gazed and we drank old fashioneds under the shower, staring at each other in anticipation, in wait, in brimming bliss of the moment about to be until we wrapped our bodies and tongues and oozing parts together, entangling our most intimate, soft, and ripe desires into one.

And I was right.

She was better and more beautiful than them all.

Afterwards, I stared at my clothes sitting in a mushy pile on the cold bathroom tiles. This very moment did crash into my mind when I walked fully clothed into the shower, but I didn't seem to care, still glowing inside, riding that wave of happiness since my baptism with Margaret in the shower. Should I have felt bad she was probably drunk? Should I have cared that her advances to me were probably on account of whatever the hell Nick's betrayal was? Should I have been concerned that I only had a goddamn towel to wear home?

Yea, probably.

But I didn't.

The taste of Margaret was still in my mouth and overruled

all ugly realities.

"I'll go see if someone's got some extra clothes," Margaret said with a smile and bounced out of the room.

I went and lay down on the bed, not knowing whose room I was in or when, or if, I'd ever even see her again, but before long she popped back inside and handed me a brand-new polo dress shirt and a crisp pair of pleated Dockers slacks. While strapping on my pseudo Long Beach Third Reich uniform, I was reeling with questions.

"Where did you get these, they're brand new?"

"Oli said they have a stockpile of extra clothes for...I don't know...situations like these I guess." She laughed as she cracked open a bottle of Fiji water.

As I looked at the crisp clothes and at the pristine ocean view and that perfectly chilled Fiji water, I couldn't help but wonder out loud, "Who pays for all this?"

She shrugged like it was obvious

"Max does. With his podcast. He's super popular. They have like millions of followers."

"All this? With a podcast...I don't think so."

"I'm starving. Get dressed and come meet me downstairs." Her hunger was clearly far more imperative than the truth. She walked over and kissed me on the lips before prancing out of the room.

When I got downstairs the party had ramped up. It was dark now. The booze flowin'. People were dancing and the place looked like a nineties' beer commercial. White. Drunk. And horny. Still, there were pockets of staunchy fellas in the corners talking all serious. As serious as young rich guys in their twenties can appear to be, anyway. Max was among one group. A pack of eager beavers listened to him prattle on about the failures within Marxist socialist ideology.

I looked around for Margaret but didn't see her. This was fine at the moment given I'd come here for one sole purpose that my lust had completely derailed. So I mixed myself a drink and tried to think straight.

I ambled over to Max's corner. They were just talking football now. I didn't think he even noticed me till he looked me right in the eye and asked flat out, "Still here, Sam? Enjoying yourself?"

"Hell of a party, Max."

"It's not just a party. It's a way of life. This. Now. Here. People think this is some kind of utopia. But it's America, man. This is your country. Imagine this—everywhere you went. Where like-minded, smart people like you, Sam, can feel empowered by the people and environment around you."

I sipped some booze and looked around. "I don't know...still just feels like a party to me, Max."

"You're absolutely right. Because this is a party. A party of ideals. A party of people who have come together, who believe in something. Do you know what a theocracy is?"

"No."

"A theocracy is a system of government ruled by a theology. Are you familiar with Mount Athos in Greece?"

I shrugged no, ready for the lecture.

"Mount Athos was built on an ideal. It's a pure monastic state—right in Greece, embedded inside the European Union—but which operates independent of the government. A self-governed community, with their own values. Their own laws and infra-structure that all grew from male-driven Christian principles.

"To us, Patriot Strong represents an ideal. What we've started here and what we are destined to become. See, we believe in something powerful. And it unites us all. And this utopia around us? This place, this feeling, this experience you have— *right now*—is going to grow and grow and grow until all of America sees and realizes it, too, can become a utopia."

Some folks actually started clapping.

I nodded and pretended to be pleasantly amused at his little speech. "I wanna believe it. I do. But think it's gonna be hard to get like, say, Muslims and socialists to buy in, amigo."

"Unless we divide into ethno-territories."

"But that's divisive, isn't it? I thought you were all about uniting people?"

"People with sound principles. We're not ignorant to think we can unite every religious fanatic or left-wing socialist but we're a tide of growing wisdom that more and more people are welcoming. Because they want to return to traditional values. Where men run the world. Where women can nurture children like they are born and bred to do."

I vowed to stay collected. "You don't think this messed up planet would be better off if it were run by women? If they can nurture a child, why can't they nurture a civilization? But hey, I wouldn't be here if I weren't at least intrigued. Truly. I just think at the end of the day…it's like, you all were talking sports earlier, right? Well, Giants fans are Giants fans. Dodger fans are Dodger fans. And that's fine. I like the Dodgers, and I hate the Giants. But if people wanna live their life loving the stupid Giants, as they have every right to, then they should be allowed to. Go right ahead. But don't tell me I gotta be a Giants fan. The Giants suck."

All eyes turned to Max, excited for a punishing retort but he only laughed. Like he might actually appreciate the analogy.

Then his eyes got tight. "Have you enjoyed yourself this evening, Sam?"

"Yeah."

He kept grinning at me, like he'd won some bet. It was only then that I caught him eyeing Margaret behind my shoulder across the way, catching her eye.

She smiled at Max.

Then at me.

And it all fell into place.

Sitting here, wearing their fresh clothes, this uniform, trippin' on their booze and all freshly fucked. This utopia.

I'd been played.

This was their bait. How they wooed us over. Their game. It racked me right. I couldn't talk or think of what to say next and drowned out the world. I'd been infected. Margaret wasn't so beautiful, after all. Margaret was a soldier and as rotten as the rest of them.

My face burned hot and I wanted to torch the place down. But Max just smiled, had the audacity to start asking me about the Dodgers, gabbing sports like we were old pals.

So I steered the conversation my way, rambling on about how living in Glendale made going to Dodger games easy with the stadium was so close.

"You ever been up to Glendale, Max?"

"Of course. We speak at colleges all over LA. I love it up there."

I was legit surprised. "Really? You love Glendale?"

"I love the people," he corrected. As if they were vastly different than the chiseled faces listening in. Which, to his credit, they kinda were. My Glendale, anyway. I knew my next question was dancing dangerously close to the edge of cover but, with the help of some really poor judgment and hours of drinking, let it fly.

"Yeah. The people are great. You ever meet a girl up there named Josie Pendleton?"

His face didn't betray whatever feeling he had. "I meet a lot of people, Sam."

"You might remember this one. She was murdered recently. Josie Pendleton?"

All those sets of eyes stared back at me, curious if this was some kinda weird inside Glendale joke. But they got their answer real quick looking at my steely resolve.

"Rings a bell." Max was on autopilot. Unflinchingly calm.

"Someone raped and murdered her. In the back of a beige Camry. Is that ringin' them bells, too?"

The air got tight just like Max's lips. "Why are you talking about this, Sam?"

I grabbed my phone and pulled up a picture of Josie I'd saved for this very moment. Pointed it at Max. "I was just curious how well you knew her."

Max stared at the face and his righteous mug cracked. Like I'd damaged his armor. He stood up and walked away. The faces surrounding me went dark and cold and angry because I'd obviously pissed off their king, and pretty soon they all moved away, trying to process this ugly turn of events.

I'd rattled his cage legit.

He *did* know her.

This was a major victory.

I wanted to chase him.

I wanted to hound him on all things Josie but the longer I stuck around, the longer I felt in real jeopardy of getting my ass kicked.

I texted Nick but he didn't respond. So I grabbed my soaking wet clothes from upstairs and made for my car.

As I walked out of that magnificent hellhole, I thought about Margaret. I wanted to say goodbye or confront her or deal with her motive and intent.

Or was it all in my head?

Maybe it wasn't a play, maybe they just smiled.

I was spinning bad theories, walking to my car when I heard someone following me. I turned around to find Max and all of his six feet five inches or whatever mountain he was with those ugly tattoos and shining evil teeth coming into focus out of the darkness. Like some demon.

He was alone now. For the first time all night.

"Why were you asking me about Josie?"

"Because I know you two were seeing each other."

"Who told you that?"

"No one. I just figured it out."

"How?"

"I'm smart."

He sized me up, trying to land that.

I stayed on him. "Things she said. People she talked to. Am I wrong?"

"Why do you care?"

159

"Because I care about what really happened to her. Am I wrong?"

"We all know what happened to Josie. She was killed by a serial killer."

"Were you with her that night in Glendale, Max?"

"No." Then, his face twisted under the streetlamp, like it should have occurred to him earlier. Realizing.

"You think I killed her?"

"Did you?"

Unlike before he didn't seem to boil at the suggestion.

"Josie came here one night. A little over a month before that night in Glendale. Most people who come down here want an answer to something. They're usually lost. Or they have an agenda. Or they just wanna get laid. But Josie was different. She had this sparkle. She didn't belong. She didn't want any of that. She was...I couldn't figure her out. And I've made a distinct powerful living, working throughout this country, figuring and mining the depths of people's wants." He trailed off. Like he remembered something perplexing.

"But Josie wouldn't give. And she kept coming back. And I couldn't figure out *why* and I couldn't resist her."

"Even though she represented everything you hate?"

"*Because* she represented everything I hate. So I kept up with her. Respectfully. From a distance. We got to know each other. But eventually I seduced her. She said she never told a soul about us. But *you* knew. So imagine my surprise."

I was getting tired of listening to his pandering voice. "So what was she doing here? If she didn't like what you and everybody else were about, why was she here?"

"I don't know. At first I thought she was out to take us down. Like some spy. But after getting to know her, I let go of all that. It seemed impossible. And then, that night in Glendale hit and, the whole thing, the whole time with her felt like some kinda dream..."

The man looked genuinely racked thinking about Josie's fate.

I kept on his eyes, trying to discern if this was some bullshit yarn when Nick came booze bounding around the corner, relieved to see me.

"Aw sweet, you're still here. They told me you just bailed. I need a ride back, man!"

Max turned around, surprising Nick with his face.

"Oh. Wow. Hi, Max...I'm...Nick". Like he almost forgot.

"I know." Max turned to me, that grin growing back on his face. "See ya around, Sam. Come back soon."

But something furious welled inside me and more words bubbled out

"She had scratches on her back. Was that you? Did you scratch her?"

He clocked me a perplexed look then shrugged arrogantly, grinning. "She enjoyed it when I did that..."

And then, Magnet Max disappeared into the night.

We piled into the car and Nick hammered me with questions.

"Scratched who? Who did he scratch, Sam? And why in the hell were you having a private conversation with Max?"

I drowned out his pestering, reeling the entire way back as the headlights hit my face one after another along the interstate. I now understood why Nick fell in with this fraternity. He wasn't some loyal soldier, fighting for the cause. He was just a pawn they plied with pussy and promise. A loser with weak ideals in search of tail. He'd been lured and bit by the likes of Margaret.

Just as I had tonight.

Saturday, August 22nd, 10:09 a.m.

I got home.
　　I slept.
　　I woke up and stared at my article.
　　I hit send and held my breath.
　　I hit up the Volt for some cash.
　　I missed my crew at the bar.
　　I missed the smell of her shirt.

Saturday, August 22nd, 4:51 p.m.

For all its depressing spirit, insufferable lonely souls, and bad oxygen, after a night at Patriot Strong, walking into The Damned Lovely felt like burst of beautiful sunshine.

I regaled the troops with the latest sordid tales of Sam the sleuth. They lapped it up.

The mansion.

The wealth.

The ladies and drinks and free food all wrapped around a demented wild man people called Magnet Max. I kept a tactful lid on the Margaret chapter but hinted at glory and rounded it off with the payoff sting: the smile on Margaret's face behind my back that shivved my heart.

They wanted the next chapter. *What now, Sammy?* Hell if I knew.

I was bent. Happy to hit pause and drink for two days. I needed to step away from those roaches in Long Beach. But deep down I knew that wasn't gonna happen. Because, deep down, there was a blinding problem.

It was Max.

It was that I believed every goddamn word he said.

I believed they were together. Why else would he come at me, so charged like that?

I believed he seduced her. And that Josie was probably ashamed to be with a man like him. Ashamed for being so attracted to him. That's why she was so secretive. Why she never wrote about him, or talked about him to her friends and family.

I believed he scratched her up. And worst of all, I believed she liked it.

I believed she had an agenda, just like he said, but I still didn't know what it was.

But above all of that, I still believed he killed her. Or someone in his circle did.

I just didn't know how the hell I was going to prove it...

I needed some professional advice and laid it all out for the aged-out fuzz. Jiles chimed in, said it was a no brainer. And, he added, never as interesting or compelling or dynamic as you wanna it to be:

"Money. It's no secret. If it matters, there's money. It's always about the money. Money's at the heart of everything."

But even I knew that was only half the equation. "You mean money and sex?"

"Money *is* sex," Jiles barked as he filled some pints. "It's power. People want money so they can eat fine food and fuck the people they wanna fuck. Money buys CLASS. Cases like these? A mansion in Long Beach? Rich and crazy young people? It's always about the money. Sex *always* comes second to money."

Slice tagged in, "It's true, chief. Except in the case of psychopaths and sociopaths who throw a wrench in the system. That's why they're so fascinating and people come up with stupid stories and dumbass movies about 'em. And why they got even dumber super detectives like Sherlock Holmes."

"And if you don't buy Pinner's theory that this was a serial killing, you don't need Sherlock Holmes to solve this case. Guaranteed it's just about money," Jiles eagerly pointed out. "Which is good for you, cuz you're no fuckin Sherlock Holmes. You're fuckin' Sam."

These guys.

No wonder I loved 'em.

They backed my play. I don't know if they believed me. Hell, they probably backed Pinner's theory, too, when he was buying a round for the bar, but I knew they weren't out to mess with me.

Then something weird happened.

My phone rang.

It was Daphne. My agent. I didn't recognize her voice at first because she wasn't all bitter and rushed.

"I read your article. It's fantastic. Who have you sent this to?"

"Nobody."

"Perfect. Don't. I wanna run with this before it gets published. But, first, I need to ask you and you need to be honest with me: is this actually real?"

"Yeah."

"This man…Slice? He's real?"

"Yeah."

I turned my head and stared at the glassy eyed drunk sitting next to me, picking his fingernails.

"Do you own his life rights?"

"His what?"

"I'm gonna presume that's a no. Well, leave that with me for now. I'll cross that bridge when it's time. Anyway. Good job, Sam. I think we can sell it and set something up. Make some real money. I'll be in touch. Don't show the article to anyone."

She cut off the call and my eyes hit a stain on the wall behind the bar. I stared, transfixed, almost confused.

Slice and Jiles stared back, wise that something was up. "What gives, chief?"

I wanted to jump and shout and buy rounds for my allies but knew in my jaded—call it cynical, call it wisdom-filled—heart that this was nothing more than another phone call loaded with unbankable promise. And I was so tired of promise. I can't live off promise. Which means I have to live with Nick. I needed money and action, and a contract. I needed free lunches and an expense account, not more promise.

So I took a sip of booze, and answered honestly.

"Probably nothing."

Saturday, August 22nd, 10:58 p.m.

Six hours later I was still perched on that stool. A filthy, unattractive stint. An ugly admission of vice. That said, it was damn productive. A couple hours in, I'd cut out to do some research in the box. If Jiles and Slice were right, then I needed to learn more about the money trail attached to Patriot Strong. But I couldn't pull any leads off the web. Margaret had said that Max's podcast paid for the operation which always seemed highly improbable. I mean, it's a goddamn podcast. Two guys ranting in a studio. And they didn't have millions of followers on any social media platform. I listened to an episode of Max interviewing some fanatical pastor outta Memphis and there were ads peppered in but all from local businesses clearly grasping at straws to beef up sales. There weren't sponsored by any big national brands. Which meant they couldn't have been reaping cash off that outlet. And as for the mothership, Patriot Strong only had a bare bones website listing its mission and players and standard contact us drivel. There were no visible sponsors or entities willing to publicly back them. But someone had to be forking over a lot of money to keep the lights on and the fires burning over at the mansion of hell.

So who was it? Was that what Josie stumbled onto and threatened to expose in that email she sent to jimmyface999? It was by far the most promising avenue of investigation. But how the hell was I gonna figure it out?

I stared at that denim shirt, soaking up Josie's spirit, praying for inspiration, but the smell of my beloved had started to fade.

I refused to layer on detachment metaphors and kept drinking back at the bar.

Some luck came my way in an alcohol-induced *aha* moment of clarity after Jewels crossed behind me holding a tray of pints, her shapely tattooed arm held high and mighty. *Impressive*, I croaked, and she clocked me a genuinely kind smile that, for the sick reason of simply being a man, reminded me of sleeping with Margaret. Which led to the moments *before* sleeping with Margaret when I stumbled into their office.

The office. Those filing cabinets. Computers. Accessible, ripe intel.

It was a terrible plan.

It was a long shot.

It was dangerous.

And it ran counter to everything I swore I wouldn't do: go back to Patriot Strong's headquarters. But, I liked the idea. I wanted to steal from those bastards. Right out from under their nose. Steal their precious list of donors and leak it wide, forever ruining anyone attached to that cancerous ideal. And then I pretended this had nothing to do with wanting to see Margaret again. Pretending not to think about her wet skin in the shower. Of touching her again. I did a good job, convincing myself she had nothing to do with this ugly, dangerous plan of attack.

Friday, August 28th, 1:00 p.m.

Six days later I still hadn't heard from Daphne.
    Nothing
    Not a squawk.
    Promise.

Saturday, August 29th, 6:22 p.m.

I was back on the 5. This time, without Nick yapping in my ear. But thanks to Nick I'd learned they were having another bender to celebrate some Southern Confederate loser on this night. My ass tightened just thinking about the fire I was about to march into. The pain of the ignorance I was about to be subjected to.

But once again, good ol' race-forward thinking Oli was workin' the front door and greeted me with nothing but smiles and genuine kinship.

"Welcome back, amigo!"

I played the part.

I graced curious and wide-eyed.

I smiled like a good soldier.

And the party was pumping. On the surface it was nothing but pretty faces and booze. *Cheers!* and *Cheers!* with happy white people uniting. I didn't see Max but I could feel him. Channeling my inner liberal-ass Jedi power like I'd sensed his presence...He was *near*. I truly wondered if he could he feel me back.

I grabbed a Bud Light, intent to stay sharp, and ambled through the proceedings. I talked with Oli who was glad, or so he claimed, to see me once again. As he applauded my return, I saw Margaret across the pool. She was talking to a face I recognized but had to run it through until—bam! Yellow Beamer. Penis Boy. Cigarettes in the kitchen. Nick's alpha mates drinking rum. I wasn't surprised to see them but wanted to steer clear knowing they would only draw attention. I needed to get into that office

169

and get out fast. So I buried the burning desire to talk to her and instead slunk to the edge of the yard, chatting with some college students outta Chatsworth. I peppered them with questions to take the focus of myself and it worked until before long a hush fell over the crowd and the man himself, Mr. Magnet Max, emerged, welcoming folks, talking up his podcast and the night's celebrated guest.

This was my time.

I edged out and found the stairs to the third floor.

I passed a couple girls coming out of the bathroom who looked guilty of doing blow as I walked down the hall. When I reached the office, it was locked.

I hadn't counted on that. I considered trying to use a credit card like they always do so easily in movies, until I saw that the lock had a childproof pinhole access in the middle of the knob. I rushed down the hall and found an open empty bedroom with a desk that had some pens inside its top drawer. I grabbed one and rushed back to the office, pulling out the thin black ink cartridge tube. Then I jammed in the plastic tube to try to unlock it, just as I'd seen my buddy Roger Morfidis do in eleventh grade when Sarah Wheeler passed out after barfing and locked herself inside his mom's bathroom. As I fished around, trying to unlock it, I wondered whatever happened to Roger. He was super cool. Always had the cleanest, crispest baseball hats that—

Click.

The lock let loose and I stepped inside the dark office. Afraid my phone's flashlight would draw too much attention, I waited for my eyes to adjust, and after what seemed like a goddamn eternity, was able to make out the surrounding dark room. I started by waking up the computer but as I suspected it was password protected. Next up were those filing cabinets. I opened them slowly and quietly, then rifled through the files. They were mostly filled with boring appliance manuals and extermination contracts. But I kept digging until finally a folder titled FUNDRAISING EVENTS caught my eye. The docs inside

listed itemized groups of entities who'd contributed to the fraternity.

I buzzed with victory.

I took out my phone and snapped pics. But then quickly
realized the folder was at least thirty pages thick and there
was no way in hell I wasn't gonna risk the time it would take to
get a shot of each page. So I shoved the entire folder into the
small of my back and covered it with my shirt.

Then, I inched open the door and the hallway was clear. I
edged out, jacked with adrenaline, praying to god I wouldn't see
anyone, when instead I found myself face to face with Penis Boy.

I kept my head low and booze-slurred hard. "...*heeey man,
do you know, know where the bathroom is?*"

He pointed down the hall and stepped aside. My performance
was both natural and compelling. There was no way in hell he
recognized me as I shuffled into the bathroom and waited a few
moments. Then, with no sign of Penis Boy still in the hallway, I
shuffled down the stairs and made for the exit near Oli's perch.

"That was quick, bro! Going so soon?"

"Yeah. I'm not feeling well. Something just hit me."

"Oh, that sucks. Well, feel better—hope to see you again."

I kept walking, out the front and down the outside steps until
Oli's voice called out one last time.

"Hold up a sec' dude!"

I stopped. Turned and saw Penis Boy talking to Oli. He was
nodding his head.

"I really don't feel good, I think I'm gonna be sick—"

"HOLD UP, man!" My gregarious race-forward thinking
padre was advancing now, flanked by Penis Boy and two hulking
male beasts.

I could've run.

I needed to run.

Run!

Right now!

RUN!

Do it now!

But no. My petrified feet stayed tight to the ground as a swell of testosterone surrounded me.

Penis Boy piped up, "Yeah, he was coming out of the office. And the computer was on."

Oli was legit angry and put on his bad cop pants.

"What the hell were you doin' in there?"

"Nothing...I got lost. I thought it was the bathroom."

"Then why'd you turn on the computer?"

"The computer? I don't know, I musta knocked a chair into the desk and it woke up or something..."

Oli eyed me skeptically just as Penis Boy realized the inevitable.

"Wait...I know you. I was in your house. You're Nick's roommate. You were talkin' shit about us that night. What the hell are you doing here?"

"It was a mistake. I feel really sick, can I just go please."

"Not just yet. Feels a little weird, bro. Just chill for second." Oli was going all good cop now. "You didn't do anything wrong, right? We're just talkin'."

And then Max emerged from the side of the house, his lieutenants whispering in his ear on approach, eyeballing me with ugly curiosity.

"You're back," Max oozed. "And snooping inside our office?"

"I wasn't snooping, I got lost and—"

"Did you search him?"

"No."

Max nodded to one of the beasts. "Mario. Search him."

Mario started patting me down. I looked at the pavement and stared at his ugly ass steel-toed cowboy boots and, as he felt the crisp file-folder wedged against my back, a small dribble of piss leaked outta my dick. I clenched and barely managed to jam the pipes shut in time. As if that was going to make anything better.

Seeing the folder, they got quiet and cold, surrounding me now.

"Should we call the cops?" Oli asked, as he handed Max the folder.

"No." Max slowly leafed through the papers. "Why did you take this?"

I tightened up and let loose. "Because I was paid to. Someone contacted me anonymously. Someone named Rose-bowl2003@gmail.com Venmoed me two hundred bucks upfront and said they'd pay me another three hundred upon delivery for a list of anyone responsible for contributing money to Patriot Strong. I was to drop any information into a garbage can in front of the House of Pies at Vermont and Franklin at one a.m. tonight. But I don't know who they are. I'm broke. I needed the money. It was a stupid thing to do, and I'm sorry—I shouldn't have done it."

Max blank-faced me and dug my phone from out of my pocket, coolly asking, "What's your password?"

"Nine-two-nine-nine."

More piss pushed through. But my story felt solid just like I'd rehearsed it on the drive down. Except for the sorry part which I added cuz that was true at the current moment. *Did they buy it? What is Max doing now, anyway?* I edged up my eyes and caught a glimpse of the screen.

It was my Venmo account.

"You didn't get paid two hundred bucks." Max said smoothly.

"No, see, here's the thing—"

I lunged and pushed through the hulking monsters, desperate to escape when a fistful of nails scrapped my ribs and shirt and pulled me back into the scrum where some knuckles ripped into my face. The world flashed white and stinging tears and blood exploded out of my face. I balled a fist and let loose on some-one's jaw before a second even stronger fist smashed my ribcage. Then more pain tore inside as fist after beastly fist pummeled my liver and kidneys and spleen.

I crumbled to the ground, as the beasts went to work, those

steel-toed cowboy boots busting my face and bones and entire body until my world went black.

Saturday, August 29th, 9:18 p.m.

Pain tore through my spine and ribs and face when I finally regained consciousness. My left eye had swollen completely shut but I could make out a crack of reality through my right one. I was hunched behind the wheel of my car. The sonsofbitches had the decency to decimate my body, unlock my car, and then politely place my sticky, half-dead carcass behind the wheel. And then they smashed up the front of my car to make it look I'd gotten into an accident.

It hurt to breathe.

It hurt to move.

It ALL hurt.

I opened my mouth and let out a gob of blood-filled fluid that dripped off the edge of my seat. I needed water. I swiveled my eyeball around and found a half-drunk bottle of Arrowhead in the console. I inched my arm over to it and slowly lifted it up to my lips, sucking back the liquid. It was cold and godlike. Then I saw my face in the mirror. At least a part of my face. The other part was purple, yellow, and puffy bad. I kinda looked like Popeye. All round and chinny. I pretended to find it funny and laughed like this was just a little bump in the road. Like I was gonna be okay.

And my feet hurt. Both of 'em burned something fierce. What the hell did they do to my feet? I couldn't bend over to see cuz it hurt too much.

I thought about driving home but everything wailed in agony so I closed my eyes, hoping the pain might get better with sleep or something.

It didn't.

I woke up later.

Same agony.

But I knew I had to get out of there. If not to a hospital, somewhere better than this trashed car on the side of a road on these pretty Long Beach streets in the middle of the night. Thankfully my keys and phone were still in my pocket. The beasts were so kind as to let me have them. Rich pricks probably laughed at the sight of my outdated iPhone.

I pulled out my phone.

I shoulda called an ambulance.

I shoulda called for help.

But, no. I punched the ignition and said to hell with good reason and my seat belt. They had smashed my front window, but I could see through the spider web cracks enough to make my way down the street. I knew I wouldn't be able to rip sixty-five miles per hour down the I-5 so stuck to surface streets, streaming through the empty, foggy roads.

As I puttered home I thought about my options. A wise man would go to the hospital and get checked out. Look at the X-rays. Check for internal bleeding. Cranial fractures. Concussive somethings.

This man would also wisely have good medical insurance.

I was not this man. I was not wise. And I did not have good insurance. But I did know a good doctor.

Well, I knew *a* doctor.

Saturday, August 29th, 11:18 p.m.

I couldn't wait to see the look on their faces. Really.

I was broken, bleeding, and in a baaad way. But they were gonna love it. Not the fact I was busted but the drama. A change in pace. Something they could see just sittin' on the stools. Like fresh chum in the water. And they were gonna feed off this tale for months. *The day they broke Sammy.*

I pushed open the door but nobody turned my way. It felt like time got all stuck as The Ovations were crooning about blue skies and the day we all fell in love.

Jiles finally looked up from cutting some limes and bellowed, "Oh Jeezuz. Slice, Jewels—help him out, will ya?!"

They shouldered my crippled body straight into the box, peppering me with questions along the way. I gave them the base facts.

"Got in a wee tussle."

I could hear Jiles shouting, "I just saw him. Well, find him! He's around here somewhere, for chrissake!"

God bless that man. He got me. He got my ticket.

They lay me down on the stinky loveseat in the corner. It felt close to heaven, lying down like that finally.

Slice chimed in. "They did a number on ya."

"You should see the other guy, Slice."

"Yeah, buddy. I know it."

Jewels stared at my face and started to cry some. "Sam. What happened, Sam?"

"A little nudge on justice, Jewels."

She held my hand and I loved her for it.

"What the hell are you doing here? You need to go to a hospital."

"Where's Pa?"

"Stop it. You need proper care, you need—"

"I can't afford proper care, Jewels!"

Jiles ushered Pa into the box. He looked a little wobbly. He looked right wasted. Who could blame him, it was well after six p.m., after all.

The old timer angled up and tried to focus on my face. I'm pretty sure he could tell it was me as his bushy eyebrows bounced, surprised but concerned no less.

"What happened, Sam?"

He started touching my face. Those smooth cold pads actually felt nice.

"They got me good, Pa. Four of 'em, I think. At least four. We didn't see eye to eye tonight."

"What hurts?"

"All of it. My face. Hurts to breathe, too."

Pa unbuttoned my shirt and felt around my chest and guts. "I think you have a broken rib. Maybe two. Have you been coughing blood?"

"No. I don't think so."

"Good. That means it didn't puncture your lung. What time did it happen?"

"I don't know...eight thirty maybe?"

Pa looked at his watch all wobbly, in and out from his face for focus.

"It's eleven twenty!" Jewels barked.

He rocked the math. "Right. We still got time. Jewels, where's the first aid kit?"

"He needs to go to a hospital and see a real doctor!"

"I am a real doctor."

"My insurance is shit and I'm broke, Jewels."

She huffed off.

She was right.

She was the best.

"Your eye is busted open pretty good. I'm gonna have to suture it up."

"You sure you're okay to do this?"

He grinned a toothy smile. "Are you kidding? Like riding a bike. Jiles, do you have any superglue?"

"Superglue?" Slice weighed in like the wary assistant coach.

"Same as the hospital uses. They just got a fancier name. Binds the skin."

Jewels raced back in with a metal first aid kit ripped straight outta the 1970s. The rust alone made me shutter.

Pa said he was gonna go wash his hands. Thank god.

I edged Slice in closer. "How far in is he, Slice?"

"What do you want me to say? It's almost midnight."

"You think he can handle this?"

The man weighed in. "He seems confident. But sounds like you don't have a lotta choices here. Pony up for a real doc or take Pa. But I mean...you gotta fix that eye one way or the other."

When he came back in Pa was barking to Jiles like something wasn't right. Before long they pulled in Lily who was clasping a purse-sized emergency sewing kit and she saw me all laid out. "Ohmygod Sam. What've you done?"

"I nudged justice, Lily. You'd be proud..."

I'd rehearsed the "nudged justice" line on the drive in, knowing I'd be hit with questions. I like the way it sounded. Lily didn't seem to at all. She just looked sad.

People kept coming in and out. Jiles rolled back in with some fresh white bar towels and a bottle of bourbon.

"All yours, kid. On the house."

I took a deep pull and the warm booze glugged down my throat. It tasted beautiful and sweet and wrong. But it felt good, like I needed the liquid. Any liquid.

Pa walked back in with dripping hands and wiped them on the fresh towel. He looked me square in the eyes with surprising focus.

"You sure you wanna go through with this?"

I knew this moment would come. Before the pain. I'd wrestled with that very question driving back from Long Beach when I couldn't see much but knew my face would need stitches. This meant going to a doctor or a hospital. This also meant with my garbage insurance I would need to pay for a doctor or a hospital. This absolutely meant I would be forced to call my father for money. I would hear that deep breath of air before he answered, that sucking back of oxygen where his loathing, his disdain of everything I'd NOT become would woosh up into his body, then get pushed out into the world and onto me with a pained hate as he would utter, "Okay, son."

So it was in that moment, *that* moment driving in, when I'd already answered Pa's question.

"Yea. Lemme suck back some of this bottle and let's get it over with. But pass me that denim shirt."

Jewels handed her over and I pressed it to me like some kinda shield. Then, I plundered the booze and, as we waited for it to smash my bloodstream, Jewels had the good sense to tell Pa to drink some water while she walked two blocks to the CVS and bought some numbing cream, rubbing alcohol, tape, gauze, and a bunch of other stuff that looked like a right blessing.

At one point even the Rooster walked into the box. He took in the scene with unflappable poise. Like this was exactly what he expected to see.

"We'll hold you down," Jiles said. He seemed almost excited. As if moments like these were his rebellion against the slow death of retirement.

Jewels was about to step away, but I asked her if she'd stick around.

"Why?"

"Cuz you're prettier than all these slugs and I gotta focus on somethin'."

She was still none too impressed that they were gonna let Pa, our in-house disgraced inebriated ex-surgeon, sew up my face, but I smiled at her and she got cool.

Out of the corner of my eye, I saw Pa wave a needle through a lighter's flame.

"Tell me again about those tattoos, Jewels."

The booze was going to work and Jewels got the drift, and out of pity or friendship or mercy or a mix of 'em all, accepted that we fools were gonna actually do this so she may as well help.

She came closer and lifted the underside of her arm, the soft white side, and she started telling me about her aunt and a crow—that was the tattoo: a woman and a crow intertwined with a vine. And as she rattled on, Pa dabbed my face with rubbing alcohol and numbing cream, and Rooster and Jiles clasped my hands down hard, and the drunk surgeon pierced my swollen flesh with a razor hot needle and I wanted to scream and punch and rail but I bit down hard on my tongue and pretended to really really really care about Jewels's aunt and the stupid crow who represented death as the pain screamed through my face and Pa squawked that I was doing good Sammy, doin' real goddamn good and we're almost through now and for the first time I felt he, this drunk mess of a man, actually knew what he was doing, like the ol' chap was in his element as the bourbon hit me just right and a wave of this IS gonna be okay rippled through me and Jewels god bless her cuz she was crying now and in that moment I realized that these people, these imperfect, odd, wary, uneven, unaccepting addicts were dear to me and beyond chums on the stool, beyond kin faces, they were something like friends and confidante souls I adored and valued more now than my own family because they were holding me down and operating on my Nazi-busted face like we were in fact bound by something like love or something even stronger I wanted to believe and did until I saw the Rooster look pale and nervous maybe cuz Pa was starting to sweat ugly, like something was wrong type sweat, cuz he was biting his lip and shaking and I could feel the tug and pull of the suture and the old man's fingers pushing and pinching and someone else started cursing and this was not good and the pain kicked up fierce and now Jiles was yelling at Pa and it started to hurt baaaaad and I could see the blood soaking the towels and Jewels was playing it cool with the aunt and the crow but Pa was yelling back at Jiles like it was all gonna be okay but it wasn't okay and I ripped my hand away from the Rooster and I needed to know what the hell was happening until the pain wrecked me right and I started breathing hard and harder and harder and I got mighty scared until the world went rushing white red and all quiet black.

Sunday, August 30th, 1:25 p.m.

Sunshine filled my world.

The day was bright and piercing when I woke up in my bedroom.

I needed water.

My face burned.

My chest hurt.

Everything hurt.

Real hurt. This was next-level, WWII hurt.

I got to my feet, not knowing how the hell I got to my bed in the first place but could reasonably square that someone, probably Jewels, helped me home after the horror of the box surgery.

I sucked back water straight from the tap, careful not to touch my swollen face to the faucet and sink.

And then, I looked into the mirror.

It was better than I suspected. My right eye was bloodshot, black and yellow, but there was a big ass bandage covering the left side of my face. Wow. They really went to town on that bandage. I debated pulling it off to see how long the scar was gonna be but had the good sense to know the damage was done. Let it go. Let it heal, you moron.

Superglue.

Did he really ask for Superglue?

I washed. I washed around, anyway.

It still hurt to breathe. But I was gonna be okay.

Josie was still dead. But I was gonna be okay.

I walked down the stairs.

Nick saw me coming. He was confused like *why's Sam wearing a pillow on his face?*

Then he saw.

Saw the shape I was in. He didn't make a snide comment. For Nick, this was superior behavior. The man was genuinely concerned. Like seeing my broken face was beyond his realm of trash-talking.

I laid it out. From the beginning. The Josie hook. The Magnet Max connection. The stolen file. Pa. The stitches.

He stared. Gobsmacked. I kept waiting for Nick to make a jab at my stupidity. But he didn't. He just shook his head like he was sad. Concerned even.

My actions had silenced the unsilenceable fuckin' Nick.

I shoulda been happy.

I'd dreamed of this moment.

But it was all just a glaring reflection of how bad things had turned out. The Josie rabbit hole. This chase, this terrible mistake, no, all these terrible mistakes I'd made in my life. Sitting there, the sun piercing through, making it bright and clear how bad it'd all got. How hard it was to breathe.

Just to breathe.

I had to make some changes in my life. I couldn't keep doing this. I was broken and broke and all of this was going to kill me.

Nick offered to make me a coffee. I was happy about that.

Monday, August 31st, 12:03 p.m.

I picked up my car outside the Lovely but didn't go in.

I needed a break.

So I drove to my mechanic on Hyperion. He looked worried. He fixed the car and gave me a wrecked-face discount. I shoulda found it funny. But I was too gracious and rattled. The repairs cost me my $466, and I filed the accident report with my supervisor, hoping she'd allow to me work the roads again.

Her name was Greta. She had concerns about my wellbeing. Really though, about their clients' wellbeing. Could I even see okay to drive?

Yes, I assured her and left out the part about how it hurt to breathe.

She was rightfully dubious, so I sold her a sob story that I'd been ruthlessly beat up at a party, aka the truth, and was desperate to get behind the wheel to pay for my medical bills.

She bought it.

Thursday, September 3rd, 10:18 p.m.

I drove four days straight.

I didn't drink.

I hadn't been back to the bar since.

No one asked or called. That was fine with me.

Changes.

I thought about her denim lying lifeless in the box. The smell of it.

Nothing but trouble, Sam. That was the voice rattling around my stupid head. Nothing but trouble come outta there. If I was gonna make some changes, I needed to stay away from the goddamned Lovely.

But first, I owed them a thank you.

Friday, September 4th, 12:58 p.m.

They cheered.

They howled in victory.

Like a soldier back from war. Clapping at my ragged face.

No one's ever clapped for me like that.

I tried not to cry but couldn't stop it.

They howled harder.

Jiles cranked some Otis Redding and Jewels hugged me like some kinda proud sister might. Relieved.

Those tears kept rollin' hard. Thankfully half my face was still covered in bandages.

And Slice grinned fierce.

"You look great, kid."

Except there was Pa. He was in the corner, sipping soft and timid. I walked up and said thanks.

But the old timer just shrugged, like he didn't to wanna talk about it. I respected his wishes and ordered a Sprite from Jiles who didn't seem at all surprised. Word came down that he was the one who drove me home that night and got me to my bed.

"Did you brush my teeth, too?"

"Hell, no. Helped myself to some pretzels on the way out the door though cuz I was so damn hungry."

I plied him for more details. "As far as I can remember, it got kinda rough before I passed out. What happened?"

He glanced at Pa down at the far end of the bar, still awfully quiet, and leaned in.

"Pa got kinda rattled. Not sure what happened but you

started bleedin' bad and something in him just snapped. Like he had some sort of PTSD. Got all wide-eyed and totally locked up. Eventually we had to pull him back cuz there was just so much blood and his hands were shaking. We were gonna call an ambulance but Lily was ahead of the game. After she saw you come in, she called her brother-in-law, some doctor who lives in Echo Park, so he zipped on over and stitched you up right."

It all kinda made sense.

I looked over at Pa, suckin' back that gin, alone, as Jiles continued, "The sonofabitch was right about that superglue, though. Doc stitched you up and lathered that stuff on. Tightened you up good. You believe that? Superglue."

I walked back over to Pa. I wasn't mad. I knew it was my own stupid fault for putting him in the crosshairs. He did the best he could. He tried. He *cared*. He wanted to help me so bad. And I loved the old bastard for it. So I just told him that.

"I love ya, Pa."

I put a hand on his shoulder. He didn't turn around or get all soft, instead he tapped my hand with his soft smooth palm and kept to his gin with a slight sad smile.

I went back to my stool and waxed Dodgers with Slice. The wildcard race was brewing and he bubbled up stats. Eager to share. But before long, he was on me about what was really on his mind.

"So what are you gonna do now, Sammy? What about the case? What about Josie?"

"I'm done. Who was I kidding? All I was doing was stirring up shit. With Max and those pricks. With Glenn. Lying to Susan Glasser. Pissing off Pinner. Lyin' to Allison...Nothin' but trouble, Slice."

The news put Slice down like I'd robbed him of some kinda hope. But I could tell he understood. I finished my Sprite and told him I was in the red and needed to make some cake. The old-timer looked like an abandoned dog, and I felt bad in a way, but Slice wasn't my problem right now.

I walked over to Lily and said thank you.

She just straight-faced me and said, "You're welcome…Be smart, Sam. I know you are."

That was it. The woman practically saved my life. But she just went back to reading a brief.

I gave a salute to Jiles and walked away without the denim. Then I drove to get a burrito and some water.

I was gonna be on the road all day and night.

Friday, September 4th, 2:03 p.m.

I peeled the bandages off my face. The cut was long and ran from above the edge of my left eye, down the side of my face towards the bottom of my ear.

I always thought it would be cool to have a scar on my face.

Like a warning about how dangerous I could be.

This just reminded me what a failure I was.

A weasel thief.

A spineless sleuth.

A luckless avenger.

An alcoholic.

I wasn't drunk when they hit me, but I was drunk more than I shoulda been. I wouldn't be cut if I'd beat the urge to booze at the Lovely, day in and day out. Never would have met Josie, I figured, anyway.

I snapped a shot of my new charming scar as some kinda reminder to be a better man.

I swiped some earlier pictures and stared at an odd shot of an Excel spreadsheet. At first I thought someone else musta pinched my phone and snapped something but then I looked closer and saw the contents. It was a list of companies and financial contributions to Patriot Strong.

Then I remembered.

Before I stole the file, I'd taken some pictures in the office and they were still on my phone. Those Nazi pricks never figured to check my pictures.

I felt a spike of adrenaline.

And then I pushed that stupid spike down, down, down.
Nothin' but trouble.

Friday, September 4th, 5:22 p.m.

I got back on the road.

It was the first time I'd driven someone without my bandages on. I picked up two teenagers. Guys. They were about sixteen. Tom and his buddy, Alec. Sounded like they were going to their friend's house party. I remembered being a teenager. Going to house parties. Getting into delicious trouble. Acting like those house parties were just a steppin' stone to a greater, more rewarding life. When really, those house parties were the treasure.

That was a long time ago.

I don't think they noticed my chewed-up face.

Saturday, September 5th, 10:19 p.m.

The next night, I saw Josie on a sidewalk boulevard. I knew she was dead, but I picked her up, anyway, and asked where she wanted to go. She said she needed to go to the ocean. This made absolute sense so I pulled into traffic. I drove silently, staring at her in the rearview mirror because she was alive and beautiful wearing her denim shirt and she smiled at me too and now I wasn't driving because I was sitting next to her in the back seat, just inches away, and I reached out to touch her hand and she took my hand in hers and smiled and she whispered gently, almost softly into my ear—

"Thank you, Sam."

I jerked awake.

I was behind the wheel.

I'd been driving for over twenty-seven hours but wide-awake now thanks to that image of Josie. Staring at me.

Thank you, Sam.

I sat behind the wheel. Stone-faced. I knew it was just a stupid dream.

Nothin' more.

Nothin' but trouble.

I could see her so close to me. I held her hand. It meant something.

It was just a stupid dream.

Nothin' more.

Nothin' but trouble.

I yelled hard. I didn't know why or at what. But it felt right.

Be smart, Sam. I know you are.

"I know, Lily." I said it out loud.

I yelled again. Harder. Better.

Thank you, Sam.

That face.

I needed to sleep. I needed to rest proper.

No, I needed to make more money.

I turned on my app and before long picked up three new rides. The last one was a girl named Tanya. She was black, with extremely dark skin and a swirl pattern shaved into her hairline. She was attractive. She clocked my gash. I think she was frightened. I couldn't blame her. We both kept quiet, a silent tension in the air. But I liked having her in the back of my car.

She was so beautiful.

That's how it works, I guess.

Eventually, I pulled over and she looked concerned, wondered what was happening. I started to cry again.

"I'm sorry. I'm so sorry. You just reminded me of someone. I can still drive you, I just need a moment to—"

She opened the door and got out of the car. Fast. Walked away.

Then I got out, too.

Felt the night on my face.

I opened the back door and sat on the back seat. Across from where Josie sat in my stupid dream.

Her face was here.

I could see her. Hear her say thank you. Over and over.

I guess I felt haunted.

I guess that's how it works.

Then I felt stung. Stung ugly with determination.

Saturday, September 5th, 10:58 p.m.

I rolled back in to The Damned Lovely.

Like a moth to a flame. And just look how that turned out, Samuel.

There were no claps. No hugs. There were some twists on the stools and a coula of *heya look, Sammy's back.*

Only Slice looked at all happy to see me.

But I didn't saddle up. I didn't order a drink. I went straight to the Rooster and handed him a piece of paper.

"What's this?"

"It's a list of companies."

"What kind of list?"

"That's not really important. I just need to know everything about these companies. Who owns them. How much money they have. And what they do with it. Anything I can't get on Google. I'll pay you a hundred bucks a company. And if you feel that's not enough, like some companies you gotta cast a wider net, come talk to me and I'll up the ante."

"I don't get it."

Jiles said I needed to follow the money. I didn't have time to spell it out but this was my only lead from the file. And considering I got my ass handed to me, figured it was worth at least using the last piece of intel I had left.

"I'm in need of information. You're the master at finding it online. Can you help me?"

The Rooster shrugged indifferently. "Two hundred a company."

195

Where the hell was this jab coming from? I guess it was fair but came outta left field.

"How about one fifty?" I countered.

The Rooster wavered.

"I'm still paying off my face those guys busted up. And my car. Please?"

He looked at me, nonplussed. "Jewels is a bitch."

Ah. Coming into focus now. "Didn't pan out, huh?"

"She said she's got a boyfriend." He leaned in, all dramatic, all squinty-eyed. "She doesn't have a boyfriend. I checked. She's a liar."

"I'm sorry, man. That sucks. I tried."

"Okay. One fifty."

"Thanks."

Nearby Slice was watching like a lab on a leash. "What's going on, Sammy? Where you been?"

"Working. Trying to buy back my life. Make some money."

"Have a drink."

I ordered a Sprite.

Slice grunted and pressed if I'd heard from my agent.

"Did she call ya back yet? On the article?"

With all the madness last week, I'd kinda forgotten about the article. Forgotten insofar as chosen not to trust my stupid agent would ever actually do anything with it.

"No, Slice. And to be honest I don't ever expect her to. I wrote that thing on a whim. For my portfolio. The chances of it actually getting published or seen or read by anyone are pretty slim."

It was kind of a lie, but kind of the truth.

Again with that crushed dog look.

Maybe I underestimated how important this was to him. That maybe this article was his last bastion of hope. That the world might finally understand or celebrate or love him.

"I'm just saying. I don't want you to get your hopes up. It might happen but if it doesn't that's gotta be okay, too. All right?"

He filled his chest with air like it was no big thing.

"Just askin' is all."

We sat all quiet and maybe I felt bad for stringing him along or felt annoyed that he kept on me after all the crap I'd been through.

Tom T. Hall cooed on the radio singing about Memphis.

I looked around. Saw the usual faces. Jewels. Jiles. Lily. The Rooster.

I looked around and it was the first time I ever felt cold and uninterested in the world around me. Those faces. The sounds. The smell. The characters comin' in the front door. I was indifferent. Numb. Maybe my time at The Damned Lovely had run its course. Maybe it was time to *change* course.

I started thinking about my options, where the hell I might set up shop. I'd rather burn to death before writing at a Starbucks. Home would have to do until I could find another box somewhere. Then I remembered a guy named Todd I'd met at Covelle years back. His folks owned a bunch of buildings in the neighborhood. Old money. Maybe he'd remember me. Let me rent out a space on the cheap. I considered looking up his number in my phone when the Rooster walked my way.

He looked different. Probably because his face wasn't lit up by his computer screen, but it looked like he was almost smiling underneath his blank stare.

He flashed a phone's screen in my face.

"You see this?"

It was a Twitter blast. KTLA breaking news:

All grabbed up! Police arrest alleged serial killer, the Glendale Grabber.

Below the copy was a picture of Pinner marching a man I'd never seen, never thought about, never considered, into some government building.

It was posted fifty-seven minutes ago.

"What is it, Sammy?" Slice obviously saw the look on my

face but the shock stopped me from speaking.

The Rooster chimed in. "They got that serial killer."

Slice perked up. "The Glendale Grabber?"

Jiles walked over now, too. The Rooster turned the phone and showed the guys.

"Sonofabitch. They got him!" Jiles said. "Look, there's Pinner. Wow. They finally got him. That's great!"

I shoulda been happy.

But it didn't make sense.

I couldn't believe it.

Why wasn't I happy? They finally got the guy. Without me. It wasn't Max. It wasn't Glenn. It was a just some guy with a beard I'd never seen before.

I shoulda been happy.

Why wasn't I happy?

I needed to know more.

The Rooster let me use his computer. We dragged the net. Guy's name was Louis Ullverson. An ex-con outta Lompoc who was on parole, working as a janitor at a medical facility off Central Street. He'd done time for assault and robbery. But the breaking details were scant. No mention on how they connected him to the Glendale murders.

I needed to talk to Pinner. God bless Jiles who was already on the phone. When he finally got through, word came in that Ullverson was being arraigned on Tuesday at four p.m. downtown at the Temple courthouse.

I wanted a drink to celebrate.

I resisted and walked outside into the night.

Tuesday, September 8th, 3:33 p.m.

Slice shuffled uncomfortably down the hallways, leading me through the barren, government arteries filled with suits on both sides of the law.

Orange jumpsuits.

Lawyer pinstripes.

Power pantsuits.

Pinner told us to be on the second-floor lobby around the elevators and he'd come find us.

And so we waited.

Slice kept his head low, like he was wary of anyone seeing him back on his old stompin' grounds. In these here halls o' justice. He looked shaky. But no one made him. No one cared who this man was.

Pinner squeezed out of an elevator and greeted us with his signature smarmy grin.

"Toldja we'd pin him, Sam."

I shoulda said congrats and thank you and good job. But I wanted information.

"How did you find him?"

"Police work. Like I told ya we would. DNA found on the vics' clothes and in the cars matched Ullverson. His deck was in the system. Took some time but once they had the full work up from the rape kits, it was an easy pin."

"Then why'd it take so long? I mean, if you had Josie's DNA and the guy's DNA on file—"

"Because it wasn't just Josie," the cop barked. "Three vics.

Three cases. You think closing a charge on this happens overnight?"

"No, of course not."

"Do you know how many people we had on this?" he said,
growing louder now. "How many hours of lab work we're
runnin' down? How many grunts scouring street cams?"

Pinner slugged Slice a look, like who the hell is this chump to
question him. Here. Now.

"I can't even imagine. Lotta work." I backpedaled, trying to
buy it all back. "So, but in the end, I'm just curious what DNA
did you get off Josie? Cuz I remember at the autopsy there was
no semen. In the rape kit, right?"

"I can't get into all this now, I have to be in court."

"Congrats, Pinner," Slice chimed in, trying to smooth it all
over. "That's one helluva good grab. Good day."

"Yeah, great job," I padded.

Pinner eyeballed me. Almost angry. "Why you look so sad?"

"I'm happy. Happy you got him. I'm happy he's off the
street."

Pinner shrugged like he'd heard that clichéd drivel before.
But he was right. I didn't feel happy. I felt overwhelmed. Or
something like that.

"Well, he's gonna be arraigned any minute now. Over in
Rhodes's courtroom. It's down here on the right."

He swiveled his girth and lumbered towards the courtroom
without waiting for us.

"I'll come by the Lovely and give you the download. I just
don't have time right now."

As repulsive as that man was on so many levels, he was good
at catchin' bad guys. And for my money that was the penthouse.

Slice and I walked into the courtroom presided over by Cecily
Rhodes. She had a tight, tough, old face that had obviously seen
a lot of tragedy. We slunk into the back. There were no reporters.
Just a couple of cops and clerks.

I nudged Slice wondering if this was a private arraignment

and he figured it couldn't be if we were there.

"Where the hell is everyone?"

Slice was straight-faced. "It's Glendale, Sammy."

Yeah. This wasn't a splashy Brentwood O.J. celebrity scandal. This was a dirty Glendale rapist. And nobody cares about Glendale. Even me, and I lived there.

Slice was taking in the scene. It was odd seeing him so keyed up. Getting a taste of the old days. The juice.

Before long someone I finally recognized walked in. It was David Pendleton. Josie's brother. He looked worn out. Saw me and tried to square it but I kept my eyes low.

A bailiff marched Louis Ullverson into the courtroom. He had a lawyer with him. A young guy who couldn't have been more than thirty we pegged as the public defender but he had a nice suit. Rhodes blared the charges.

Murder in the first degree. Three counts.

I stared at Ullverson. The man looked ragged and unhinged and exactly what you'd expect a serial rapist to look like. Unattractive enough. Unpowerful. Unphysical. Sick on the inside, plain on the outside.

Scary sick you can't detect.

There was a lotta courtroom banter but I just stared at this man. He was wearing a brown jumpsuit and it bothered me. I wanted orange. I wanted impact and resonance.

I thought about Josie's skin on the slab.

I thought about this due process.

I thought it was bullshit. I wanted this man to burn. I wanted the old days where we hang 'em up and snap that neck. Let those eyes bulge out. Let the world see what happens when you violate a woman.

They said some more stuff and walked him away.

Due process.

Slice stared at me. "Happy now?"

I think he smiled a little. Like he knew how insignificant the process felt compared to the pain.

"Sure, Slice."

As we walked out, I tried not to look at David, though I could feel him staring at me. Still squaring it all friend or foe.

I broke away from Slice and marched up to David, tired of defending myself inside.

"I just miss her. I'm sorry you lost your sister."

I walked away and hoped to never see him again.

Tuesday, September 8th, 5:16 p.m.

I drove Slice back to the Lovely.

I locked myself in the box.

I tried to write. About the arraignment. About Ullverson.

But Josie's blue face on the slab kept creepin' in. The smell of her shirt. I couldn't shake it.

I hit the road.

I needed to numb myself with strangers' faces and mindless banter.

With stops and starts and flashing traffic lights.

Thursday, September 10th, 2:11 p.m.

I slept.

I avoided Nick.

I hit the box.

I let my face heal.

I stayed away from booze. I drank Sprite and cursed.

I thought about burning Josie's shirt.

I wrote random short stories.

I distanced myself from the slugs at the bar and missed Jiles.

Until someone knocked on the box door.

So I opened it and saw a smile. It belonged to Allison and she handed me a Sprite.

"Bartender said this is your drink of choice now." She stepped in, and I was worried the room smelt like the worst of me. "Nice office."

"I call it the box."

"Kinda stinks...Not a lot of fresh air in here. Not a lotta light." She looped around in a figure eight.

"So, thanks for the orchid."

I shrugged and shoulda said you're welcome but was still processing what the hell she was doing here. And how good it was to see her.

That smile.

"It's good to see you. Didn't think I ever would after the last time."

"You started it!" she barked with a grin.

She glanced at my computer and I got tight.

"What are you writing?"

"Nothing important."

"You obviously *heard*. About this guy they got."

"Yeah."

We just looked at each other and it felt good until she saw the fading bruises and scar around my eye.

"What happened to your face?"

"I got beat up."

"Who beat you up?"

"Nazis."

She didn't believe me, like it was some joke. "You beat those Nazis back?"

I shook my head and instantly realized how much I truly liked this woman. "You wanna get outta here? Grab some food?"

"I can't. I just came by to say hi. But I was thinking of you with all the news about Josie. And...that orchid."

"You like orchids?"

"I like the one you gave me. I also like to think how stupid you were to ask me here and ask me all those questions when you didn't even know Josie. Or me. I guess you really cared about her."

She made for the door.

"I've been listening to Lou Reed. You were right. Something about his voice...it's infectious. Been dancing around my apartment all alone with Lou keeping me company."

She danced a little jig and flicked up her skirt, exposing a piece of her thigh.

"Gimme a call next week. Don't text. Just call me."

And then she was gone.

It was a bona fide skirt-jig hit and run.

I mean. Just the smell of her changed everything.

She smelled like hope.

Thursday, September 10th, 2:27 p.m.

I walked outta the box and Team Lovely looked my way like they wondered what kind of mischief with Allison went down behind that door. I dashed their dirty expectations and told them it was all clean and friendly.

Pa laughed. "It was awful faaaast."

The Greek chorus chimed in at my expense when my phone rang. I figured it was another solar energy company or insurance racket and answered without saying anything—waiting for the din of the call center and the *hello Mr. Samuel* before hanging up.

But instead a women's voice told me to hold for Daphne.

I got tight.

My agent Daphne clicked on. "Sam?"

"Daphne?"

"We sold the article. You're gonna make some money. Pretty sure we're all gonna make some money if you don't mess this up cuz I slipped the article to an exec at *Stake*."

"*Stake?*"

"Yeah, the magazine. But they're expanding. They have a partnership with the Alden group—this big French firm with European money who are helping them launch a content division. They're looking to create a whole brand—starting their own streaming platform and have been desperate for sort of, macho, male-driven content. Pretty much the opposite of what everyone else wants. Anyway, they purchased the rights to the article outright and are gonna publish it."

"Wow. Wait, they just bought it?"

"It gets better. The exec slipped the article to David G. Frazier. Please tell me you know him?"

"Kinda..." I lied.

"He's a writer. Producer. Done a ton of stuff. Studio guy— worked on the *Thrasher* franchise. And he's got three shows streaming right now. Look him up. Anyway, he's got a first look with *Stake*. He LOVED the article. Loved the voice. Wants to meet you right away and talk about developing it into something bigger."

"Bigger what?"

"They wouldn't say. That's what he wants to talk about, I guess. And by all accounts he's a super nice guy. Canadian, I think. He suggested the bar, The Damned Lovely, you know, the one in your article. His office will reach out with times. Okay?"

"Okay."

"I got you six grand for the article up front. That's five times what most publications would pay for something like this. If Frazier wants to develop it, you'll retain the rights so presuming you guys can work together, we'll all make some real money. But that's down the line. Anyway. That sound good? What are you writing next?"

"I don't know yet."

"Send me some ideas..."

"You always say that and then you hate my ideas. Then I end up hating them or hating you."

"That usually means the ideas are inherently problematic. Look, you can write, Sam. You've proven that. It's time we started to work together from the beginning and really develop your voice. Just tell me what you're thinking. Maybe we can find some development money for you. Get you out on some generals."

"Okay. Thanks, Daph—"

"You're welco—"

The line went dead before she finished.

Onto the next kill.

207

I stared at the phone. This portal of highs and lows that just detonated my life with information. Yes, yes, we all create our own destinies but it just rings and *boom!* the sum of all my self-loathing, of fear and nights of panic of why do I even bother typing these words anyway...all of it changed in a burst of words through this little glowing beacon.

We *like* it.

We want to *buy* it.

And for that, I could buy better food and shelter and booze and feel better about myself.

It was only six grand. But it *was* six grand. And it was the best damn six grand I would ever earn.

And then those stupid tears hit. The stinging kind. The kind that reminded me what a fuck up I was NOT, after all. After wrestling those failures, pinning them down against the floor of my conscience for another burst of something, some inspiration, some fuel in the tank. Those stinging tears dripped out and I didn't care if Jiles and Jewels and Pa and Lily and the Rooster saw. They were *earned*. They were stinging victory tears, my friends, so bottoms up.

They all wanted to know what was going on.

I wiped my face.

I kept quiet and coy.

Wait till I tell Slice.

"Nothing."

I kept it close for now.

For me. I bought them a round instead. They were thrilled. They smiled and said something like *Sammy's back*.

So I asked Jiles to pour me some bourbon.

Thursday, September 17th, 8:27 p.m.

I called Allison.

I bought good wine and we hit Abbott Kinney's finest for dinner.

We walked the streets of Venice. I marveled at the beautiful faces and the smell of the air.

We talked and smiled, all in sync. I held back about Max. About the jerks who beat me up.

She never asked about Josie.

I never asked about Josie.

I felt like holding her hand but was afraid to kill the buzz and have her shake loose.

I asked her if orchids reminded her of a woman's labia and by extension were not great gifts.

She laughed magic.

I drove her home and walked her to her front door like it was the fifties.

She invited me in and we danced to Lou Reed in her apartment.

I could smell her neck.

I swelled with willpower and chose to leave before messing it up. I thought about her neck and how sweet she smelled driving home.

The traffic sucked coming east. Even at midnight.

God, how I loved this messed up town.

Friday, September 18th, 10:11 a.m.

I considered telling Nick I was gonna move out. No, I dreamed of telling Nick I was gonna move out. Literally think I had a dream and woke up bright.

Was six grand enough? Always said that if I was gonna move west, I had to make it worth my while. Like it was an achievement, like it meant something bigger creeping closer to the beach.

Like my life had improved.

I checked rent in Silverlake. I found a little guesthouse overlooking the reservoir for twenty-one hundred.

I got wise.

I held back.

Six grand was a drop in the bucket.

But for me it was a grand slam. My own golden ticket assuring me this chase, this painful pursuit, was worth *something*.

My meeting with Frazier was coming up. My future was wiiiiiide open.

Friday, September 18th, 5:23 p.m.

I figured it was time.

I gave Slice the article, careful not to watch his face as he read it sitting at the bar next to me.

When he was done, he threw it back in my face. Like *actually* threw those papers at me until they scattered around and fell to the sticky wet floor.

"I bare my fuckin' soul and this is what you do to me? Cut into me like this?"

I sucked back oxygen. Suspected he'd be ruffled but didn't anticipate the disappointment behind his eyes.

"It's all true, isn't it?"

The man hated it. Said I'd left out all the good parts. The badass cop stings. The Vice busts. Those hero moments. Instead it was mostly all about how sad his life had become swilling booze in Glendale most afternoons.

"This is what you think of me, Sam?"

I didn't have a safe answer for that.

"You think I want people to read this?" Then, he added softly, "My son?"

Slice looked cut up. Like I'd never really seen. He stood and walked outta the bar.

I shouldn't have been surprised.

But it wasn't a puff piece.

It was a *character* piece. Meant to cut to the truth. I never exposed his great sin outright, but Slice was a fallen soul. It was *his* fault. I didn't shoot a guy, I just wrote around it. And he

211

knew all along that was gonna come out. Why else would he have told me? Why would he have told me if he didn't want it coming out?

Screw him. I mean, I love the man. But I got nothin' else. The article was about to get published and it was my ticket to a better life. So yeah, that's how I justified it when I asked Jiles to pour me a double.

I wanted him to see my side of things but the bartender just grunted.

"I don't know. The man's been through it."

"Yeah and that comes out in the article. I think what he is, what he did is tough but noble and ugly and a dark shadow—"

"Doesn't matter. It's still a cut."

"A cut?"

"There's a code. With cops. A bond. An unspoken oath. And what you're doing? Cuts in. We call it a cut."

Jiles was rampin' up. I could see the engines charging. Like he often did when talking cops.

"Meaning?"

"It means we don't rat out our own. One of us fucks up, we own it. To each other. Not to a judge. Not to our wives. Our kids. To each other. Because we understand, only *we* understand what it's really like to go out there every night and put our body up for sale. Now I know you've heard that talk before but think about it. *Think about it*, Sam. Every night, a part of us believes: this might be it. This might be the night some crazy on meth catches me off guard cuz for him, I'm a demon. That's what we do. It's not a stupid TV show or a movie. It's what we actually do on Tuesdays and on Wednesdays, on every day. So when we mess up. And we *do* mess up, we got two choices. You can own it. You come right out and say, yeah. I messed up. I hit the guy. I pinched the money. The gun went off. I shoulda known better. And for that? You burn. Your pension burns. Your family burns. Or. You bury it. You hold the line and tell 'em nah, fuck you, I did my job. You keep quiet and tell yourself you were the good guy. There were casualties but for the greater good you did what you had to do.

"Some skate by. Some don't and get called into court. But either way, we know. *Cops know.* On the inside. Cops know when other cops mess up. And at the end of the day, we decide when it's too much. When the line has been crossed. When there was no greater good there was only you and your own messed up demons burning inside that you couldn't keep in so someone else had to hurt. *We decide.*

"What Slice did? In the court of cop opinion was in the greater good. We let it slide. We knew the facts. The monster he took down. The ugliness of it all and it *was* ugly and he made a terrible choice that day but he didn't need to burn for it. He needed to go quiet. He wasn't coming back after that. But the man didn't need to go to jail. He wasn't a threat to society. He was damaged. So we kicked him to the curb. Let him sit with what he did. On the *inside.* He's been broke ever since. It was the right thing to do."

"You decide?"

"We decide."

"What happens when guys like Slice push back?" I asked. "When they don't go quiet?"

"Then we step in. You'll never read about it. Or hear about it. But we right the wrong. On our own terms. In the interest of the people. Because we already know the system's broke. And most cops would rather take a bullet than face the bars."

"You say so, Jiles."

"That's just the way it works. Always has. Which is why you've put Slice in a jam. You're exposing him, the system and how it all really works."

Jiles turned and saw a brunette with an empty wineglass waiting impatiently at the far end of the bar. He set off to help her but rapped his hand a couple times on the bar, like some judge banging a gavel on this disturbing session.

Jiles always spiked the drama when it came to cop talk. I just couldn't buy it. I'm sure it went down sometimes, but I'd read enough dirty cop headlines to know they didn't always *decide*. Right?

I swilled the bourbon and planted my flag. Maybe I'd betrayed my friend's trust but Slice was broken and it was his own fault. Maybe he *wanted* those sins to come out. Why else would he have told me? Hanging off my elbow asking when the article was coming out. Maybe he *needed* to get locked up.

That's what I told myself when the Rooster approached and cooed close to my ear.

"You owe me twelve hundred dollars."

He placed a black USB thumb drive on the bar and walked away. *Twelve hundred bucks?* I didn't owe him—

Then it hit me. I never told the Rooster to stop. That I didn't need the intel on the Patriot Strong financial donors now that they'd snatched up the Grabber. I clenched my hands against the bar till they got hot and white. Twelve hundred dollars for an Excel spreadsheet I didn't even need. I stared at the little hard drive, laughing at the terrible pun. The amount of hard driving I would have to do to pay it off.

Rooster would hack and destroy my life faster than Jewels kicked him to the curb if I didn't pay him back. I sucked it up and told him I'd step out the payments in three chunks over a few weeks' time. He shrugged which I presumed meant that was cool.

I stared at the drive.

Did I really want to open up this wound again? They caught the guy. I didn't need this shrapnel. I had *traction*—a girl like Allison, a bon-a-fide paycheck and the promise of a better horizon.

I stared at the drive.

I thought about Josie.

I thought about her skin on the slab.

The denim I couldn't bring myself to burn.

I wished I was stronger.

I had to scratch.

Friday, September 18th, 6:01 p.m.

I hit the box and plugged the drive into Benny. Figured if I paid for the information, may as well see what he dug up. Maybe I could write an article exposing the scum who funded an organization like Patriot Strong. Earn a few bucks from some blowhard liberal publications.

The Rooster had dug into eight different private companies with mixed results.

Capital 7 Partners LLC.
Unlimited Reach LLC.
Optimize RD.
JD Assets LLC.
Blue Whale Inc.
Global Road Inc.
Excel 96 Inc.

Capital 7, Unlimited Reach, and Optimize were all owned by big-wig real estate cats out of Houston. A conglomerate of land-owning, aged-out, rich, right-wing white guys with dubious moral standards. The numbers were staggering. The wealth. So many commas. They'd each lobbed close to thirty grand a month at Patriot Strong. The flagship funding. JD Assets belonged to an ex-Brit out of Silicon Valley named James Devon Ingram who, at not even thirty years old, made a killing selling encrypted software data storage programs to governments all over the world. He was pouring in a steady ten K every month. Blue Whale was the book name of a company owned by a ninety-year-old fast-food chain heiress. She was tossing in over six K a month. Global Road was a nondescript LLC shell company out of Fresno with a single principal by the name of M. N. Sandoval. They'd given steady chunks of five K a month but there was very little clarity on who or what they represented. Similarly Excel 96 was shoving over erratic cash anywhere from a couple hundred to twenty-two K. The principal of the company was Rachel McSorley. The Rooster couldn't find much on these folks outside of the deposits. Or never bothered.

I printed out the list and pinned it on my corkboard of ideas. For a rainy day in Glendale. Maybe I'd dig it up after my meeting with Frazier. Circle back on these sharks and write up a hasty exposé, revealing their true colors to the world. Spin my twelve hundred outta the red and add to my escape fund.

Friday, September 25th 3:20 p.m.

The day finally came.

I shaved and could see my face healing nicely. Nicely enough with a huge scar down the side of my eye.

I hit the bar, ten minutes early.

Gained my bearings.

Rehearsed my compelling tale for the meet. Who I was and how I came to this moment in the world. The general meeting highlight reel.

David G. Frazier breezed in fourteen minutes late. Annoying. But I cut him some Westside slack.

I recognized him from the Google images shots. He was tanned and much taller than I expected with a full head of black hair and aviator sunglasses that sat on a tiny nose. He was about fifty, looked rich and comfortable in a button-down shirt and jeans but walked with an awkward gait. Almost cautious. Then again, it was my home field advantage.

I introduced myself and he lit right up. All smiley, healthy Brentwood white teeth beaming out. He seemed genuinely excited to meet me. Even more excited to see the bar and meet Slice, who wasn't around.

He ordered a Diet Coke and offered to buy me a drink.

I ordered a Bulleit. No way I was putting on airs for this man. He called the meet. I may as well get a free drink outta this if nothing else. We rocked the usual opening banter. Traffic and heat. He was curious about the scar on my face. I spun a terrible lie about cutting it on a busted coat hanger in a dark closet.

As the chatter slowed down, Frazier looked around the bar and asked about the history of the joint. I waved Jiles over and Frazier started up about what a great writer I was.

I let it play.

It felt odd and glorious. That admiration.

Jiles shot me a look like a proud father and regaled Frazier with the bar's history. The chain of command. The players. The space.

Frazier said the article rang true and did the place justice. "No pun intended," he mused. Then he started up with his vision. "With what it could be."

I was a little lost. Vision? "What *what* could be?"

"The article. I wanna turn it into a TV show. You've got all these burnouts—what a great cast. And the cop thing. It's like *Cheers* meets *Murder, She Wrote*. But newer. Cooler. Every week the characters, the ex-cops, will solve a crime. With Slice blazing the trail. You know, the disgraced ex-cop with killer instincts that everyone underestimates. It could be a fun crime show. A dramedy. But with heart. Whaddya think?"

Dramedy? I covered the pain with a foggy look. Tryin' to square the nonsense. "Did you say *Murder, She Wrote?*"

"That's a dated reference. But you get the idea. Course we might have to change some stuff...maybe set it in Venice or Culver City. Get some women in. Make it more diverse. Make Jiles Asian or something. You know." He looked around the dive bar. "Yeah. Brighten it up a little."

"That show from the eighties? With Angela Lansbury? You wanna turn Slice into Angela Lansbury?"

Frazier cocked me a guarded look. Like that tanned skin wasn't used to people pushing back on it.

"I think your article is a great jumping off point, has a great engine for a show and it's a fun little nugget of IP to help launch some content. But, to be candid, it needs an overhaul for the medium. A TV facelift."

"No, it doesn't. This place is a gem. Just the way it is. If you're gonna write a show about this joint then, write a show about this joint. Tell it like it is. Warts and all. Tell it *because* of the warts. Make it real."

Frazier was nodding his head. "I agree, and it would have the *spirit* of this place...the spirit of Slice and his life as a cop. About a man who gets a second chance in life and helps the new young cops solve crimes from his stool. That could help us access a younger demographic. Anyway, it's gonna be great. I can see it. Might have to make Slice a little younger though. And I'm not really sold on Glendale...There's nothing sexy about Glendale. I see it more like Culver City."

"Culver City?" I looked around the room. "This ain't Culver City. This is fuckin' Glendale. You wanna make a show about a bar in Culver City with Angela Lansbury what does that have to do with my article or this place?"

Frazier started brewing when Slice bust through with a slab of Porto's chocolate cake. I introduced Frazier and the old coot lit right up, smearing a piece of cake off his upper lip.

Frazier peppered Slice with adoration and questions. How excited he was to finally meet him. He asked the ex-cop about his son. About the beat in Vice. Bustin' streets in nineties' LA. Even about his old man and listening to the fights on the porch. Slice rambled, eager for the ear, and Frazier lapped it up.

I watched from the sidelines. *Am I supposed to be happy?*

I bubbled up a laugh as they exchanged war stories and hated myself for it.

Frazier wouldn't even look at me.

I ordered another drink and hit the box. Happy to be alone and away from his tan and perfect teeth. His Hollywood schlock and pandering.

Culver City.

Friday, September 25th 4:24 p.m.

When I came back out Frazier was gone. Slice was yappin' with Jiles, still riding high from the pomp.

I told him about Frazier's idea. Culver City. *Cheers* meets *Murder, She Wrote*.

"You believe that?"

Slice didn't get it. "Who cares? It's a TV show. About us?! I think that's pretty great."

Jiles shrugged. God bless that man. He didn't seem to care either way.

Slice kept trying to tell me how great it was gonna be. That I was gonna be rich and famous like that was gonna solve all my problems.

"What problems?" I asked, genuinely curious.

The man roared with laughter. Rich, unironic bellowing. Even Jiles chuckled.

I sipped my booze.

I burned furious.

As if on cue, my agent called.

Daphne was wicked sharp. Said I'd pissed off Frazier. Said I'd screwed the whole thing up.

I argued he was gonna turn the article into a stupid Angela Lansbury show about a fake version of a real cop in a fake Culver City bar that had nothing to do with the real me. Or Glendale.

She railed. "Glendale?!! Who cares? And this isn't about *you*! It's about Frazier! All you had to do was nod and say yes and what a great idea Mr. Frazier, and then we're all friends and then we get the money and then we drill down on the creative and then we can fire Frazier cuz remember we're all friends. Of course we were smart so we'd retain the rights to the article. But now, no. Now he's either gonna dump the project, or more likely, he'll just go over your head. He'll get the magazine to sell him the rights and cut us out, altogether. You just buried us. THIS is why you're not getting anywhere. THIS is the problem. YOU are the problem. Not the writing, YOU, Sam."

She hung up.

I kept drinking.

Did I really just defend Glendale?

Friday, September 25th, 8:10 p.m.

Chalk up some more pain.

The Pluckin' Strummers were hittin' it hard that night.

Pinner waddled in.

I'd never been so happy to see his ugly face. After the Frazier debacle and the stinging call with my beloved representation, I needed to get my mind off the article and I hadn't seen the cop since the arraignment. He'd been dodging me and I was still buzzing with questions.

The man was riding high and mighty. Pinner was a veritable toast of the blandest town for catching the Glendale Grabber. All he wanted was to drink and be merry with his fellow cop-o's but I wanted details. There wasn't much more in the press about the get on Ullverson. The *Times* said they "used a variety of methods to narrow down the search including a DNA match to the victims, surveillance cameras and eyewitness accounts that all contributed to the arrest."

But I squeezed Pinner for the real juice.

He started up about the exhaustive search and hours of ugly police work he and his brethren had put into finding the monster. Days of digging into rape kits across the country pinged a match with a John Doe offender outta Detroit from 2013. Oddly the DNA wasn't in the system but the officers recognized the MO. Death by asphyxiation in a stolen car. Turns out because of a processing backlog of over three hundred cases, they never even processed the DNA since the vic died, but Pinner persisted and made some calls. Pressed some crisp suit to push through the data. When they finally did, it matched Ullverson who had just recently been sprung from a four-year stint in Lompoc. Then, the real get was scouring security cams. Seventeen cameras and over three hundred hours of footage finally turned up Ullverson strolling past an ATM cam only blocks from the car at the first victim's crime scene. From there it got easier, and they matched the DNA to the second girl.

"Amazing," I geeked out, sopping up the details.

"We worked our asses off and it *paid* off." Pinner beamed, taking in the audience. "And then we caught a break when a gas station clerk, our one eyewitness, Antonio Yuarez, pegged Ullverson for the third murder."

"That's fantastic," I nodded but didn't totally understand. "You mean as well as the DNA?"

"DNA came up empty on the third case. So thank god for Antonio."

"The third case? You mean Josie?"

He nodded but I was still confused. "So...you don't have any DNA connected to Josie's murder? Or in the car?"

"No. But we got an eyewitness who saw the bastard three blocks from where we found the car that night."

"Three blocks?"

Pinner was no fool, picking up my curiosity. "He was in the vicinity. And he killed two other women with the exact same MO. You think that's a coincidence?"

"I think I'd wanna be sure." I blurted it out.

Pinner put down his drink. Barked at Jiles to pour me a stiff bourbon and put it on his tab.

"I am sure. I've been doing this for over fifteen years. Trust me."

Then he glared at me. "Drink your drink, and mind your place. We got the guy."

The Strummers panged hard.

Pinner talked to Jiles and pretended to ignore me.

I felt the disconnect brewing deep in my gut.

This was all supposed to be over.

Monday, September 28th, 9:49 a.m.

For three days I tried to wash off the stain of Josie's murder. They finally had the guy in cuffs and I should've been happy but my gut rumbled dark.

An eyewitness account. A convicted sex offender guilty of raping and killing two women spotted only blocks away from Josie's crime scene. Was it enough? Of course, it was.

On paper.

Jiles always told me cops think in straight lines. Direct connections. Past cases. Similar MOs. Repeat offenders. Hard stats. But if Pinner had told me they had DNA and a cop saw him do it, I'd still wanna be sure. I *had* to be sure and his collar only scrambled it all up. Maybe he was right. Maybe I was overthinking it, looking for some victory in place of my own life's failure, but I didn't care.

I couldn't shake it and went back to the well. Laid it all out from scratch. Everything I had on my whiteboard in the box:

Josie was at the bar.

Josie was raped and killed in a car.

Josie had scratches that came from Max. Check—most *likely* Max.

Josie said in her emails she was going to bring down a powerful organization. Presumably, Patriot Strong.

I didn't know how.

What did I know?

They had dispositive evidence on the first two killings: Ullverson's DNA.

But not with Josie. Josie was different. A different killer? Made to *look* like the Grabber? A targeted hit to take out Josie by Max?

The MO was the same.

What was different? Specific and unique to only the third murder.

The night.

The place.

The car.

The night. I couldn't find any significance attached to the night of July 6th. Birthdays. Anniversaries. The stupid moon. I scoured online for close to an hour and nothing popped that connected in any way to Patriot Strong or Max.

The place. I looked up all things connected to the intersection of Maple and Central where they found her, but from the jump this didn't track. Why would you kill someone somewhere that meant something? The smart play is to make the location random. Untraceable. Not outside your apartment. Or job. Or anything that can connect back. Results were thin.

The car. I went back and looked at my notes on that beige Camry. Cops said the car was stolen, just like the other two murders. Pinner had told me it belonged to Sally Harnell. She was seventy-two and lived in Eagle Rock but I'd been unable to find anything on her. Still, I went back in. Who the hell was she? I powered through a twelve-page deep Google search and came up empty on anything connecting dear Sally. So I hit up some images. Mustang Sally. Sally Field. Lay down Sally. Endless faces and cartoons and useless pics of cowboy boots and random celebrities.

I typed in: *Sally Harnell Organization* and went seven pages deep hoping to see if anything connected to Max but nothing popped. Just more of the same random images.

Until I saw the sweatshirt.

It was yellow. With cursive blue writing and a crest, worn by an elderly woman with grey hair, smiling next to a group of old folks on a playground. Those sharp blue letters blazing on Sally

Harnell's chest:

Backyard Dreams.

Something like electricity shot through my spine. I tried not to freak out but this was the wrong organization. I was supposed to connect Max and Patriot Strong, not the charity helping children at Backyard Dreams.

I punched in: *Backyard Dreams Sally Harnell.*

The same grey-haired, pleasant-looking woman's face popped up. I clicked through the endless wormhole of information on all things Sally Harnell. There were Sally Harnells in Hartford, Winnipeg, London, Bangkok, and a slew of other towns but none of 'em seemed to be connected to Backyard Dreams. I burned hours trying to connect Sally to Backyard Dreams but nothing popped.

Then I remembered my dad's fishing mantra he'd blast with a smile when we'd be skunked on the boat for hours, swapping out flies: *Never change a winning game, son...always change a losing game!*

I pulled a one-eighty.

I was gonna dig back into Backyard Dreams. Come at it the other way. Maybe Sally was connected to them.

Fourteen minutes later I found an online volunteer sign-up list. Sally Harnell's name was listed to help set up tents and lay out food at a fundraising run. There were some pictures in the margin of helpful volunteers smiling wide. Among them one of Sally next to Susan Glasser, Glenn's assistant. The happy-go-not-so-lucky exec assistance/ex-actress working at Backyard Dreams. The bird girl. The one who gobbled down my Proof bakery scones and left me to slave doing her grunt work moving into that North Hollywood office. Intrigued, I dug deeper and hit up Glasser's Twitter feed. That's where I saw them. Those three beautiful words from Susan to Sally in a public post only three months ago: *Happy Bday Aunt Sally!*

Susan Glasser and Sally Harnell were related.

My mind went rowdy, swirling with theory.

226

It was Susan.

Of course it was. The unsuspecting, lovable, disgruntled worker who killed her younger more beautiful counterpart to sleep with the boss. It suddenly all made perfect sense. Glenn admitted he was in love with Josie. Susan was probably in love with Glenn and knew as long as Josie was around, he'd never see her for who she really was! So she stole her aunt's car from Eagle Rock and...and then...raped Josie? Strangled her to death so it would look like the Glendale Grabber?

It all fell apart. Made absolutely no sense. Susan didn't rape Josie. How the hell did that fit in? But this *was* something. It had to be.

I needed counsel.

I needed the man behind the bar.

I needed another drink, bad.

Monday, September 28th, 11:42 p.m.

It was close to midnight and the joint was way quiet. Slice was slurring words with Lily next to some strange faces in the corner. I ambled up to the bar and found Jiles, eager to lay out my dynamite connection.

But the ex-cop just winced. He agreed the Harnell/Glasser car connect was peculiar and even nodded with cred at my digging, but for his money that was the end of the line.

"I just don't buy it, Sammy. And neither do you—I can tell. You got no motive. The pieces don't add up. And your gut's sayin the same thing, isn't it?"

The ground was an easy place to keep my eyes. Circling through theories.

"Maybe she had a partner. Someone who did it for her?"

"Pinner's a pain in the ass but he's a good cop. He wouldn't have been drinking here, celebrating, if he felt they got the wrong guy. Maybe it's time to walk away from all this."

"Pour me a Bulleit please, Jiles."

But he just stood there. Looked kinda sad, like a tired dog. Checked his shoulder.

"I love ya, kid. You know I do. But where's this all getting you? Look at your face. You've been chewed up. Inside and out. Why don't you give it a break? Go hide behind a computer and write something. Something to make yourself proud or smile or I don't know. You're obviously good at it. You're just tripping yourself up with this Josie dirt. I get it, you've put a lot of yourself into it, but at the end of the day, where's it really getting you?"

I appreciated Jiles's little monologue, but all I wanted now was a stiff drink not some stupid Dad advice.

"Can I please have a bourbon?"

The man shrugged. Whipped up my amber delight and left me alone. I sat stung and solo but the silence and cold booze helped figure out my next play.

Tuesday, September 29th, 7:12 a.m.

The matching Land Rovers were parked in the driveway. Perfectly parked in front of Glenn's perfect big house, his perfect-looking family all likely resting inside.

I parked across the street, staying low in my car, watching, waiting for him to emerge. Figured Glenn to be an early bird type-A guy. But it was his beautiful wife who burst out the front door wearing headphones and splashy orange workout gear. She stretched her quads and bounded down the block.

Inside the massive house, the little girl was drifting from room to room. Finally, Glenn emerged in his kitchen, staring at an iPad. I considered waiting until he emerged but didn't want to corner him next to his daughter.

The house felt even bigger standing on the front porch. I rang the bell and Glenn looked out a window to see who the hell was on his front porch so early in the morning. I wondered if he'd even remember me. He opened the door with a tight face and his daughter hiding behind his legs.

"What are you doing here?"

"I'm not here to bother you. And I'm sorry for showing up like this, but I've discovered something sensitive I felt you should know. It's about Josie."

His face softened and the little girl smiled from behind her dad's leg like she was playing a game.

"They already got the guy."

I wound up and laid it out. Practiced on the way over. What to drum up, what to omit. No way was I going to mention Patriot

Strong or Max but reminded him that Josie said something was rotten about his charity. Then teed up the Susan Glasser connection. The aunt. The car, the crime scene. The ugly coincidence. How Glasser chose her aunt's car cuz she was suffering from Alzheimer's and probably wouldn't connect any dots.

His daughter wandered off, confused and bored. Glenn took in the tall tale and spewed it back.

"You think Susan Glasser killed Josie? The woman who has worked tirelessly with me for over seven years? For hardly any money, helping to make kids' playgrounds a better, safer place? You think she raped and murdered her friend and coworker?"

He stopped talking and let that impossible truth sit in the air. "She wouldn't do that."

"Unless she was in love with you. Or feared Josie knew something, something rotten about your charity and was going to—"

He started to shut the door. I doth protested with a softening plea and wedged my foot inside the path of the door. It didn't hurt which was cool.

"I know. I agree some the circumstances feel...uneven...but maybe Glasser was doing something behind your back, Josie found out and was going to tell you so she had to stop her. Maybe Glasser had a partner, someone to help her and that's who raped her and together they—"

"You need to leave. Right now. You ever come near me again, come near my family, near my house, near my charity, I'll fucking destroy you."

He wound back the door so I moved my foot before he slammed it shut. Seconds later, I could hear him explain to his perfect little daughter that the man was trying to sell him something and to never open the door to strangers.

Like you do.

I shuffled back to my car. Hit the ignition and drove out fast.

Moorpark was stacked with commuters and slow going. I considered rerouting until I saw those orange workout pants in the distance.

Mrs. Glenn was running fast and hard.

I wanted to scream at that pretty face that her perfect husband would have cheated on her with Josie Pendleton if only Josie'd let him. He was probably already cheating on her.

Thankfully the scar on my face in the rearview mirror reminded me how stupid I was sometimes. And the way she was running, hard and pounding the concrete with each stride, somehow reminded me that people with perfect houses can have shit lives, too.

She hit a red light. Kept those knees bouncing.

I pulled up next her and lowered the window.

She caught my eye and looked away.

I bellowed.

"I hope you trust your husband."

She wouldn't look, but she could hear me. The light stayed red. The knees bounced higher. Gaze locked straight. Focused and determined.

Ignoring the LA crazy.

The light burst green.

She hit the road hard.

I sat. At peace with something, watching her run away as a chorus of horns blared behind me.

Like I'd taken some kinda stupid higher road.

Thursday, October 1st, 5:33 p.m.

The Damned Lovely was lit up. People were buzzing and the jukebox blazed some fierce brass soul. Lily nodded, and the rest of the liquored cheeks angled my way.

But it all got quiet as I stepped up to the bar.

"What's what?"

Slice edged my way.

"That guy Frazier called me. He wants to buy my life. You did it, Sammy!"

"Whaddya mean he wants to buy your life?"

"I don't know but he had me on the phone with this Beverly Hills lawyer. They offered me ten grand. You believe that? All cuz of you. Jiles set him up—on me!"

"So that's it?"

"What's it?"

"You're just cuttin' me out?"

"What? No. Not at all. Don't get all paranoid. I asked him, I made sure of it, he said he'd get you in. Help consult on the show. He even said that word. 'Consult,' I mean, come on, it was your article. We can't do this without you. And get this, he said I'd be a producer. You believe that? I'm a producer now."

My head shook like a depressed parent. "You actually believed him, Slice?"

He stared lost and muddled.

I laid it out.

"Once you sell your life rights to Frazier, he's just gonna go around me and you and make his stupid show without us. He's

233

paying you off. He's got no reason to give us anything."

"Na. You'll see. He's a good guy. Canadian. Didn't he tell you that? C'mon have a drink—let's celebrate. You know how hard up for cash I am. Without this money...it wasn't lookin' good, Sammy. This really saves me. And I have you to thank for it. Lemme buy you a round."

Maybe I shoulda been happy for the old drunk but...I was too angry.

"So you're not worried?"

"Worried? I just landed ten K for nothin'. Not exactly cause for worry, bud."

"About the truth coming out. About what you did."

He hit me with a cold glare. "Why the hell do you think I spend all my time in here, Sam?"

Slice had had enough of me and turned around. Joined the rest of the smiles his newfound bounty was feeding.

I wanted nothing here.

I stormed out.

Right after I took a piss.

And after a shot of Maker's. Change it up.

And after asking the Rooster for a small favor.

And then I asked Jiles for the rest of the Maker's bottle to go.

Thursday, October 1st, 6:13 p.m.

The streets were jammed.

Cars locked in snarling heat and crawling over asphalt at a painfully slow clip.

My head was ripping fast.

My fingers were tight on the wheel with ugly white tips.

Slice had betrayed me.

He didn't care about my article. He cared about his glory. His pay out.

Did I have any right to be angry?

Felt like it. It was *my* article. My initiative. My work. My content. My sweat and time pushing out those words. And I walk away with six grand minus the Rooster's fees and agent fees and car repairs and this feeling in my gut.

And Slice gets ten grand.

No wonder betrayal made for ripe art.

I was ready to destroy something.

My muse had betrayed me.

My friend, too.

I smashed the horn and yelled like a man in a movie.

Thank god I had a bottle of Maker's.

And a goddamn mission.

Thursday, October 1st, 6:39 p.m.

Susan Glasser shuffled out of her car and hustled up to the rusty gate of her apartment complex carrying three heavy canvass bags. I hadn't seen her since my volunteering stint at Backyard.

She looked the same.

She looked plain and soft and unhappy, even from across the street.

Cars hurtled past the Victory Boulevard apartment complex. I was valley deep. Burbank deep. Where ugly KTLA headlines broke. A healthy mix of porn, mayhem, and too much sun.

It was an old building but looked well maintained and functional. The Rooster had slipped me her address back at the Lovely. Free of charge. I suspected he could smell my pissed-off stink and threw me a freebie like a pal might. Oh, no. Was I really becoming friends with the Rooster now?

I snapped back in.

Glasser was my target.

I needed to focus. I had a mission but lacked any kind of plan. For now, figured I'd sit on her house a while and drink some bourbon like this might make a difference.

Forty-seven minutes later she burst outta the complex carrying a yoga mat wearing a red tracksuit. She waited for the light and then walked west along the boulevard, disappearing around the corner.

I swilled some Maker's. Ready for battle.

Glasser's name was listed alone on apartment 109.

I buzzed 109 at the front gate and no one answered.

Then I pulled out my phone and pretended to be on a call until finally two dudes emerged from within the complex, not giving me a second glance as I edged in, arguing with someone named Ron about a missed doctor's appointment while the gate locked behind me.

A truly incredible performance.

I weaved around the old-time lima-bean-shaped pool in search of 109, trying to recall if Susan ever mentioned a roommate or a dog, but came up empty. Except for Montgomery. Her beloved green parakeet. I remembered Montgomery.

I braced my broken face and knocked. Montgomery squawked.

I knocked again.

And again.

I checked my shoulder.

I checked for ways in.

There was a private patio nestled behind some potted trees six feet away with a sliding door that looked out onto the pool. I slipped through the plants and tried the door but it was locked. Then I saw the frosted window. It was higher up, protected with a dusty screen, but open a crack. I grabbed one of her patio chairs and stood on it, reaching up, and managed to slide back the window. But I was gonna need to break the screen open if I wanted to get inside.

I cranked back my hand, ready to bust it open but stopped short.

Was I really gonna break in to this woman's place? Because now would be a good time for a sharp realization, a moment of clarity to highlight how stupid this whole charade had become. Now would be a good time for a wise voice to scream out and tell me to stop.

What you're about to do is illegal.

Are you really that stupid?

All because of a Twitter birthday message.
My fist smashed through the black screen and ripped away the mesh, as I hoisted my body up, into her apartment.
I chose to ignore that voice. Instead I listened to Josie screaming out inside me.
They got the wrong guy, Sam.
They got the wrong guy.

My feet were dangling until I lowered myself down onto the back of a toilet, kicking away bottles of moisturizers and exfoliates for somewhere solid to land. The cramped bathroom was brimming with creams, lotions, and conditioners of all kinds. Daytime. Nighttime. Face-mask creams. Jade rollers. This woman really cared about her skin.
I crouched quiet and on edge in case someone was inside.
But only Montgomery was squawkin' nearby.
The bird was wise. *Trouble brewing.*
I edged out into the main living space. The parakeet was flappin' fierce but I didn't see any alarm motion sensors.
It was a small one bedroom with faded paint and tired furniture. A pleasant kitchenette with some dirty dishes and fresh yellow lilies on the table.
The place was clean and bright.
Except for the pictures of Christ everywhere.
Above the TV. On the table. On the walls. Glasser was JC deep. And the images were dark. Not the happy Christ with angels and sunshine. This was the tormented and pained JC. Caravaggio style. The ones with blood in his palms and dripping out of his body. Shredded flesh. Sunken eyes. On the cross. Taking our sins hard. I never did buy into the racket that we were brought into this world unholy, wrong, and sinful by birth. I'll own up to my mistakes and faults and wrongs but don't tell me I'm rotten just for being born.
Anyway.

Those searing images gave off the feeling that Glasser was full of pain, like maybe it was hard to be Susan Glasser, the chipper assistant with a parrot.

I found a desk with a stack of mail and an old MacBook Pro. The computer was password protected so I rifled through the mail. AT&T bills. Coupons from Big 5, Bed Bath & Beyond. Some church mailers. The usual bent. There was a bulletin board overhead with an old headshot of Susan from the nineties in the corner. Dreams in her eyes. Yeah. I'd pegged it. Talent run rot. And there were a bevy of other pics of her at a picnic with Backyard Dreams folks and broken kids. The smiling faces reminded me she was probably a really decent person at heart and the chances of her actually killing Josie were slim.

I shook off the guilt and scoured the drawers. There were tax returns. Saved birthday cards. Appliance warranties. An old diploma. Class of '90. Just another woman's life.

Montgomery had stopped flappin'. But he was eyeballin' me hard. I volleyed a scowl. Right back at ya, Montgomery.

I hit the bedroom. It was clean and barren. The bed made with tight corners. I rifled through her drawers, curious but not excited at the idea of digging up any of porny secrets. There was the expected battery-operated pleasure rod hidden deep at the back. God forbid JC see her enjoy herself. Or allow her to be human. Next to the vibrator I found some faded hardcopy pictures of a guy. He was tall, Latin, and wore cheesy nineties' Oakley sunglasses and a loose red tank top revealing gym-built pecs and shoulders. He had his arm wrapped around Susan and the little woman was practically glowing. He looked familiar and I tried to square where I'd seen him when I was at Backyard Dreams, working on the office. I couldn't peg it and figured he was probably among those hapless friends and family faces in the crowd who get sucked into doing charity work. So little Susie Glasser had a crush on Mr. Latin Oakley Sunglass? Well, God bless her and that private rod. He was a good-lookin' soul. A woman's got needs, JC. Ain't nothin' wrong with that.

The rest was bunk. Underwear and headbands and everything else you'd expect to find.

Each minute grew scarier inside and my conspiracy meter was losing juice. The whole mission was feeling more and more like a big ol' bust. I couldn't connect a goddamn thing to Josie's life. And now I needed to get the hell out of there. I peered out the window, pulling back the lacy curtain—eyeing the surroundings just like they'd do in the movies.

There wasn't a soul in sight. The idea of going back out the screened window flashed past but in the end figured I'd only draw more attention and opted to just sail smoothly out the front door rolling through my made up back story in case I ran into any trouble.

(*Who, me? I'm Colin. Colin Patterson from San Francisco— just visiting my good cousin Sus' for the week. What, the screen? She forgot to leave me her key. Wouldn't pick up her phone. That is SO Susie! Anyway, nothin' to see here...so...*)

Light burst inside as I cracked open the door. Montgomery got all uppity, flapping into high gear.

"Adios, Monty."

I walked outside and closed the door firmly behind me.

I walked past the pool.

I walked towards the front gate.

I opened the gate and hit the pavement, breathing a sigh of epic relief. Until I heard—

"Stop right there. Hands wide and out."

I spun around and two large black cops in those crisp and intimidating LAPD uniforms were drilling down on me.

I fanned out my hands where they wanted them.

"What's your name?"

"Sam Goss," I croaked. So much for the Colin backstory.

"Where were you just now?"

"A friend's place."

"Who's your friend?"

"Susan Glasser—she lives here. Apartment 109." I rambled

good, clean, hard facts. We worked at a charity together. I was in the neighborhood. Popped in to say hi but she wasn't there. Then, I cranked up the deer-in-the-headlights confusion. "Is something wrong? Did something happen?"

They laid it out. A neighbor made me. Saw me bust open the screen. Saw me rifling through dear Susie's life. And. They could hear Monty puffing and flapping like something was wrong.

They snatched my wrists together.

I was cooked.

Thursday, October 1st, 8:16 p.m.

The ex-cops at the Lovely had always pressed rule number one into me with their tales of cuffed fools in the back of their squad cars blabbering on about their innocence and only sinking deeper into trouble with conflating facts and truths.

KEEP YOUR MOUTH SHUT.

I failed proper and rambled on hard.

"Pinner? Detective Pinner? You don't know him? He works Glendale PD but I know he does crossover work with the Central precinct. He knows me. He'll vouch for me. This is all a big misunderstanding."

I sounded like a bad *Law & Order* day player.

But this was real. My hands were actually handcuffed and digging into the car seat.

I was one of *them*.

A threat. A bad guy. The guy on *COPS* without a shirt and face all blurry and shameful.

That was me. Right now. Except for the shirt part.

"What about Jiles Johnson? Or Gregory Baskin, goes by Slice? They're ex-cops. Friends of mine. They'll clear this up."

The boys upfront ignored me.

The radio squawked.

I prayed for a breaking hostage situation. A freshly shot cop. One of those, "We got bigger fish to fry, kid!" moments where they let me go with an afterschool special *stay outta trouble now* so they can save the world from a *real* bad guy. Not me.

Not Sam from Portland after a few swigs off a Maker's bottle in my car.

Oh no.

My car. I realized the Volt was in a residential no parking zone after eight p.m. For some reason this felt particularly infuriating. Not the arrest for breaking and entering with possible jail time and permanent criminal record. They were gonna tow my car. More money gone. That really burned.

I looked out the window and caught the stare of a curious woman. She was about forty. Had a son in a car seat behind her. She flashed a wary glance, as if she was looking at some kinda monster who might lash out and hurt her little boy at any moment.

I would never hurt a little boy.

Thursday, October 1st, 9:00 p.m.

They guided my head outta the car and into processing. I knew the routine. I'd weaseled my way into some ride-alongs thanks to the boys at the Lovely and had seen how they book 'em. There was no fanfare or flashbulbs like some exciting bust. It was all ugly routine:

Name and address. SSN.
Personal effects
Fingerprints.
Mugshot—I straight-faced best I could. As best I could push down the shame.

They led me into a holding area I'd anticipated would be filled with bottom feeding scum who, albeit worst-case scenario, would bust my face and want my bum.
Only I was alone.
And it was quiet.
And cold. And I'd hoped there would be others whom I could compare and easily convince myself by saying, *See? I'm not nearly as screwed up as all these other lost souls. I'm just a little crooked. Like, inbounds crooked.*
The arresting officers were grouchy dogs. No one talked to me. No one told me what was happening. I was sobering up fast. My mouth was dry and I asked for some water but they didn't care. They were busy. Staring at their phones and tssking the white boy in the cell.

244

But I knew my rights.
I'd get the call.
And I knew just who to call.

Friday, October 2nd, 1:09 a.m.

The locks buzzed.

A fresh-faced police officer waved me up and led me into an interrogation room.

The sight of Lily with her worn out briefcase and unimpressed scowl was a beautiful thing. She shook her head and stared like a broken parent.

Rescuing her rascal son who'd gone off the rails yet again.

I said thank you and lauded her with pleasantries but she was already into business.

"Did you steal anything?"

"No."

"Did you damage anything?"

"No. Wait—maybe some bottles of moisturizer."

She was scribbling notes.

"So...why did you break in to this woman's apartment?"

I laid out my theory. How Josie was found in Glasser's aunt's car. How Josie was volunteering at Backyard and musta got wise to some crooked shenanigans at the charity so the woman had to silence her. Or someone at the charity did. But it couldn't be Glenn cuz he was in Buffalo. And there was no one else I knew of yet but was on the scent.

Lily looked confounded. Then got back to business.

"Were you drunk? Just tell me the truth, it's only gonna make your life harder if you don't."

"I mean...just the usual."

She needed clarity and hit me with the Lily look.

246

"I'd been drinking but I wasn't drunk."

"How much had you been drinking? It could help us."

"Half of a bottle of Maker's."

"Were you driving?"

"Yea."

Her shoulders dropped. "Okay."

Reset time.

"Have you ever been arrested before?"

"No. I've been held overnight a few times but that was in college. Years ago. Just drunk college shit. I was never charged."

She clocked me that parent look again. Like I should I know better. "There's a pattern."

"It was college. Gimme a break, Lily."

"You need to stop drinking, Sam." She said it matter of factly, like it was no big thing, then carried on, "Jiles said they caught the creep who killed this girl so are you lying to me? I don't care why you broke in—I don't care if you just wanted to…smell her panties or masturbate in her bed. I just need to know you didn't trash the place or have some vindictive motive that's gonna bite us later on."

"No. No secret agenda. I'm telling you the truth."

"Okay."

She stood up and knocked on the door. We waited in silence. She appeared to be thinking and I didn't want to interrupt but couldn't help and blurted out—

"Thank you, Lily."

She nodded and looked almost empathetic. Almost.

"Lemme see what I can do."

The same fresh-faced cop brought me back to the holding fridge.

I sat on the hard bench, waiting. It was quiet and calm and felt like the night would never end. Seeing Lily made me think it might all be okay. I closed my eyes and tried not to think about the pressing piss in my bladder. I tried not think that maybe Lily was right.

* * *

The locks clinked open.

My eyes blasted wide.

Some different cop with a snarl waved me out and led me down the hall towards Lily. She forced a tight smile and handed over my wallet and belt and keys and phone.

"We can talk in the car. Let's get outta here."

Lily led the way.

God bless that force of a woman.

Friday, October 2nd, 8:39 a.m.

Lily laid it out.

Glasser was pressing charges, second-degree breaking and entering. In California that carries a maximum of three years in state prison and a ten K fine.

That was the ugly part.

The not so ugly part was she got the name of the judge assigned to my case and called Jiles right away. Pamela Moyer. Jiles knew her. Pinner did, too. They both put in a good word this morning. They vouched. Got me released with only a two K bail.

"Who put up the two thousand?"

"I did."

"Thank you. I'll pay you back. Work it off. Whatever it takes."

She didn't slow her stride.

"I know. Once they assign the prosecutor, we can discuss a potential plea. Or you can get a different lawyer. It's up to you. But right now, you should go home and get some sleep."

"Yeah. Can you drop me?"

"Of course."

She dug out her keys from somewhere deep in her purse. It was quite possible she'd been up the entire night helping me. Helping *me* instead of her daughter.

"I was serious about what I said. You need to stop drinking, Sam."

Friday, October 2nd, 11:09 a.m.

Nick was buzzing around the kitchen. He made me a coffee like it was just another Friday cuz it was just another Friday for him. But I caught him looking at my scarred-up face. Like he was ashamed of something. It was a helluva price to pay but getting my faced smashed up did wonders for my roommate's manners. Nick was almost tolerable.

I looked up my checking account on my phone: $1306.88. Rent was coming fast, due in eleven days. I still owed the Rooster. Now I was in the hole with Lily. My agent wouldn't talk to me so it was impossible to know when my six K was coming. If at all. I had fierce doubts it would even happen. And now I needed a lawyer for my case.

My case.

I was out on bail.

I was one of those people. I would have to fix that.

But first, I needed my car back. I needed to make money.

Friday, October 2nd, 11:36 a.m.

It was a beautiful day in Los Angeles.

I ordered a ride, waiting for Peter in a black Ford Focus.

We drove in silence.

As we approached my destination and I looked for the posted tow-away contact number, something beautiful happened. My Volt was there. Parked all quiet with nary a ticket. She looked like a little victory. Like I'd finally caught a break.

The engine charged up and we hit the road. I was eager to get my mind off things, eager to make some cash and think about a better tomorrow.

I powered on my app, ready to go when the yellow flag dropped. My account had been frozen. The arrest had obviously triggered some safeguard installed by the company to protect the public from men like me.

I called my supervisor Greta but couldn't get through and left some words on her voicemail.

This was all a terrible misunderstanding.

I had to believe my own lie.

Friday, October 2nd, 11:58 a.m.

Greta called back.

Greta didn't buy it.

I couldn't blame her. She looked the other way after the boys busted my face and smashed my car, but this was a step too far.

"You willfully broke the law, Sam," she reminded me.

I reminded her about the whole innocent until proven guilty thing, but she got quiet and unimpressed.

There would need to be a review before I could start driving again.

This was gonna take some time.

I didn't have time.

I needed money.

I needed an alt.

I needed what I always needed in this moment.

I needed a drink.

Friday, October 2nd, 12:11 p.m.

No doubt word had spread.

Gather round, everyone!

No way even Lily, known for keeping her cards close, could resist spinning this yarn. *Lemme tell ya who I just bailed outta lockup.*

The slugs lived for that juice.

I would need to own it. Damn right I broke in. Had a lead I couldn't shake. Jiles would understand. Slice, too, but I didn't care about him right now. That's what I kept telling myself, anyway.

Nina Simone was wailing on the jukebox as I pushed through the door and waddled in all full of shame and indignation. The mood felt tight and a hush rippled out across the bar.

Slice was at his usual post so I hit the opposite far end of the wood. Jiles greeted me with a smile that reminded me of my father.

"Rough night, eh, Sammy?"

"So it goes, eh, Jiles?"

"How'ya holdin' up champ?"

"You know me, still swinging for the fences."

"Atta boy. You write it down?"

"Not yet. Needed one of your tonics first."

"Why don't you go write about it. You always feel better after you write it down, get it out of your system. It makes you happy."

"I will. Need a drink first."

I rapped the bar with my knuckles and could feel Slice staring at me as Jiles just stood there, with his back straight.

"May I please have a drink, sir?"

Jiles shimmied off and returned with a clear bubbling liquid adorned with a lime.

Nina Simone wailed about praying and running to the river and running to the lord and to help me.

"What is this?"

"Sprite."

"I don't wanna Sprite." Jiles could smell the hate glaring behind my eyes.

"Best I can do. For now. Like I said, why don't you go write it down?"

"I'll just go to another bar."

Jiles shrugged like this wasn't his real concern, like he was trying to help me and my disdain burst up and hard out of my throat.

"You're supposed to understand! No one else. But YOU'RE supposed to get what this is really about, Jiles!"

I swiped the glass off the bar with the back of my hand and it shattered on the ground.

It hurt my hand.

It hurt even more to hear it shatter like that.

Jiles got tall and looked like a real cop again.

The slugs got tight.

The place got quiet. Nina wailed about a Sinnerman. Running to the river.

So I walked out.

Friday, October 2nd, 12:32 p.m.

Thank god.

There was a Cheesecake Factory seven blocks away.

I saddled up and ordered an old fashioned and a zitty twenty-something kid behind the bar had to look up the ingredients. It tasted like watered-down booze syrup.

I smashed three of them.

I needed to talk to someone.

I thought about calling my sister but she could always tell when I was a few drinks in.

I thought about Margaret.

I thought about Allison.

I called Allison.

Allison was pure. Allison was beautiful.

Allison wasn't currently picking up her phone but I liked hearing her voice coo on the message. "This is Allison. Leave a message thanks byyye."

She had a swell singsong bye that reminded me of a Southern bell.

I rang it again for the byyye when her voice suddenly clicked on:

"Hello?"

"Oh. Hey, it's Sam."

"I know. I'm at work and I can't really talk, what's up?"

"Uh, just...nothing. You good?"

"Yeah...is that it?"

"Yeah."

"Where are you?"

"I'm at the Cheesecake Factory in Glendale. It's beautiful in here. Kinda orange and dark. They got music. Air conditioning. And they got so many things on the menu. Wanna come meet me? We can have pad thai AND enchiladas—they got 'em both, Allison. Pad thai and enchiladas. And you should see the portion sizes. This place is magnificent."

"Sounds like you need some water, Sam."

"They got that, too!"

"I have to go. I'm at work—"

"I like your voicemail message."

"Sam..." She sounded disappointed.

"Oh go fuck off," I snapped. "Not you, too. Please not you, Allison."

The line went dead.

I shouldn't have cursed.

I really shouldn't have cursed.

I ordered another drink. And zitty boy had memorized the fillings. If nothing else, I'd educated a young man on how to make a proper old fashioned.

"Easy on the bitters, mate."

He smiled like a nice guy and the drinks improved.

She was right. But I was committed to drive this painful day into the ground.

I was committed and smiled.

I railed at the injustice. The conspiracy that robbed this world of the once beautiful Josie Pendleton!

I wanted to smell her shirt.

I was asked to lower my voice.

I requested Sam Cooke. Wilson Pickett?

I was asked to *please* lower my voice.

I requested Otis Redding. Roy Orbison. Aretha Franklin something, please god, with soul, with intent. Something, anything better than nineties' soft rock.

I was asked to settle up.

I owed $131.27. I tipped zitty right.

Then.

I cursed and railed. This vapid, soul-sucking excuse of a watering hole.

The manager escorted me to the nearest exit, guiding my arms, and steering me out. The tourists and students staring.

I was no longer welcome at the Cheesecake Factory.

I walked into an alley and pissed like an animal.

I walked further on enjoying the sunshine and found Pacific Park where a T-ball team was practicing. Some moms with strollers strolled clear wide. Some dads with visors and pleated shorts eyed me suspiciously.

There was a beautiful water fountain and I sucked back the liquid that tasted like metal. I waddled to the top of the bleachers and watched the children play ball. The hunched-over coaches poking and prodding the little tykes. Clobbering an outfield field grounder like a pack of hyenas. The little fellas didn't even know where to run, where second base was. Little misguided souls.

I said it out loud, "*Misguided souls.*"

Friday, October 2nd, 3:55 p.m.

"Hey man. Hey. Hey. Yo. HEY."

A man was rocking my shoulder back and forth, waking me from my passed-out slumber. His was face silhouetted with the sun blaring behind a palm tree over his shoulder.

He was unhappy. Just like the guy next to him.

"This is a family park. YOU NEED TO GO."

They were the T-ball coaches, now coaching me off these bleachers as their wives and kids looked on uneasy.

I straightened up and saw that I'd pissed myself.

I pretended not to care.

I got to my feet and shuffled off the bleachers, down to the water fountain. Took a long pull and walked away, embarrassed.

I dug through a garbage can and found a plastic bag that I filled with leaves, then held it in front of my crotch hoping it would cover my piss stain as I walked back to my car.

My phone buzzed in my pocket.

I pulled it out and wiped drips of my own urine off the glass screen, relieved it wasn't damaged. The incoming 415 area code felt suspicious and I wasn't wild about touching the wet device any more than I had to, so...let the call go to voicemail.

Then it rang again.

And *again*.

I accepted the stupid 415, pressing the piss-soaked phone against my temple, pretending to be all cheery like everything was rosy.

"Oh hello?!"

"Sam? This is Glenn Royce."

I stalled out. Why's Glenn calling me?

"From Backyard Dreams? I just heard about what happened at Susan Glasser's apartment..."

He stopped talking and I tried to square why the hell he would have any reason to call me other than to lash out. But he wasn't mad. He sounded concerned, but not mad.

"...I'd like to talk to you. In person. I know this is a crazy call to get out of the blue but...can I come meet you somewhere? Wherever you are. It's urgent. Is now a bad time?"

I could smell my own urine on the phone and stared at the bag in front of the stain on my pants.

I doubled down with glee. All in.

"Now's a great time, Glenn! I'm in Pacific Park in Glendale. Off San Fernando. You know it?"

"No, but I'll find it. I'm on my way. Leaving from North Hollywood now."

I waited in the sun.

I thought about my old friend Slice and how much he'd love today's episode of the Sam show.

I almost missed him.

Friday, October 2nd, 4:33 p.m.

Twenty-nine minutes later Glenn's sparkling white Land Rover pulled up. I'd seriously considered getting a Lyft, going home, showering and returning, pretending to be clean but...

Fuck Glenn Royce.

Let him see the real me.

The me with Cheesecake Factory piss on my clothes. I didn't owe him anything. I never hurt him. And what the hell did he want, anyway?

He got out of the car and legit double-taked at the sight of me crumpled on a bench.

He approached with caution and genuine concern. "You okay?"

I flashed a phony LA smile, "Right as rain, Glenn."

"Thanks for meeting me. Look, I just wanna say...I'm sorry for what happened to you at Susan Glasser's apartment."

"Why would you be sorry about that?"

"I don't mean to be coy but...can you keep a secret?"

"I can. Unless...you know, I can't."

He seemed content with that flippant bark and carried on. "After you showed up on my doorstep, with those crazy accusations that Susan was stealing from me, I couldn't shake thinking about it and...it kinda rattled me. So I took a closer look at our earnings. You were right, Sam."

I stared.

Incredulous.

Me?

260

"Right about what?"

"Susan *has* been stealing from me. From the charity. For a long time. I had no idea. She was smart. Secretive. Played me completely. Buried it in phony corporate tax laws. Funneled our earnings into some bogus shell corporations. Spliced profits to take care of made-up zoning laws and fake insurance permits and office accounting fees. It's a disaster. I trusted her completely, and I can't believe I was so blind. That's why we kept losing money, why we had to downsize and move offices to that dump in North Hollywood. I think it's been going on for years..."

He shook his head, burning mad.

I should've been happy. Vindicated. But I sat there, empty.

"How much?"

"Hundreds of thousands of dollars. More maybe. I don't know the full scope of it yet."

He looked at me now, square in the eyes. "You were right." He said it again like he couldn't believe it. "I'm sorry for not believing you. I want to thank you, really. And...I want to help you now."

"You wanna help me?"

"If it weren't for you, none of this would have come to light."

"Josie was the one who figured it out. I was just following her."

"I want to know everything. From the very beginning. How you got onto this, how Josie got onto it...who else is involved...How you figured out it was Susan's aunt's car she was killed in. All of it."

I rolled back to day one. Seeing Josie at The Damned Lovely. Seeing her at the morgue. The funeral. Josie telling Allison there was something rotten about his charity. Magnet Max. Ullverson. All of it. He shook his head, incredulous but all lit up. "So you think Glasser was working with this guy Max?"

"Or someone there. But Josie must've figured out that Glasser was stealing money from your charity and feeding it to Patriot Strong. That's gotta be the reason she got hooked up with those clowns before Max sunk his claws into her."

"I know for a fact Susan's not Josie's killer. Her alibi is solid."

"Which means it has to be someone connected to Patriot Strong. Someone connected to the money who knew that Josie was gonna blow the whistle, who felt threatened that if word got out, they'd be left without a chair when all that music stops."

We sat in silence awhile until Glenn pegged his next move.

"I'm gonna hire a private investigation firm. If people discover their money's been syphoned out of my charity into Patriot Strong, it'll take me down for good. I need to get it back, but I have to do it discreetly. Whoever I hire is probably going to want to talk to you. Would that be all right?"

"Yeah, fine." I shrugged. All he cared about was the money.

"I have to do this quietly. Can I trust you won't sound any alarm bells here?"

"Yeah."

"I was serious before. I wanna help you, Sam." He looked at me as if he was embarrassed or something. "Kinda looks like you need it."

"I need money. And a lawyer."

"You're in luck. I'm a rich lawyer."

I stared at his perfectly clean, shaven face. His white teeth and perfect jaw line. His suit. That shiny car behind him. This was usually the part where my disdain bubbled up but that all kinda melted away.

"You really wanna help me?"

I caught him staring at the fresh scar on my face and wondered if he could smell the piss on my pants.

Friday, October 2nd, 5:44 p.m.

I wouldn't let Glenn drive me back to my car.

Some righteous piece inside didn't want my piss on his car seats. Bigger part of me was straight-up embarrassed. But I did take the $310 cash offered that he had on him. Along with the promise to help me with my mounting legal woes.

The walk back was slow but overwhelming.

The Glendale sunshine actually felt soft and warm on my cheeks.

Welcomed almost.

With each step I heaved fresh oxygen and self-purchase. Purchase that my mission and goal and intent and everything I wrapped my pride around, hell, my entire identity as a man of tremendous ill judgment, was more than just a sham.

I wanted to bust down the doors and holler hard at the slugs hanging off the bar. Spit my victory in Jiles's righteous mug. Rail with Slice over icy bursts of bourbon and glory. *We was right after all, amigo!*

But that wasn't going to happen anytime soon.

That place was dead to me. My time at the Lovely was past.

I shook off that ugly reality and considered next steps.

Angles and plays. Options.

I came up empty.

How the hell was I gonna to chase this connection between Backyard Dreams and Patriot Strong without sounding any alarms?

Then it hit me.
Jimmyface999

Friday, October 2nd, 7:22 p.m.

My body smashed into the desk, waking up my computer with a jolt. I punched in jimmyface999 and quickly found Josie's old emails I'd been looking for.

——————Original message——————
From: jjpendleton98@gmail.com
Date: Wed, July 01, 2018 at 11:11 p.m.
Subject: story
To: jimmyface999@gmail.com

You in town? I'm working on something you're gonna like.

——————Reply message——————
From: jjpendleton98@gmail.com
Date: Wed, July 01, 2018 at 11:11 p.m.
Subject: Re: story
To: jimmyface999@gmail.com

Yeah I'm around. Can you give me a bite? Big or small?

——————Reply message——————
From: jjpendleton98@gmail.com
Date: Wed, July 01, 2018 at 11:11 p.m.
Subject: Re: story
To: jimmyface999@gmail.com

I'm gonna blow the lid off a very powerful organization...and I'm gonna need your help once I got the goods.

————————Reply message————————
From: jjpendleton98@gmail.com
Date: Wed, July 01, 2018 at 11:12 p.m.
Subject: Re: story
To: jimmyface999@gmail.com

C'mon at least give me a taste? Corporate? Local?

————————Reply message————————
From: jjpendleton98@gmail.com
Date: Wed, July 01, 2018 at 11:12 p.m.
Subject: Re: story
To: jimmyface999@gmail.com

☺

That smiley face.

It was all crashing back in.

Back when, Slice agreed the guy sounded like a reporter. If that was the case, jimmyface999 might still be interested in a good yarn. And now I had the answer he asked Josie for.

Glenn had asked me to keep quiet about all this, and I intended to. But there were angles to play. I didn't intend to expose him or his organization, but I needed to move on Josie's case. Nothing was going to stop me now.

Except maybe going to jail.

Whatever.

That reality seemed impossible, so I wrote to jimmyface999, shrouding my identity and exposing only pieces of my legwork. Instead I hit him with the truth explaining I knew what organization Josie was gonna blow the lid off of and that I suspected that was what killed her, not some terribly named Glendale

Grabber.

I hit send and took a shower. By the time my ass plunked back on the chair there was a bold message in my inbox from jimmyface999 asking for more information I ignored cuz I saw three delicious words at the bottom:

Can we meet?

Friday, October 2nd, 9:22 p.m.

The Americana fountain was in full ridiculous swirl.

The open-air mall was brimming with horny teenagers and rich Armenian dudes. A public place felt like the right way to go meet some anonymous would-be reporter I'd found by hacking into a dead girl's email account. I waited anxiously on the edge of the fountain watching moms push strollers and kids shuffle into the Pacific theater. It was cool out and the longer I waited the worse my expectations dragged.

Maybe this was a big mistake.

Maybe jimmyface was actually a political titan with deep pockets out to protect the radical right and this was all a trap. I'd fed right into his hand! The bad movie clichés were hard to escape until I saw an Eastern European woman in her early forties with dark glasses wearing a leather jacket approach. She had that *I'm smart* and *busy* look on her face that made you wanna get the hell out of the way.

"The pistongame?"

"Nine-nine-nine?" Then, added awkwardly, "My name's Sam."

"Ellen." She sized me up with a lackluster smirk. "So...what's your story?"

She had an East Coast no bullshit air I found extremely appealing. Decisive and all business. Like her existence on this planet had a purpose. Like she didn't belong at the Americana in Glendale on a Friday night. But before unleashing my tangled tale, I wanted more on her.

"How do you know Josie?"

She laid out the past. They'd met at a Backyard Dreams event years ago. Ellen worked at the *LA Times* covering soft civic functions built for the frothy California section. River clean-up festivals. OC parades. Downtown art walks and the like.

They hit it off.

Ellen admired Josie's spirit for goodwill and continued to come out to Backyard events through the years. They'd catch up. Josie went to art school. Ellen survived some cutbacks and got pushed to work the obituaries. It was a thankless gig, but she caught a spark. Some forgotten obits caught her attention. A string of homeless guys turning up dead in South Gate. She dug deeper and flagged trouble. Worked the story with a crime guy from Metro and uncovered the real killer. The story put her on the map and it was a welcome pivot to the crime beat. She'd lost touch with Josie and seemed genuinely rattled when news broke of her murder. She even went to her service.

But none of this made any sense to me.

"Josie said she was gonna blow the lid off a big organization, turns up dead right after, and you—a crime reporter—you don't even look into it?"

I could see her jawbone tighten.

"You think she's the only person to send me an email teasing a big story? I get messages like that all the time. 'Trust me, Ellen, this is the one. Pulitzer Prize stuff.' And yes, I was concerned when she was killed but I talked to the detectives and they were convinced it was the Grabber. And then they found the guy. What was I supposed to do? She was dead and didn't give me any details. I can't chase down every half lead I'm fed no matter who it's from or how important *they* think it is. What I *can* do is show up at the Americana on a Friday night when someone emails me out of the blue claiming to have some valid information. Now...you said you knew about this 'organization' Josie was gonna supposedly blow the lid off of? Is that true?"

"Yes."

"Yes and? Who was it?"

"There were two. One of them was Patriot Strong."

Ellen laced a tight poker face except her eyebrows danced up like this obviously struck a chord.

"And the other?"

"I can't get into that yet."

"Okay. But you believe this led to her death?"

"Yes."

"Why? What was so important she was going to expose?"

I laid out the money trail. Threw in enough coded speak on Backyard I could only hope she'd buy. "So you think whoever killed her just pretended to be the Glendale Grabber?"

"Exactly."

"Do you have any proof, Sam?"

"I've connected the car she was killed in to the organization she was going to expose."

Ellen leaned in, sniffing some chum in the water. "Do the police know this?"

"Some of them. But they wouldn't take me seriously." That part was true. I left out the other stuff about getting drunk and breaking into a woman's apartment. "Believe me, her death had nothing to do with the Glendale Grabber, other than whoever was behind it was smart enough to use his MO as cover."

I could see her eyes twinkle as they danced around my face looking for lies.

"Who exactly are you in all this? How do you know Josie?"

I laid out the facts enough to sound legit.

But she pegged the truth. "And lemme guess that 'other' organization. Was it Backyard Dreams? I mean...it kinda lines up."

So much for shrouding the truth.

"I'm not gonna comment on that but lemme tell you," I backpedaled hard, "You don't wanna rattle any cages on that front. They've got deep pockets and will end you if their name gets out into the press. And me, if it comes out I was your source."

She laughed and softened like she'd heard that line before. Or heard enough to maybe trust me.

"How did you get my email? That was a personal account."

"I can't really tell you that."

Now she squirmed and looked me straight in the eye. Wrestling with something.

"Josie called me a few days before she was killed, wanted to ask my advice about something."

This now, my chum.

"About what? "

"She was pretty vague but maybe..." She trailed off and for the first time Ellen looked stung. "I should've taken her seriously. It literally never even *occurred* to me that Josie Pendleton would be chasing something legitimately dangerous. I mean, she was a fine arts major who volunteered at a kids' charity."

"What did she ask you?"

"Just some advice. On getting information out of a source without them suspecting anything. She played it off like it was no big thing. Said she was following someone. I thought she was talking about a boyfriend or something."

"Did she say who it was?"

"No. Just that they hung out at some dive bar. She said it was around here actually, in Glendale."

My world stopped.

My heart pounded real.

I went into lockdown.

I stared on the fountain spewing water and forgot to breathe.

Ellen kept speaking, needling me with questions. "Does that mean anything to you? Do you know where she could have gone around here?"

I put on my very own jimmyface and finally looked her square in the eyes.

"No."

Saturday, October 3rd, 12:07 AM

No one could be trusted.

I would reset and align.
   I would be clean. Sober.
   I'd pack a smile and blast them with respect.
   I'd look them in the eyes and listen like we were friends.
   And then, I would strike.
   For Josie.
   "For Josie." I said it aloud, lying in my bed, stirring through the night.
   I vowed not to let down my ghost crush.
   Josie had been on the scent the whole time.
   She was after someone at the Lovely.
   Someone there was connected to Patriot Strong. Which meant someone there was lying to me. Probably in league with Glasser.
   No wonder Josie was at the bar.
   Alone.
   Reading a book.
   In stealth.
   She was *hunting.*
   And now, so would I.

Wednesday, October 7th, 5:16 p.m.

I worked strategy and outcomes. Pitfalls and options.

I refused all calls.

I ran data from my room.

But mostly, I cleaned up. Scrubbed the filth from my body. Scraped a razorblade across my face eager to shed some kind of slimy preexisting condition.

I slipped on my good black jeans. My rowdy orange socks.

I pinned on the crisp, dry-clean-only grey button-down shirt from Barneys. The shirt that fell just right and angled my shoulders as close to a movie star as I'd ever be. My confidence shirt.

I took deep breaths and went over the plan in my head.

I had done my homework.

I felt numb with determination. Armed and loaded with the truth about the demon who'd been sitting at the bar next to me this whole time.

But I still had no idea who it was.

Wednesday, October 7th, 6:01 p.m.

My hand pushed open the brass handle and I stepped inside The Damned Lovely. The Van Dykes cooed some doowop gold.

One by one, my flock found me.

Jewels crossed directly in front of the door with a tray of martinis and grimaced as if she weren't sure whether to be happy or sad to see me.

Behind her, tucked in the far-off corner behind the jukebox, the Rooster peered up from his computer, letting the light from the screen shine off his dirty glasses. He stared. Dead-eyed like a savant streaming a billion thoughts all without showing the least bit of emotion. Then instantly returned to whatever shadiness on his screen I'd interrupted.

Jiles smiled from behind the bar. Like he wasn't the least bit surprised to see me. Like a part of him wanted to. Like my own father looked on a holiday.

Then there was Lily, who caught the look on Jiles's face and craned her head along with some tight cheap pantsuit, to see who'd earned the king's guarded attention. Seeing me, she huffed some air out of her skinny nose.

Slice spun on the stool and hit me with his toothy smile before reining it back in, remembering he was supposed to feel upset or something towards me.

"Hiya, Sammy,"

It was Pa.

Pa bellowed a frothy hello as he glanced up from today's soggy Sports section. He sounded like he never got the memo on my sordid exit. Or he just plain forgot.

No one could be trusted.

I threw up my hands in mock surrender. "Yes, yes, I'm back. And I'm sorry for being an asshole. Jiles. You still got some Sprite back there?"

The words cut through the tension and the slugs softened.

Lily piped up. "'bout time you came home. We were getting worried about you."

"Oh, you know me, Lily. The relentless bad penny."

"That was a hell of an exit," Jiles bubbled as he handed me the frizzy excuse of a drink.

"I'm sorry, Jiles. I was outta line." I held up the soda. "Won't happen again."

I walked over to Slice, who was pretending not to watch or care.

"Heya, Slice. Just so you know, I'm cool with whatever you wanna do on the article. For real. It's your life, man. You've earned it. No hard feelings."

"Thanks, Sam. Appreciate that."

"So?" I asked, "What's happening with it?"

"I haven't heard squat."

"Well, fingers crossed. Like I said, you've earned it, champ. Really."

I settled in and hit a stool. The same stool Josie had taken. Sitting here listening in, pretending to read Virginia Woolf's *To the Lighthouse*, eyeing the crop.

I was a spy now.

Seventeen hours earlier I'd decided Jewels would be my first mark. Not because she was a lead suspect but because for one, I felt she'd be the easiest to break. Truthfully I adored the women. And she'd been nothing but a champion of mine throughout all these raucous ups and downs. But she was also the softest mark. The easiest to flip. Compared to ex-cops like Jiles or Slice or a lawyer like Lily who understood interrogations and how to deflect guilt, Jewels wasn't engineered to understand and covet the art of innocence. At least that was my impression.

So bring on the dance.

I played it slow. Sipped my Sprite, smiled and added to the standard ramblings. About thirty minutes in Jewels sauntered by and I angled up.

"You movin' them rocks, Jewels?"

"I sold two pieces last week. That ain't nothin'."

"Congrats. And how's the rest of it? How's life treating you?"

She shrugged like she always shrugged. "You know…"

"Yeah."

I'd done my homework on Jewels. Holed up in my cage the last couple days, I did as much digging as I could online. She had a private Instagram account. An abandoned Facebook page and no Twitter or LinkedIn. There just wasn't a lot to find online.

In all the years I'd been coming to the Lovely, Jewels never dug all that deep. I knew surface Jewels. I knew she hated booze. I knew she was from Florida. I knew she lived near the 170 on a street called Banning next to a park where she walked her dog Nico. But she always kept any political talk quiet. It was either cuz she was hiding something and didn't want to offend customers, even me, or she really just didn't care.

Or she had a dark secret she didn't want to get out.

I gazed at her large soft eyes and laid out the speech I'd practiced back home, eventually coming around to the big ask: "So I guess, I don't know, having tasted a bit of success on Slice's article, I wanted to do more of that kinda profile journalism. Could I interview you? Write a piece on all things Jewels? If you don't want to, I totally understand but…hey, maybe you can option it and make a few grand like Slice did?"

Confusion quickly morphed into flattery. Jewels cocked her shoulders in surprise. "Me? Really? I mean…yeah, okay."

"Just so you know, I might ask some of the others, too." I lobbed on some emotional juice. "I feel like you guys are kinda family to me now in a weird way." She nodded but you could tell she was already thinking how odd this advance was.

The backhanded agenda felt kinda mean but hey, *For Josie.*
For Josie, so the chorus sang.

Jewels offered to sit with me that night after her shift. Like
our own little date, we found a corner in the back. Jiles eyed us
all screwy but not enough to really care at one in the morning, so
he asked her to lock up. I dropped my iPhone on the table and
recorded every word, pretending to revel in all things Jewels.

She grew up in Florida and bounced from one dysfunctional
roof to the next. She'd been dealt a bad hand, with what sounded
like inbred, bottom-feeding losers for parents. There was hitting
and screaming and a whole lot worse I didn't want to dig up.
Jewels managed to escape to Houston at eighteen and then LA at
twenty, thanks to god knows what luck, cash, and happenstance.
I angled the conversation to any fun prejudices she might have
absorbed along the way, but she didn't have a dog in the fight.

"So long as people don't hurt people, I don't care who they
sleep with or what god they worship. Should be that simple, if
you ask me."

Jewels was the poster child for simple but wore it sweet. Not
naïve or ignorant but sweet. Like she'd just seen too much pain
and hate at the hands of her own father. So when it came down
to politics or the white nationalist bent or any of the creed
shared by team Patriot Strong, Jewels couldn't care less.

Unless she was lying.

I nudged her to be honest and share even any unsavory feelings
she might harbor against liberal mucks like myself. White or
black. But she shut me down as only Jewels can and by the end of
the night, it was impossible to believe this woman harbored any
passionate hatred like the cats at Patriot Strong. That she was
anything more than a broke, simple-minded jewelry maker
slinging drinks to make ends meet. I'd been drowning in this
Josie pain long enough to sniff out a lead, and after talking to
Jewels for all of ninety-two minutes, was convinced the girl was
innocent.

That, coupled with access now to one of her private Instagram accounts revealed she was at the Lovely only twelve minutes before Josie was killed. She'd posted a shot of some random high school friends who'd popped into the bar for a drink. The image could have been staged or fabricated by someone remotely but that would have been a deeper technical game Jewels was in no way capable of engineering.

Nevertheless, it was touching to discover the past of this woman I'd seen so many days and nights, slinging all those drinks and putting on a brave face for drunk slugs like me. She told me her real name was Maisie.

I smiled and told her that was a beautiful name.

Thursday, October 8th, 9:16 a.m.

Nick was lonely and looking to joust. Talking headlines and upcoming elections and the tail he'd been circling.

I had time to kill before my next round at the Lovely and pressed him for any updates on Max and Patriot Strong.

He skirted details. Said he'd been steering clear of his miscreants.

"Why the change of heart?"

He shuffled his feet and rambled on about being busy with work and other stuff that in no way seemed to justify his change of course.

I wondered if he'd had a change of heart since they beat my ass.

I wondered if Nick was human, after all.

I buzzed caffeine and holed up in my room looking at printed pictures of the regulars at the bar that were now taped up in my room. Jewels. Slice. Pa. Lily. Jiles. The Rooster.

No one could be trusted.

I scrawled notes under Jewels's pic from my interview.

Florida. Houston at eighteen. LA at twenty.

Real name Maisie.

I was gonna do the same with Slice. But thanks to the article, I'd already spent days digging deep on the ex-cop and never witnessed a shred of any fanatical righteous hate. I would have to dig deeper but right now felt pretty confident I could put both Slice and Jewels at the bottom of the list.

Pa would be next. Then Lily. Then the Rooster, who scared

me. If he was tied up in all this and found out I was chasing him down, he'd hack hard into my life and destroy me. So I wasn't exactly in a rush to put out that fire. Then there was Jiles. The notion that Jiles could be the one attached in some way to Josie's death stung my soul a little. He'd been like a father to me and I worshipped the man. I tried not to consider that reality and chose to focus on finding all that I could about Pa online before approaching him at the bar later.

Friday, October 9th, 5:33 p.m.

The old buzzard was sucking back his third Beefeater martini at the far end of the bar. I slid up next to Pa and he smiled. His signature soft boozy glaze that the world was working out just fiiiine, thank you much. Then he stared at his handiwork on my face. Even tracing the scar with his wobbly smooth cold fingers.

"Lookin' good, Sammy. Lookin' good."

I thanked him again for his help that night. He looked touched, but even sad some and offered to buy me a drink.

I ordered a Sprite.

He dished a cold side-eye.

I was ready to lay in my pitch about writing an article on him, but the lonely coot was game to gab, already rambling on about some friend of his from the eighties who turned up in the obituaries. And some devious scam in Tarzana he caught spear-headed by a crooked veterinarian bilking clients for cash.

"You read the *Times* today, Pa?"

"Cover to cover."

"Ever hear of that organization called Patriot Strong?"

"Those bastards." To my surprise, Pa shook his head, well up to speed. "The scourge of our nation."

He expounded on his hate for white radicals and their ugly principles. It was pretty compelling.

But he could've been lying.

So I grilled him for another fifty-seven minutes. He sunk another martini and still looked stony sober. I caught Slice watching us from across the bar, and suspected Jewels mighta let slip my interest in writing a piece on her. Now Slice was sizing me up like I was betraying him. As if we were exclusive and that I had promised to only article-fuck *him* in the bar.

It kinda brought me a sliver of joy. Like putting aloe on that knife wound he'd slashed into my back.

Anyway, I tuned out Slice and dug into Pa's past. There was nothing to mine on the net back home except for a few articles on his soured medical career. He told me he grew up in Indiana and moved west with his parents and four sisters when he was six. They set up shop in Hancock Park and Pa's life played out pretty smooth. He was good at sports and got good grades. Went to UCLA and found medicine. Got married at twenty-seven and set up a practice in Eagle Rock. Had some kids and life was lookin' swell until his thirst for Beefeater reared earlier and earlier in the day.

After an early Tuesday lunch and two fat martinis, he cut up a girl on the job. Knicked her kidney and sewed her back up without even knowing it.

Til later.

Til it all got ugly fast for Pa.

Got pretty easy to fill in the rest of the blanks. Why his wife divorced him. Why he lived alone in a one-bedroom apartment in Glendale. How he chose the bottle over his family.

On paper, of all the players, Pa actually looked pretty damn good for raping and killing Josie. A dirty old horny alcoholic who resented the world that shut him down. Who mighta seen those legs at the bar and fantasized about her insides. Who mighta followed her to a dark corner and couldn't help himself.

The only trouble was...

Pa was a soft soul. We've all got some kinda monster inside but in all the years of coming to the Lovely, I'd never seen him cut Jewels a dirty-old-man look or lash out at the world. He wasn't an angry, tormented drunk. He was gliding through, happy to swirl down the drain of life with a smile and a martini. But more than all that, with his leftist bent, there was no way he fit the Patriot Strong mold.

So, I took a different tack and just out and asked him.

"Do you know Susan Glasser?"

"Susan Glasser?" There was no flash of *oh shit*. No stutter. Or uneasy breath or what's the plan b. There was only, "No. Who's that?"

"Did you kill Josie Pendleton?"

"I don't think so. Who's Josie Pendleton?" He asked all curious without a hint of guilt or remorse or flash of any memory.

"Forget I asked."

It wasn't Pa.

I knew it wasn't Pa. But I had to ask. And secretly I hoped it had been. Cuz now it was time to hunt Lily, Jiles, or the Rooster.

Saturday, October 10th, 7:12 p.m.

Lily found me at the bar, sitting alone. Drinking Sprite. Scribbling thoughts on my worn-out Rite Aid notepad.

"What are you doing, Sam?"

I stared at her ruffled brow. *Is she onto me?* Maybe Lily was the demon. I'd told her everything in lockup. She knew all the pieces. All the players. Maybe that's why she agreed to help me. Friends close, enemies closer style. Yeah, maybe that's why—

"Did you hire another lawyer?" she asked.

"No."

"Do you still want my help with your case?"

"Yes, of course."

"Then why haven't you come talk to me? It's been over a week. You're facing some very serious charges. What's going on?"

"I've just got a lot on my mind."

She clocked the Sprite and looked at me like I was actually telling her the truth. "Well, I'm glad you're taking my advice at least."

"Sound legal counsel, Lil. Did they set the hearing date?"

"Yes, it's in twelve days. I'm going to try to talk to Susan Glasser's lawyer and see if she'd consider dropping the charges."

"Lily, have you ever met Susan Glasser?"

"No. Why?"

If she was lying, Lily held the world's most formidable poker face.

"No reason."

She clocked me another one of her signature disgruntled brows.

"Sorry. I'm all..." I wheeled my fingers, pretending to be all churned in the head. "I will pay you. I'm just trying to figure out how. Actually, about that. Could I write an article about you? I need to make some more money and the truth is, I really admire—"

"Absolutely not. I'll let you know what happens with Glasser's lawyer." Then, she touched my shoulder with her pale hand like Lily's cold-ass version of a hug. "Just get your life together." Then she moved off.

I listened to Derek and the Dominoes riff into the night until—

"So you're trollin' the waters, eh, Sammy?"

Slice ambushed my flank. "Heard you're writing some more articles." I turned on my stool and faced my old pal as he continued. "Jewels said you're digging into her life. Pa, too. Lookin' to make some more coin?"

"Why not, right? Pa's got a helluva story to tell. Not quite as colorful as yours but...I'm guessing a more noble ending."

He shrugged, taking the dig on the chin.

"What's going on with the big show, Slice?"

"Haven't heard a peep." He didn't look sad, just bored. And lonely. Like maybe he even missed me, though he'd never admit it. Truth is, I missed him, too. I wasn't even mad at him anymore. And boy did I have a yarn to spin. He'd howl hearing about my little escapade in the T-ball park. Pressing the piss-soaked phone against my face with the call from Glenn that ignited my investigation back to life and essentially justified my existence on this planet. The old coot lived for it. It was probably the reason he was even hanging out in this joint. A drunk suckin' up people's lives filled with pain and humor he didn't have the courage himself to endure.

But I had to be smart. I could trust no one. Figured I had Slice on the line and should sniff around. So I played into his ego, asking for some advice.

"What kind of advice?" He was all keen to share.

"Feels like someone might be following me," I lied.

"Who?"

"Someone from Patriot Strong."

He straight-faced and dug in on tactics. Write it all down. Faces. License plates. Times. Wheres and whens. Pick up on patterns—that'll help pin it down. Keep things credible.

I cut him off. "You know much about that organization?"

"No, just the stuff in the paper." Again, straight-faced. "And what you told me."

But I pressed him for details. Chance encounters. Third-party connections. Despite the towering whiskey in his hand, the coot sounded clean sober and, as I suspected in my gut and from everything I knew about him, Slice had nothing to give. No tell to show.

I still didn't trust him but kept things light for now and asked if he'd been watching the boys in blue as we railed on the Dodgers for an hour.

Something about it all felt wonderful.

Sunday, October 11th, 12:01 p.m.

I stared at the pictures tacked against the wall in my room.

I stared at Jiles.

The man's face loomed large.

Now that Pa was behind me and my soft-pedal stab at trying to pin down Lily failed that left the Rooster and Jiles. A wise and intelligent detective would have looked at the Rooster next. He fit the bill. Awkward. Secretive. The man was so withdrawn he had a crush on a cocktail waitress struttin' around him in the same room for years and he still didn't have the guts to strike up a conversation with her. For *years*. That was the kind of pent-up shyness, resentment, and self-pity that led to raping women. That led to the hate bolstered by Patriot Strong.

The Rooster was the intelligent play.

But I am not a wise and intelligent detective.

I am Sam. A failed writer trying to feel like a wise detective cuz I can't write one truthfully. A guy out on bail, scarred up and scared broke. An intelligent detective acted in the best interest of solving the case. I was acting in response to an ugly dark fear that the man I most revered, an ex-cop who'd battled years of terror on LA's darkest streets, a man who had shown me great decency and respect when most men wouldn't, hell, more than even my own father, a man…a man who…

It scared me.

Because deeper down, in some sick ugly way, Jiles made sense. Jiles was smarter than all of them. He wasn't a drunk. He would know how to throw off the cops and make it look like the

Grabber. He understood crime scenes. He would know what they would be looking for and how to cover his tracks. And Jiles was an obvious closet right winger. He never talked about it because it was bad for business. But he was a traditionalist. A blue-collar cop. And more than that, for Jiles, after so many years of chasing evil day after day, of witnessing the pain caused by humans writ large, it was no secret the experience took a toll on the man. I'd catch those side-eyed glances overhearing civic cats discussing liberal criminal reform programs or the plight of those poor souls in overcrowded prisons. As much as I loved the man, his hardened old school values aligned with Patriot Strong more than any of the regulars in that den. Not the hardcore "West is best" bent but enough to overlap.

The one part I couldn't square was the rape. But then, Jiles was a man. Men, in their darkest hearts, are all monsters. Maybe that was enough. Maybe he felt he had to conquer her insides in some sick way just so the cops would match the MO. Like some kinda necessary evil.

I needed to know.

I needed to make a run at Jiles.

But first I smashed a Fred 62 black and white milkshake for lunch. The finest in East LA.

Arming me for battle.

I would be ready.

Sunday, October 11th, 1:01 p.m.

Jiles usually got to the bar around eleven. I'd give him some time to get settled. When I walked in, the joint was pure Damned Lovely. Pa, Rooster, Jewels, and Slice. The regular faces save for Lily, which was normal for Sunday.

I found Jiles reading the Business section at the side of the bar. He didn't look up but just handed me the Sports.

"Mornin', Sammy," he grunted even though it was after one p.m.

I picked a down beat and greased him with the wind up. "Jiles...you know how much I admire you...respect your story. Your perseverance...Maybe I could write an article—"

The man squinted. Skeptical.

"What do you want?" He cut the talk and squared me with those dark eyes, like a cop sniffing a lie.

"Money," I lied. "I've got some legit legal fees. Figure if Slice's piece went well, why not tap the well again?"

His eyes got all squinty. "How long's this gonna take?"

I smiled victory. The old man's hubris reared its ugly head.

"When it sucks, we'll stop. How's that sound?"

He nodded but looked more annoyed than anything. So I pulled out my phone and a notebook. Then, he waved me off.

"Not here. Let's hit the box."

Sunday, October 11th, 1:07 p.m.

Jiles looked around the box. Taking in the scraps of papers and gnarly old coffee cups like he hadn't been in the room in a while. He pulled a dusty, chipped black stool from the corner and sat across from me as I pushed aside a bunch of research files. Jiles glanced at the Rooster's list of companies I'd dug up from Patriot Strong along with some old pamphlets I'd pinched on Backyard Dreams.

"Why you hammering on the regulars? No way you're writin' articles on Jewels and Pa. *Or me*. So, what's what?"

I shoulda known he'd call my bluff on the article.

"I need to ask you some questions."

Jiles shrugged. Happy to get some honesty out of me.

"Do you know a woman named Susan Glasser?"

"No."

"Do you know that guy Magnet Max?"

He stared, like he was curious why I'd ask him, and there was a jolt in my guts.

"Of course, he's the one that runs Patriot Strong. The guys who beat you up, right?"

"Yeah."

"What about him?"

I laughed to make light of it. "Nothing, just....What do you think of them? Patriot Strong?"

"They're all a little crazy."

"A little?" I prodded.

"Yeah."

"But you'd heard of them before all this? Before Josie died?"

"Yeah. So. Why?"

I could feel my chest tighten some. "How come you never mentioned it? After all the time I spoke about them? After what they did to me?"

"What difference does it make? I knew *of* them. Not like I'm the only one."

"But you never told me how you feel about them?"

He shrugged, like it was simple. "I'm running a business, Sam."

"Come on, it's just you and me, now."

He stared and seemed to acknowledge without looking around the room that there was no computer, no phone recording.

"I don't agree with their whole mentality. But..." He stopped like he was fighting some urge to blurt out the truth.

My heart pounded fierce but I played it light. "I'm just curious what...a guy like you, with your background, might think about them? We've never had a chance to talk without those bar slugs around."

He sucked back some oxygen.

"Wish I didn't have to but sometimes...Maybe we need to get back to dividing not uniting. All this talk and blathering. Integration. It's like...blacks and Mexicans don't get along. Never have and never *will*. That's just the way the world works. And trust me—you learn that shit the hard way. Working the streets. There's too much hate in this country. We were divided then and we're divided now, we just pretend to grind it out like that's the solution. But it's not. I've seen it firsthand, Sam. I've seen the blood justify that. Blood on the streets. Blood on little girls' clothes. Every day. Every weekend." Then, he looked at me. Like maybe he'd gone too far, realizing. "A guy like me? You mean an ex-cop with an axe to grind?"

"Yeah, I guess."

"I don't buy all they're selling but sometimes I think we might be better off lining things up the way it used to be. When everything wasn't so upside down. Like when it was okay to look at a woman and smile like it's not some kind of offense. I mean..." His nostrils started to twitch some, staring at me with a piece of contempt I'd never seen before in Jiles.

"A guy like me." He stood up, all tight. "I don't have time for this. I got a business to run." He made for the door— stopped before getting very far and looked around the room. At my work, at my face, like he was thinking, connecting some kinda dots. And then, he saw Josie's shirt.

"Is that...?" He shook his head. "You're not writing articles, Sam. You're still chasin' Josie."

I hit him with my iron poker face. "We're just talking."

"That cut on your face not enough? Getting arrested didn't set ya straight?" His head swiveled. "I think it's time for you to find another office. I love ya, kid. I really do. But this path you're on...You need to stay away from here. From this place. Get your things outta here by tomorrow night. It's for your own good."

He walked out.

I never did have a very good poker face.

Sunday, October 11th, 8:11 p.m.

I thought about the juice.

The second sip.

I thought about hitting up zitty at the Cheesecake Factory.

But I resisted.

I took Jiles's advice and got the hell out of the bar as fast as I could, reeling so hard I even forgot to take Benny with me.

I sat in my car at the curb, still shaking from my talk with Jiles.

Jiles. My north star. My badge of right.

In all my time at the Lovely he never mentioned Patriot Strong but he knew 'em well. Even bought into some of their garbage. But he kept this burning secret quiet the entire time. Josie must have connected Jiles to Glasser. That was the one piece I couldn't square but it didn't matter. It lined up just the same—she was obviously hanging out at the bar, hoping to get the proof she needed to tell jimmyface.

I sat in my cold car in the darkness listening to Sam Cooke.

I didn't want this.

I didn't want to chase Jiles.

But none of that mattered if he hurt her.

The shit stung and I needed a lifeline. Not for the chase, but because for the first time, I was scared. Jiles was smart. If he suspected I was onto him and gonna blow the whistle about his connection to Glasser and Patriot, why *wouldn't* he strike to tie up the loose end? All my information was at his place this entire time. Not to mention my constant updates on the stool.

Had he been tracking me all along?

Was Pinner in on this? Maybe they were working together, maybe that's why he chose not to chase down the lead on the car I'd found. It all started lining up.

But I bucked the fear.

I needed an ally.

Someone who understood the game.

I needed a cop.

I smiled wide as Sam cooed all feel it don't fight it.

Don't fight that feelin'.

Monday, October 12th, 8:23 a.m.

I betrayed my creed.

Slice spilled out of his house carrying a bag of garbage grumbling his way to the black bin in his lane with a slumped-over gait.

"Heya, Slice."

He turned and looked all ambushed or scared until the feeling quickly gave way to confusion.

"What are you doin' here?"

"I could use some more advice. Got any coffee?"

He waved me inside with the kind of smile that reminded me how much I missed my old, flawed friend.

"You get paid for your article yet?"

"No, not yet."

"If you're short I could float you some cash once I get a piece of that Frazier cake."

I shook my head. "Thanks, Slice, I'll squeak by. Always do."

"So what's what, Sammy?"

He poured me a cup of watery coffee and I laid it all out in his dirty kitchen. My talk with Jiles and his cagey rebuke. Kickin' me out of the box for good. Slice soaked up the yarn all nonpartisan. All stone-faced and impossible to read. All cop. Then it was his turn to hit me with questions.

"Can you put him there that night at the scene? Wherever this girl was killed?"

I'd run this through last night, convinced I'd seen Jiles at the Lovely the night of the murder. But there were pockets of time he was unaccounted for. He could have easily snuck out and come back in, with a decent alibi that he was in the office the whole time. It was impossible to know for sure. Especially how foggy I was after getting knocked out. But Pinner had said there were no security or ATM cams where she was found. I considered asking the Rooster to hack into the city's grid to try to pin down Jiles on any cameras around the area but that was one ugly, timely, and costly fishing expedition I couldn't afford.

"No."

"What about his connection to this Glasher woman? Can you square it?"

"Glasser. Not yet."

"If you can't put him at the scene or connect him to Glasser, you don't have enough. Yet. But...Let me think on this. There's a move here and we gotta act fast cuz you showed him your cards. But I need to think..."

"Thanks, Slice."

He looked me in the eye and I kinda did the same back. Like some stupid movie reunion moment where the heroes bury their hate and storm the castle for glory.

"Lemme talk to my old crew at Central. They might have a better line here. Just stay low and outta sight. I'll call you in a few hours." And then, the man inside Slice, the man who admired and knew Jiles as well as I did, took over sounding ugly sad. "Sammy. If you're right about Jiles..."

I nodded all heavy and told him his coffee tasted like dirty water.

Monday, October 12th, 4:56 p.m.

I tried to be calm.

I tried to get my mind off it.

I tried not to think about the Bulleit.

I failed hard and Nick found me thirsty, smashing BBQ potato chips in the kitchen.

He asked if I wanted to drive up to Malibu with him.

Nick would never ask me to drive up to Malibu with him if there wasn't something in it for him. Some gain. He said he was proud of me for staying dry like we were friends or something. I wasn't sure I believed him. But his usual pity should have worn off by now. *Why is he acting so weird to me?*

It didn't matter much cuz with the Jiles drama there was no way I was moving until I got the call from Slice, so Nick took off alone.

Lily called to say she spoke with Glasser's attorney and there was no way they were going to drop the charges. I told Lily to sit tight.

Lily did not appreciate me telling her to sit tight and hung up on me.

I couldn't blame her. The woman was trying to help. But with Glenn out to expose Glasser's malfeasance, I had to believe that would shine a healthy light on my charges. I just couldn't get into it with Lily yet.

I went back to my desktop computer and searched all things Jiles. I was desperate to unmask some hidden connection between Jiles and Glasser but came up empty. Wasn't all that surprised given Jiles's disdain for the internet and social media. I mean, the dinosaur still got the hardcopy newspaper.

I wanted a drink.

I stirred anxious in a bad way.

I tried to watch TV.

I checked the window, fully paranoid that Jiles was gonna show up on my doorstep and ask if I wanted to go for a drive to some place quiet where we could "talk."

I listened to Lou Reed.

I wanted to drown in booze.

I smashed more BBQ chips.

I smashed stale sour cream and onion remnants I found in a scary place in the pantry.

I felt my throat scream and wail, desperate for the drink.

Desperate for some Bulleit.

But I was dry.

Monday, October 12th, 8:56 p.m.

Where the hell was Slice?

I called and texted. I texted and called. The buzzard stiffed me.

The air was cold but I was sweating fierce.

I thought about Josie.

I thought about Allison.

Lou Reed wailed at ear-piercing volume and I hammered the bed with my fists.

I needed Benny.

I needed to get my stuff from the box before closing.

I needed a drink baaad.

I needed HELP.

I called Allison.

She didn't pick up.

I texted her: *I'm sober.*

I called again.

Her soft voice came through like a gift from god.

"Hi, Sam."

"Hi. I'm sorry for calling you before like I did. That was awful and rude and you didn't deserve it and I'm sorry. I just wanted to tell you that."

"Thank you. Are you okay?"

"Never better. Crushin' it."

The line got quiet fast. I listened to her breathe, waiting for words that never came.

"How's my orchid?" I asked, desperate to fill the silence.

"The flowers fell off. But I'm keeping it."

"How's the air out there?"

"The air?"

"Yeah. The oxygen. That Santa Monica air...It's got a taste of the ocean in it. It's so much better out there."

"The air's fine."

"You don't realize how nice that air is until you've lived in Glendale for nine years. Hey, guess what? I'm listening to Lou Reed. What are you doing?"

"I'm with friends."

"Oh. Fun. Hittin' the pier tonight? Rock the arcade and play some Galaga? Ride the coaster and—"

"If you're being honest about being sober, then I'll be honest with you and tell you, that makes me happy, Sam."

"Ya proud of me, Allison?"

"No, that makes me sound like some kinda sister." She reset. "Are you alone right now?"

"Yeah."

"At home?"

"Yeah."

"Thirsty?"

"Yeah."

"Maybe you should go to an AA meeting."

"I've never done that."

"My sister's in AA. There's meetings all over town at all times. You should try going."

"Thanks. Maybe I will."

The line got quiet again. But I stopped churning inside.

"You're really gonna keep that orchid? Even without any flowers on it?"

"Definitely, they come back to life. The trick is to soak them in water every two weeks. My cousin in Colorado does it." She carried on about her cousin in Colorado who was a magician at reviving orchids. I pretended to care about her cousin in Colorado just to listen to her soft voice like it was some kinda tonic taking my mind off the drink.

There were dudes in the background telling her to hurry up and come back in. She pushed them off, telling them to leave her alone and that she would be a minute and that *this is important.*

It brought tears to my eyes. Not big, gushing tears, but the stinging kind where your eyes just kind of fill up with water and pain. Because it was obvious her orchid cousin in Colorado was not important but something about this conversation was, to Allison, important.

Seven minutes later she asked if I was okay.

"Yeah. Thanks for making some time for me tonight, Allison. Thanks for talking—"

"Stop saying thanks! I love talking to you, Sam. When you're not all juiced up. I really do. But my stupid friends are leaving and they're my ride, so I have to go. Wanna call me again sometime?"

"Yeah."

"Good. I'd like that. I mean it...Okay?"

"Okay. Bye."

"Bye, Sam."

The line went dead. Those stupid tears welled up fierce but I didn't fight 'em off now. I didn't push the emotion down cuz it felt safe to sit in that feeling. I kept trying to boil it down to something concrete. Something I could define, what her little sacrifice meant. That moment when she made *me* more important than her real friends. But I gave up cuz the best I could do was to reduce it to something like love.

Whatever it was, was powerful.

It killed my desire to drink. My need to sit around and wait for Slice.

It killed my fear and empowered my will.

Time was running out. I texted Slice. I needed to get Benny and my files on Josie from the box. And I wasn't afraid to march back in there and get them.

Monday, October 12th, 9:44 p.m.

I pushed through the door.

I was ready for war. Ready to protect myself from whatever battle lay ahead with Jiles. So long as I was in a public place, at his bar no less, I felt relatively safe.

But he was nowhere to be seen.

The room looked the same. But everything about it tasted different.

The moment I stepped in carrying a bankers box I'd dug up from my place, the Rooster shot me an odd look. Like he knew something.

I stepped his way and he checked his shoulder.

"Word is you're moving out."

"Word travels fast." I grinned. "I haven't forgot about the money. Just cuz I may not be comin' back doesn't mean I'll flake. Besides. I know you could destroy my life with one stroke of those keys."

He smiled, like he genuinely appreciated his backdoor power.

"So, I'm planning on paying you. I mean it. I just need to—"

"Not get locked up?"

"Something like that."

"Just so you know, Jiles was in the box all day. Kept shuffling in and out, shutting the door. All day, in and out."

"Is he in there now?"

"Don't think so. I saw him go into his office."

"Thanks for the heads up. You seen Slice today?"

"No. It's weird. Haven't seen him all day."

"Yeah, that is weird." I pretended to play along. "Well, I'll see ya around Rooster."

The Rooster reached out and touched my back, with some kinda awkward pat, signifying we were something more than just strangers who shared some secrets and a drinking hole. Then he slunk back to his computer and never looked at me again.

I pushed through and made my way back inside the box. When I opened the door, my stomach tightened. Jiles was there, reading something behind the desk.

"Hey. Hope you don't mind but I've been reading some of your research."

The snake was wise.

I played it off all cool hand Luke as possible. "Nah. I don't care. I'm all done with it, anyway."

"Heard that before." He pointed at the wall. At some pictures of Glenn and Susan Glasser and the map of Glendale and newspaper cutouts of Ullverson's arrest. Of Max. And Josie. "Girl really set the hook in you, didn't she?"

My guts twisted as I dropped the box on the table. Pulled out the scraps from the drawers. Old *New Yorkers*. Gum. Masking tape. All kinds of crap I didn't need but kept me from looking at the man.

"You really went to town on all this. Reminds me of when I was younger." He chuckled like it was funny, then got cold fast. "Don't forget to settle up before you shove off."

More money. I probably owed Jiles close to five hundred bucks.

"I'm not gonna stiff you, Jiles." I kept my eyes down but he held up some papers in his hand.

"What is this?"

I took a closer look. It was the list of companies the Rooster had dug up. My empty twelve-hundred-dollar lead.

"Nothin'. Why?"

He stared at the list but then shrugged it off and walked out grumbling. "No reason."

He disappeared and I stared at all my hard work on the wall.
Then I ripped it down.
Grabbed Benny and went to settle up at the bar.

Monday, October 12th, 9:58 p.m.

Jiles hit me with a bill for $387.22.

More money. More cake I didn't have.

The number stung as I dropped my box on a stool and plopped down my card. Without saying a word he pinched it up and walked back over to the register. I looked around and caught Lily at a booth, buried in paperwork. She wouldn't even look at me. Jewels was yappin' to a couple of drunk, middle-aged dad-looking dudes and Pa was blasted, staring into the mirror.

I was gonna miss this place.

I wondered if they'd even miss me. I mean truly miss me.

Then Slice walked in.

He looked rattled and clocked Jiles a hard look as he found me at the bar.

"Thanks for the call," I snapped. "Where the hell have you been all day, Slice?"

"Sorry, but I've been workin' on it," he hissed. "What are you doin here?"

"I texted you. Needed my computer. And my stuff from the box."

He leaned in. "I talked to my guys. They did some digging."

"And?"

"And I think you might be right. They tell me Pinner's been acting squirrely. And apparently Jiles came by the station the other night. He never does that. Somethin's going on with these two. Something *off*."

Jiles was far enough away, running up my card, but still too close for comfort. I tried not to explode.

Even Slice looked uneasy. And weirdly sober. "Let's talk, outside. I gotta plan. Brought some help, too," he said.

Jiles returned, waiting for my signature. "Usual, Slice?"

"Nah. I'm not stayin', gonna see Sammy out."

Jiles squinted at this bullshit, all confused. The man knew us well enough by now and could tell we were on edge.

As we moved away, Jiles kept a tight eye on our every step out into the night.

We pushed outside and Slice let loose. According to the brass down at Central some cops were questioning Pinner's collar. Some of the pieces weren't adding up. And he said Ullverson changed his plea to not guilty for the third murder. Slice kept rambling as he walked towards a blue Nissan sedan waiting at the curb.

The car was idling, trickling fumes.

"Hop in."

A guy got out from behind the wheel and smiled at me. I recognized him but couldn't pin it. He was Latin. Tall. And built like a truck.

"Sam, this is my son, Mario."

Mario smiled and reached out a hand. "My dad's told me a lot about you. Great to finally meet ya."

"Yeah, you, too," I muttered, surprised to finally lay on eyes on the guy.

"Mario knows a lawyer named Gareth Napier." Slice kept rambling. "I think I told you about him? Anyway, Napier handles some pretty high-profile cases. We called over and he offered to meet you tonight. Mario'll introduce you. I think we should lay out what you found for him."

"Okay. Great. Thanks."

Mario walked around and slid behind the wheel. All this time, I'd pictured him as a terrified ten-year-old boy all bashed and scarred up. A kid outta Boyle Heights who loved pink lady apples. But he wasn't that at all now, of course. He looked strong. Powerful. Like he twisted that past into his own body, arming it with muscle so no one would fuck him over ever again.

I hit the back seat and Slice slid in next to me chattering on about the lawyer. We rolled north on San Fernando, soon slipping onto the 134 East.

"Where's his office?"

"His house," Slice corrected. "He lives in Pasadena."

The old coot finally stopped talking and I cracked the window for some air.

The night was cool out. Almost cold for LA.

I watched Mario from the back seat. Kept thinking about the hellhole his life had been before Slice saved the boy. I felt a bit honored to finally meet him as I caught a piece of his steel-toed cowboy boots hitting the brake.

I remembered seeing them before.

Those steel-toed cowboy boots.

I'd seen them before.

Close. In my face.

I racked memories until it all came crashing back in.

On a sidewalk.

My face against the cement.

Those boots.

Those steel-toes smashing my face outside Patriot Strong.

I straight-faced and stared strong at Mario. Swirling.

Mario turned like he felt my eyes. He smiled and I saw his teeth.

And then, I pinned it.

That face. Where I remembered seeing it.

Glasser's apartment.

Glasser's drawer.

The picture.

Susan Glasser's Latin crush.

My mind cracked.

Shit got quiet and time snapped shut.

It all synced up.

Mario Sandoval.

Mario Sandoval was one of Max's lieutenants.

Mario Sandoval was Glasser's crush.

Mario Sandoval was Slice's kid.

Slice.

I stared at the man's face on the seat next to me.

It was Slice.

All along.

I had the wrong ex-cop.

My heart hammered.

My chest wanted to explode. I was desperate to keep calm but I couldn't breathe. I pressed down the window button harder, desperate for oxygen.

Air rushed in and both men clocked a look, curious.

"You okay, Sammy?"

My lungs went deep.

"Yeah," I croaked, trying to piece it all together.

No wonder he brought Mario.

And no way they were taking me to any lawyer.

I pushed through the fear to *what the hell am I gonna do* when my phone started buzzing in my pocket. Slice glanced over as I pulled it out to see who was calling.

It was The Damned Lovely.

With his eyes all over me, I accepted the call and pressed it to my ear.

"Hello?"

"Sam, it's Jiles," he said. "I meant to tell you before you slipped out tonight but, when I was in the box today, saw that list of companies you had printed out. I kept going over it in my mind, and couldn't square it but that one company, Global Road? Pretty sure that's Slice's kid's company. Mario's." He trailed off, ready for me to respond with something like *wow* but I just stuck my eyes on the floor, listening to the dead air, trying to play it all through in my head. "You there?"

"Yeah."

"He used the bar's address and I remember calling him out on it when we got their junk mail. Stupid regulars act like it's their second home. Anyway. Just thought to tell you."

Jiles was too late. I was spinning out, racking theory. Mario was the missing piece. Glasser's boy toy was probably using her to steal from Backyard Dreams and laundering money to Patriot Strong. I just never made the connect cuz I remembered that owner was listed as M.N. Sandoval. Josie must have traced the company's address, which was why she was at the bar. Why she was soaking it all in and staying quiet. She probably thought it was Jiles, just as I did, when the whole time it was Slice.

When this whole time it was Slice.

"Got it. Thanks."

"...Okay." Jiles sounded disappointed. Like this should've been important. Or like he felt guilty for kicking me to the curb.

He hung up.

I could feel Slice staring at me, as I prayed the air screaming through the open window had drowned out Jiles's voice.

"Who was that?"

"Jiles. I forgot my credit card at the bar. We need to go back."

"We can get it after. We're almost there."

I stared at the downtown lights shimmering in the distance.

I had to get out.

I thought about opening the door and rolling out of the car on the highway. Then I thought about my skull and skin smashing the concrete at seventy miles per hour.

Slice kept talking about this lawyer, Napier. But I knew we weren't going to any lawyer's house. We were going somewhere ugly.

Mario tagged in and started up about my article on his father. How well I'd captured his spirit. I smiled and pretended to be thankful when really, I was still just trying to breathe, gaming out some kind of escape.

ADAM FROST

The car finally peeled off the 134 and rolled through the lights at the Rosemead exit. We hit the city streets and my guts got tighter with one green light after another. We hit a stop sign and in one single motion, I unclicked my seat belt and cranked the door handle, jumping free as the car started up, tripping me hard onto the cold cement. I rolled clear of the vehicle and with my heart pounding, got to my feet and ran as fast as I could.

Mario hit the brakes.

I charged down the open street and saw a red Mercedes with a woman driving, craning her neck, terrified at the sight of me coming at her full tilt.

I screamed, "Hellllppp!" but she hit the gas and sped away from the California crazy and I could hear footsteps behind me.

Mario was baring down like a bull.

I kept running, looking for an out, a save, an anything and aimed for a residential house that had a path with white daisies leading up to the front door. The lights were on and I crashed onto the front porch, smashing the doorbell furiously, pounding that door hard. I pulled out my phone and punched in my code, forgetting entirely about the whole emergency call thing and saw Mario coming at me.

The Damned Lovely popped up from my last call and I hit send.

Background noise clicked on, and I started wailing, "It's Sam! I'm with Slice. It's Slice! It's fucking Slice and his son! They're coming after me—"

But Mario slammed me HARD into the front door and the phone fell to the ground, smashing the screen to pieces as pain ripped up through my spine. I crumbled under his weight and my head buckled off the wall. I flailed my fists around like they might do some good, but Mario thundered a punch into my kidneys, dropping me to the ground. He picked my body off the ground and dragged me away. He had me by the shoulders in a wrenching headlock, dragging me by my skull and hair, up to my feet and back towards the car like he was used to this kind

310

of thing.

The door of the house finally opened and his arm tightened around my throat, crunching my airway as he bellowed to a confused Pasadena old-timer. "Sorry, sir. My buddy got drunk and your house reminded him of his ex-wife's place."

The man squinted uneasy but was happy to see us stepping away.

"I've got him under control, now. Sorry again," Mario assured the man who closed the door as I gasped for air.

He hauled me back to the car and stood me up against the trunk.

Slice was there now. Staring at me. Staring at his son.

"Jiles knows," I squawked. "He knows about Mario. Glasser. Global Road...anything happens to me, he'll chase it...it'll all come out, Slice."

Slice and Mario shared a tight look.

Then, Mario slammed his fist into my skull.

Monday, October 12th, 11:41 p.m.

I woke up.

I woke up cold and in the dirt. On a boulevard somewhere that still looked like Pasadena. My head wailed.

But I was breathing. Alive. And it all felt beautiful.

I walked along the street angling for somewhere busy, somewhere I could make a call cuz they had taken my phone.

I found a Del Taco a few blocks up. Buried myself in the bathroom and washed my face off.

I hit up a cashier named Georgina and asked if I could use her phone. She looked uneasy and I didn't blame her. I told her it was important and she bought it. I called the only number I knew off by heart in LA.

A few seconds later, the barkeep picked up.

Tuesday, October 13th, 12:34 a.m.

Jiles pulled up outside the Del Taco and I said thanks to Georgina. Told her she was a lifesaver and the girl smiled precious. I meant it.

When I got in the car Jiles didn't say much. Just looked heavy and patted my shoulder.

Then we drove in silence.

Tuesday, October 13th, 12:48 a.m.

When we pulled up outside of Slice's house, the pain in my head got sucked into my stomach, burning bad with nerves. I looked around and didn't see Mario's car.

Jiles caught my eye.

"If he wanted to hurt you, he woulda done that by now," he said. "We're just gonna talk to him, straighten this out."

Then the old man pulled a .38 from under his seat, got outta the car, and jammed it into the small of his back. It should've been cool but the sight of the pistol only made my stomach burn harder.

As we approached the front door, we could see Slice sitting in his living room, with his back to the street. And us.

He looked stone cold, in a daze almost.

Jiles didn't knock. He pressed open the lock and stepped in like he'd probably done a hundred times before. But I could see Jiles clearing the corners with his eyes as we moved into the living room. Slice stared blankly with dead eyes at his wall of history as a cop. His glory days. And the man had a deep drink in his hand.

"You all alone?"

"Mario's gone. For good," Slice said. "He stays outta this."

The air was tight, but Slice looked soft, like a wounded animal now.

Jiles kept his eyes on the old man.

"They killed Josie," I said out loud.

Slice didn't say anything when I laid out the pieces. That it

314

was Mario who was using Susan Glasser to ply money out from Backyard Dreams to his buddies at Patriot Strong.

"You got any evidence, kid?"

I nodded and Jiles almost looked proud. Like I'd done something right for once.

Slice kept silent.

Jiles looked dark.

"You kill this girl?"

Slice kept silent.

"You kill this girl, Greg?"

I'd never heard Jiles call Slice by his real name, but I could feel the anger swelling inside the ex-cop.

"He raped her, too."

Slice still wouldn't say anything. He didn't protest. He looked broken. Disgraced.

Then finally, he looked at Jiles and said once again, "Mario stays out of it."

Jiles pulled out his phone and called Pinner. Told him get over to us now. He didn't need to explain and just hung up.

"You want to beat the shit out of him, Sam? I can turn around. Or help."

I stared at Slice. This man I had trusted. Looked up to. Envied. This man who was the true source for so much pain in my life. Then I thought about Josie. Those final moments he must've had with her. The pain he caused *her*. Ripping off that girl's clothes and forcing himself inside her terrified, beautiful body. Wrapping his hands around her soft throat, crushing the air out of that throat. This man, standing right in front of me.

It wasn't anger. It was more pain and sadness.

I didn't want to hit him. I wanted him to look me in the eye. See the hurt. But he never did.

It wasn't long before Pinner blustered through the door. The cop picked up the scent in the room fast.

Saw the hate in Jiles.

The disgrace on Slice.

315

I stepped out the pieces. Laid the track for the cop as simply as I could.

After he was convinced, I expected Pinner to walk Slice out, but these men had other plans.

"Leave him with us, Sam," Jiles said. "We'll handle it."

They weren't asking. And for the first time I saw terror bleed through Slice.

Jiles handed over his keys. "I'll meet ya back at the bar."

I moved my feet and legs and pounding heart and made for the door. But I needed one more take. One more look at the monster. So I turned around and stared at Slice and those men standing over him as they closed the door when it all came back. What Jiles told me. About cops who cross the line and betray their own.

We decide.
Sometimes they go quiet.
Sometimes they don't.
Sometimes it's up to us to close it out.

Tuesday, October 13th, 1:21 a.m.

I sat down at the bar. Gutted. Swirling.

The place still had a few slugs hanging on.

The room twisted around me. Faces. Drinks. Smiles. Brassy soul music. Like any other night. Like no other night before. I don't remember talking to anyone. I don't remember much after that, I only remember someone placing a Bulleit in front of me at the bar.

And I remember taking my second sip.

Friday, October 16th, 3:19 p.m.

There were no headlines.
    No breaking news.
    No break in the case fun.
    Life went back to the same old spin.
    Jiles floated me some cash.
    Glasser dropped the charges.
    Lily waived her fees.
    Pa kept drinking.
    The Rooster stared at his screen in the corner.
    Jewels brave-faced it with a pretty smile.
    I wrote a thing. A real novel this time. With pieces of my heart on the page.
    Ullverson took the rap.
    Mario skated clean.
    And Slice vanished.

Tuesday, October 20th, 3:19 p.m.

They found his body four days later. He put a bullet through his head behind a motel off the 10 outside of Banning. Officially, they said.

He didn't leave a note.

Word ripped through the bar. Shock and tears.

What the hell happened?

Jewels cried. Pa racked numb. Even Lily cracked.

The *Times* buried the news deep in the folds. The LAPD kept mum.

When's the service? How's Mario holding up?

Jiles deflected. For weeks. But Lily and Jewels couldn't take it. They leaned on him to close the bar and pay respects.

To do the right thing for their friend.

Jiles caved. Probably to soothe something deep inside his heart, so he closed the bar early. We sat around tossing tales of Slice into the night. The good, the bad, and the lies. We raised a glass to the fallen soldier.

Jiles and I kept quiet. Playing the part. Volleying the truth behind our eyes back and forth like a dirty secret.

The place would never be the same, they said.

About a month later, Allison walked into the bar. I hadn't reached out to her since that night with Slice. Since she talked me off the ledge.

She seemed excited to see me. Less excited seeing the bourdon in my hand. I offered to buy her a drink but she declined, straddling the stool next to me.

"How ya been?"

I could smell her skin and remembered how much I liked her.

We shuffled small talk and she seemed genuinely curious about where the hell I'd been. Why I hadn't returned her texts. Trying to get the story.

I deflected with a grin.

She said I looked good.

I told her she looked better.

"Your orchid came back."

"It's really nice to see you, Allison."

"You're drinking again."

"I am drinking again. But I'm better, trust me." And I was in a way, not that I could tell her.

She looked around the joint, unconvinced. Like the place still disappointed her, just as it had the day we first met here.

"I think you can do better with your life, Sam."

I thought about Josie's bloodied shirt buried quiet in my desk. In the box, behind that door. I looked around the rest of the bar. I saw Jiles grumbling to Jewels about a customer. I saw Pa with his frosted Beefeater glee. The Rooster watching wise from the corner. And Lily glancing from afar, sipping rum, working a file, eyeing me like a raven or a mother or something. I'd always thought Jiles called this place The Damned Lovely cuz of the booze. But I wasn't so sure, anymore, seeing these faces.

So I smiled at my drink and stared at Allison's beautiful face.

"Yeah. Maybe you're right."

ACKNOWLEDGMENTS

Thanks to Amy Moore-Benson for going to bat for this little damned lovely. To the team at Down & Out, Eric Campbell and Lance Wright for your mighty support. To Chris Rhatigan for sharpening my sloppy corners. To Cooper McMains for putting up with my dirty first drafts and most of all telling me I wasn't crazy to keep going. To Novak for picking up the phone after so many years. To Glenn Cockburn and Conrad Sun for backing my next crazy play. To Jordan for all the inspiring steps. To MacDonald—my brother in artistic arms to the end. To Jamie and Kerry Rosenblatt for hosting that new year's party where I actually committed to write a novel. To Dashiell and Emmett for walking out those Saturday morning coffees. And most of all, to Nora, for always believing in me—especially when I didn't. Also to Nic—for the ten p.m. discipline, for forcing me to push out pages in my car in those blazing hot parking lots, and for seeing it through when it was nothing but a thankless word doc dream. For the armor, Nic. For the armor.

ABOUT THE AUTHOR

ADAM FROST was born and raised in Vancouver. He began as an actor and now works as a television writer and producer, best known for the crime shows *Tribal* and *Castle*. He lives on the east side of Los Angeles. He's also one helluva T-ball coach.

BOOKS

On the following pages are a few
more great titles from the
Down & Out Books publishing family.

For a complete list of books and to
sign up for our newsletter,
go to DownAndOutBooks.com.

Groovy Gumshoes
Private Eyes in the Psychedelic Sixties
Edited by Michael Bracken

Down & Out Books
April 2022
978-1-64396-252-8

From old-school private eyes with their flat-tops, off-the-rack suits, and well-worn brogues to the new breed of private eyes with their shoulder-length hair, bell-bottoms, and hemp sandals, the shamuses in Groovy Gumshoes take readers on a rollicking romp through the Sixties.

With stories by Jack Bates, C.W. Blackwell, Michael Bracken, N.M. Cedeño, Hugh Lessig, Steve Liskow, Adam Meyer, Tom Milani, Neil S. Plakcy, Stephen D. Rogers, Mark Thielman, Grant Tracey, Mark Troy, Andrew Welsh-Huggins, and Robb White.

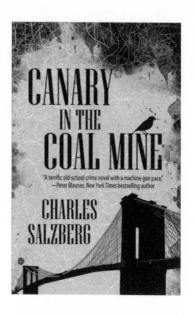

Canary in the Coal Mine
Charles Salzberg

Down & Out Books
April 2022
978-1-64396-251-1

Pete Fortunato, a NYC PI who suffers from anger management issues and insomnia, is hired by a beautiful woman to find her husband.

When he finds him shot dead in the apartment of her young boyfriend, this is the beginning of a nightmare as he's chased by the Albanian mob sending him half-way across the country in an attempt to find missing money which can save his life.

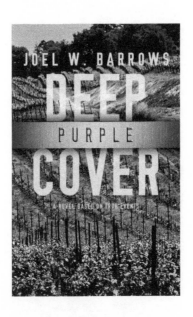

Deep Purple Cover
The Deep Cover Series
Joel W. Barrows

Down & Out Books
May 2022
978-1-64396-263-4

Things in Napa Valley are not as they seem. Everyone wants to get into the wine business, but at what cost?

When the co-owner of Pavesi Vineyards goes missing there are few clues to his disappearance. When his remains unexpectedly turn up, dark forces loom large.

FBI Special Agent Rowan Parks is assigned to the case and quickly realizes that the Bureau needs someone on the inside. There is only one person to call, her former lover, and ATF's greatest undercover operative, David Ward.

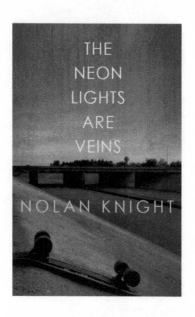

The Neon Lights Are Veins
Nolan Knight

Down & Out Books
May 2022
978-1-64396-265-8

The underbelly of Los Angeles, 2008; a place where hard-lucks scrounge for hope in gutters.

Alvi Drake is an aged pro skateboarder whose lone thrill is a pill-fueled escape from the terror of past ghosts. When news hits of the disappearance of an old flame, he sets out to find her—the biggest mistake in his track ridden life.